Valley of Dry Bones

A Medieval Mystery

Priscilla Royal

Poisoned Pen Press

Poisoned Pen Press
6962 E. First Ave., Ste. 103
Scottsdale, AZ 85251
www.poisonedpenpress.com
info@poisonedpenpress.com

Printed in the United States of America

To Lyn and Michael Speakman
With love and gratitude, I dedicate this performance to you.

Acknowledgments

Christine and Peter Goodhugh, Ed Kaufman of M is for Mystery Bookstore (San Mateo, CA), Henie Lentz, Dianne Levy, Sharon Kay Penman, Barbara Peters of Poisoned Pen Bookstore (Scottsdale, AZ), Robert Rosenwald and all the staff of Poisoned Pen Press, Marianne and Sharon Silva, Lyn and Michael Speakman, the staff at University Press Bookstore (Berkeley, CA).

The hand of the Lord was upon me, and carried me out in the spirit of the Lord, and set me down in the midst of the valley which was full of bones, and caused me to pass by them round about: and, behold, there were very many in the open valley; and, lo, they were very dry. And he said unto me, Son of man, can these bones live? And I answered, O Lord God, thou knowest.

—Ezekiel 37:1-3 (King James version)

Chapter One

The late afternoon heat settled heavily on Prioress Eleanor. Sweat wiggled down her spine, making her itch as if some impudent crawling thing were caught beneath her habit. Now her arm grew numb from holding her staff of office.

Surely it should not take this long for the party from Edward's queen to enter the priory gates. Their messenger had arrived just after the last Office. Was it not almost time for the bells to announce the next?

Beside her, Prior Andrew eased his weight to his other foot.

Her glance caught his brief grimace. "Does your leg trouble you?"

"It is nothing more than a man's impatience to be busy, my lady. I am not accustomed to standing still this long."

She nodded in response, knowing he had lied but letting him keep his pride. Her prior was a good man. His attempt at deception was innocent enough.

"Queen Eleanor honors Tyndal Priory by suggesting she might stop here on her pilgrimage route." The prior clasped his hands in a prayerful gesture. The whiteness of his knuckles betrayed the pain he was suffering.

"We received the news of her great favor with much joy." Eleanor chose to reply as if this visit were a certainty, although she knew there was a possibility that the event might never come to pass. Even if it did, Edward's wife could have some troubling reason for coming here. Honor never came without cost. Since the prioress could think of no reason why Tyndal might already have earned the boon, she concluded that any price must be paid in the future.

A shout from a lay brother, standing at the open gates, interrupted her worries before they became weightier.

Great clouds of tan dust billowed above the grey stones of the priory walls. The neighing of horses and rumble of carts on the rutted road from the west were unmistakable.

At last, Eleanor thought, and gripped her crosier more firmly. Her hand slipped, and she almost dropped the staff.

That was not a good omen. She clenched her teeth, and her heart pounded with apprehension. Then she looked at those clustered nearby. From their expressions, she suspected any misgivings were hers alone.

Standing to her left, Sister Ruth was red-faced and sweating from the heat while her square face bore an especially beatific expression. Such a worshipful look would be greeted with favor by those accustomed to the ways of a king's court. Although the sub-prioress often tried Eleanor's patience, the woman was far more capable than she of conveying heart-felt flattery, a skill that sometimes allowed the prioress to avoid attempting her own, less convincing performance.

Next to the sub-prioress stood Sister Christina, infirmarian of Tyndal's well-regarded hospital. The nun had prayerfully bowed her head, a sincere gesture as well as wise since her weak eyes often made her seem oblivious to anything around her. Even those of high secular rank, who might otherwise demand rapt attention, would never dare to find insult in such splendid faith.

"The envoys arrive," Eleanor said. With grim resolve, she tried to emulate the calm of those surrounding her.

The religious grew quiet with anticipation.

"They are accompanied by a large armed guard." Prior Andrew shaded his eyes and stared at the dust clouds.

"Let us hope they are not too numerous to accommodate." The prioress glanced at his tensed features and hoped she might find cause to release him from further attendance. During this very long wait, they had all suffered from the oppressive summer heat. When the ritual courtesies were finished, Eleanor planned to dismiss the majority so they could find refuge in the relative cool of the priory buildings.

"I have prepared for that likelihood," Sister Ruth hissed.

"Nor did I doubt that you had," Eleanor replied. Whatever faults her sub-prioress possessed, the failure to plan carefully for the comfort of high-ranking guests was not one of them.

The prioress looked again at her prior and regretfully concluded that he must stay a while longer than the others. Although she was the unquestioned leader of both monks and nuns in this Fontevraudine priory, the presence of masculine authority was expected and more reassuring to those outside the Order.

Nonetheless, Eleanor was solely responsible for assuring hospitality balanced between the monastic simplicity appropriate to a pilgrimage and the comfort to which a king's wife was accustomed. It was also the prioress who must convince these courtiers that Tyndal was prepared in all respects to welcome a queen.

Eleanor closed her eyes and prayed that Edward's wife would quite soon forget she had ever mentioned making this journey. Should God grant this plea, the prioress vowed she would not resent all the wasted effort put into planning. At least Tyndal would be ready for the burden of such an honor if the queen did arrive at the priory gates.

The first of the armed escort rode through the gates.

Eleanor squinted through the dirty haze, anxious to catch sight of the man she had learned would be leading the party.

Although she had never met Sir Fulke, she knew he was the eldest brother of Crowner Ralf, a man she called *friend*. The courtier was sheriff for this region but rarely appeared, preferring Winchester to any land populated with flickering lights known as corpse candles, stinking fens, and screeching mews.

Ralf had assured her that she had little to fear from Fulke who would be as eager to leave Tyndal as she would be to see him go. And she had no reason to believe any member of this party had a quarrel with her family or with this remote and insignificant priory.

Her apprehension diminished.

After the long journey, they surely would be grateful enough for a cool drink, a decent meal, and rest. Perhaps they all would prove as keen as she to confirm without delay that the queen's needs would be met here. Then they could make swift return to the comforts of court, and Eleanor could go back to balancing accounting rolls and estimating the wool profit from priory sheep.

She stifled a hopeful sigh.

The horsemen now drew to a halt, parted, and the lead rider approached. At last she would meet Sir Fulke.

Furtively drying her sweating hand on her robe, Eleanor clutched the crosier with determination, arranged her features into an expression of serene dignity, and reminded herself that Tyndal might gain land or some other fine gift if she handled this matter of the queen's visit with skill.

Then she recognized the priest riding behind the sheriff.

All hope of tranquility fled.

Chapter Two

Baron Otes was a very happy man.

As he rode with the sheriff through the gates of Tyndal Priory, he raised his eyes heavenward and, with an abrupt nod, thanked God for the satisfactory way in which He had answered all his prayers on this journey. Otes was wise enough to show gratitude when He did as requested, not that God often failed to grant his wishes.

The baron's only grievance today was the unrelenting heat. As he had grown older, he had gained weight in direct proportion to his increasing affluence. Now he suffered more in summer and found traveling in warmer seasons difficult. For this reason, he chose well-tempered horses large enough to comfortably carry a man of his girth without complaint over long journeys. Or so he had always done.

Otes glared down at this particular beast. Was it his imagination or had the creature given him an evil look this morning when he approached to mount? He shook his head and concluded that the heat had unbalanced his humors. After all, these animals were incapable of reason and could not foresee a fatiguing ride. Unlike Adam and Eve, horses had never eaten an apple from the Tree of Knowledge.

Suddenly he had a horrifying thought. Might Adam have fed an apple to this animal's forbearer before he himself had taken that forbidden bite?

With a grimace, Otes dismissed the blasphemous thought and forced his mind to more practical matters. He also decided that he must find shelter from this sun.

It had been a long day, and he would be glad when the inevitable courtesies were over. Sweat stung his eyes, and his fingers were so swollen that he had difficulty holding the reins. He feared that this remote priory might not possess palatable enough wine to wash the dust from his throat. Then he recalled that the prioress was a baron's daughter and grew confident. A woman of high birth would never tolerate inferior or austere food and drink.

As the delegation approached the large gathering of monks and nuns waiting to honor the queen's representatives, Otes eyed those of greatest interest to him. He smiled with delight, his spirits rose, and he grew increasingly confident that his plans would be successful.

He had been right to demand that the party delay entrance to priory grounds until he had taken time to pray. Especially after his recent and most generous donations to the Church, God should not fail to recognize his piety. A small reminder that He owed the baron a great deal had clearly not been wasted, however.

Although he knew her father, Baron Adam of Wynethorpe, this prioress was younger than he had believed. Before Otes left the court, he learned the late king had appointed her to this position because her kin had been loyal during the de Montfort rebellion. That detail meant her fellow religious had not chosen her for any demonstrated competence.

Since she had been raised at Amesbury Priory from childhood, she would also be a naïve about worldly matters. That, plus her youth, meant she could be manipulated with even greater ease than he had assumed. Oh, he had heard rumors of things she had done here and there. Those, he discounted. Any alleged accomplishments were surely the work of some monk on her behalf. In this Order of Fontevrault, a woman might hold the title of leader, but he knew at least one man must direct her.

Perhaps that man was her prior, the one standing beside her. In this, God had doubly blessed Otes, and he was eager for the moment when Prior Andrew saw him. Perhaps Andrew would not recognize the baron immediately, for they had both changed in the years since their last meeting. The prior had grown as gaunt as Otes had grown fat, and all men knew which physical state proved His favor. The baron was confident of his superior standing in God's eyes.

The dust slowly settled from the stamping of so many hooves. Otes wiped a hand across his forehead and looked with distaste at the smeared dirt. Then he chuckled. How he would savor the sight of Andrew's eyes widening in proportion to the dread growing in the wretched prior's heart. That moment was worth all the gritty dust caught in the baron's sweat.

Otes stretched his aching shoulders back. After all my generosity to the Church, he said to himself, I should not have to beg that my soul be granted but a brief moment in Purgatory. Since it seems I must, according to my wretched confessor, someone ought to pay the price for the injustice. This prior is a despicable man, one who can be cast aside and forgotten, and Andrew surely deserved to suffer for having dared to live this long.

Otes caught himself smiling at the back of Sir Fulke, the sheriff.

Now there was a fool, neither corrupt enough to succeed through fear nor so honest that he basked in the warm esteem of others. Although Otes had learned something useful about the man, the baron had found no particular reason to exact a price for his knowledge. Until now, the way the man twitched every time they met, like a mouse facing a cat, was good enough. Soon, he might have to demand something more from Sir Fulke. Others had always paid well for the baron's silence, and he took pride in getting full value for secrets. No man should ever die before gathering in everything owed him.

Pulling on his reins, Otes groaned with increasing discomfort and shifted in the saddle to ease his back. As he did, he saw Kenard walking next to the Lady Avelina.

At that moment, the servant also looked up. He met the baron's glance with a bold stare.

Otes turned away so quickly his neck hurt. The very sight of that man with hooded eyes like some malevolent hawk always made him uneasy. Why had the Lady Avelina kept him in her service? The man was mute. Perhaps he earned his keep by spying on her imprudent son, Simon.

Otes shuddered. Had Kenard been lurking the other night when the baron whispered a few words in Simon's ear and the young man almost pissed himself with terror? The baron assumed not. He had ever been careful to avoid witnesses to his tactics.

In any case, he found the servant loathsome and concluded the man needed to be reminded of his rank. Otes chose to meet the man's gaze again, then spat in Kenard's direction. The creature would not dare respond to the insult.

The servant turned his back and strode away.

Although this man might cause Otes discomfort, he knew Kenard could be punished if the baron chose to complain about some real or imagined offense. It was another member of this party who caused Otes real concern: the priest, Father Eliduc. While his voice was as soft as the cloth of his black robes, his very presence in a room made men break out in a sweat as if they suffered from a mortal fever.

Otes was not at all happy that this particular churchman was made a member of the company sent to Tyndal. A priest might be an obligatory part of the group, since the queen had proclaimed her journey a pilgrimage, but Eliduc was not the representative of God Otes wanted. The man was the one person who shouldn't learn just yet of Otes' purpose here, and the priest had a fine reputation for ferreting out secrets, a skill the baron conceded might well match his own.

"Foxes may be outwitted by clever hounds," he reminded himself, believing that his wits were surely up to the mark. God was also showing too many signs of His favor. There could be nothing except triumph for Otes' cause.

Exhaling with relief, he forced a smile. The sheriff was speaking with the prioress. Soon he could escape this heat and sit back in a chair with a goblet of cool wine to strengthen him. He sighed with pleasure at the very thought.

His horse snorted as if concurring with the sentiment.

Chapter Three

This journey had lasted far too long for the Lady Avelina. Each day, her weariness had deepened until her very bones now throbbed. Shutting her eyes, she refused to dwell on the unpleasant fact that the road must be traveled again for the return to court. Although the inns had been carefully chosen for their good fare and decent lodging, the mattresses had been scratchy, albeit stuffed with fresh straw, and she had suffered too many flea bites. Apparently none of these innkeepers had ever heard of using lavender.

She opened her eyes and gazed around at the priory grounds. To her right, she could see arching fruit trees and lush gardens, all green and dotted with the vibrant colors suggestive of seasonal abundance. To her left stood the guest quarters with stables, and in the distance she could hear the splashing groans of a mill.

"Most likely there are fish ponds as well," she murmured. "How peaceful it is here." Then she gasped as a sharp pain struck her breast.

Kenard was instantly by her side. Tilting his head, he furrowed his forehead with concern and pointed first to her mount and then to his arm.

Wincing, she nodded and held out her hand.

After easing his mistress off the mare, the man stood back and waited for further direction

Tired though Avelina was, she was too proud to lean on his arm as she longed to do. Instead, she lightly rested a hand against her damp-sided mare while noting with relief that Kenard did not walk away.

"Thank you," she said to him, her tone tender. Some snickered behind their hands that this servant might serve her too well. Especially of late, she was grateful for his gentle attendance and cared not if others made more of his consideration than they ought.

Although she had always been a strong woman, she had begun to suffer from profound weariness. This exhaustion, she concluded, must be due to the unusually warm summer. That it might have something to do with the behavior of her son, Simon, the young man who now approached, was a thought she firmly set aside.

With the annoyance of a boy interrupted in sport by his mother's summoning, he kicked at the earth as he walked. Dust swirled in her direction.

She sneezed.

"Are you ill?" Simon's expression was a mix of youth's impatience with the ways of parents and a child's fear that his mother was unwell.

She shook her head to reassure him she was sound enough, then turned to look once more at the priory grounds. Her expression grew contemplative. "When I have settled the matter of your lands and title, God might smile on me if I retired to this place."

Simon shrugged.

Hot anger at this petulant indifference flashed in her heart like sparks in dry grass, and she gripped her son's arm with such force he winced. "Ungrateful boy! Care you so little that I have forsaken any comfort for myself and devoted my life to furthering your interests?"

"Unhand me, Mother." His face reddening with embarrassment, he shook his arm until she released him. "You might as well have accepted another husband when you were still young enough to breed and gained a man's protection with a softer bed."

"How dare…"

"Let me finish. I know how hard you have labored on my behalf, and I owe gratitude, but you can never change how my sire died, nor can you erase the memory of his treason to kingship."

"We have a new king, my son, and I now serve his lady wife. Although she knows of my marriage to your father, she shows no fear when I am about her person. This proves I have reason to hope…"

"Hope is well enough for women. A man should be forceful and carve his own destiny. You would do better to find someone who would loan me money for a horse and armor. Then I might gain a fine reputation by fighting in tournaments abroad. King Edward is more likely to smile on a man who has won honor in combat than on one who waits for a woman to soften a path for him."

"Do not be so impatient for good fortune. Patience and prudence are not traits only the weak possess. They are also virtues much respected by earthly kings."

His forehead creased with annoyance.

As Avelina gazed upon her only living child, her look turned gentle. She patted the arm which had just shrugged off her touch. Although her son might not love her, and did resent this journey she insisted he take, she was relieved he could acknowledge how hard she had worked to regain what his father had lost by bad judgement.

This time, Simon tolerated her affectionate gesture. "Men with tonsures or grey beards may agree with you. King Edward is young, a crusader and not a monk. Youth is fleeting," he replied, his voice dropping to add gravity to his speech. "Coming with you has only delayed me in my quest to prove my sword arm worthy of land and title. You should have left me at court. Alone, I might have gotten the weapons I need to gain the notice of a warrior king."

His words made her shiver. "While you argue with some merit, my son, your actions contradict those fine words. Had you shown more restraint with your tongue and lusts, I might have left you behind, but you willfully ignored my warnings. Swyving willing servant girls may be one thing. Trying to force a virgin of rank into your bed is quite another."

He snorted. "So she tells the tale! She was eager enough to seduce me. To my shame, I weakened. Immediately, she pretended to protest. Lustful creature, she knew that resistance would enflame a man's desire beyond any hope of containment."

"Her mother said she screamed and tried to flee."

"You take her word over mine, as all women would."

Weary with the pointless arguing, Avelina shook her head. "Although I may own that weakness of my sex, know that fathers often believe their daughters too. If nothing else, they may seek revenge when a daughter is cruelly beaten because she tries to protect her chastity." She squeezed her eyes shut with increasing weariness. "Whether or not you understand the implications of your actions," she continued with a sigh, "I knew it was best to remove you from court for a while and can only pray the girl's mother succeeds in hushing the deed by the time we return."

Simon's mouth settled into a pout.

Avelina looked away from her son, again savoring the beauty of Tyndal's grounds and inhaling the soft scent of brightly petalled flowers and ripe fruit. Were she to turn her back on worldly matters and repent her many sins in such a place as this, she might find that peace with which she had rarely been blessed.

Maybe she should permit Simon to go his own way, as he had demanded. Doing so, she might at last cut herself free of that bitterness of heart stemming from the family's downfall. How easily prestige had been won, she thought, and then how quickly lost. For an instant, she imagined the tranquility of serving God.

Doubt began to nibble at the calm. Were she to take vows and Simon failed in his plans, falling even farther from a king's grace, could she ignore the cries of the boy whom she bore with both pain and joy? Would she stay on her knees, deaf to her son while she lifted her arms to Heaven? She knew she would cast all hopes of Heaven aside and rush to the boy's side.

"Mother."

The young man's tone was so chill that her heart clenched with jagged pain. Pressing her hand against her breast to subdue the hurt into numbness, Avelina knew she would forgive all his failings if only he loved her again as he had as a bright-eyed babe.

His narrowed eyes were not directed toward her, however. He was glaring at another, and his mouth twisted into a snarl. "Do you know why Baron Otes was included in our party?"

Exhaling in relief that she was not the object of Simon's disdain, she quickly replied, "I believe he has the king's favor."

"What a pity," the young man muttered. "I hate him."

Before Avelina could respond to those words, a lay brother appeared to take her mare, another to lead her to the chamber she would occupy for the visit.

In an instant, Kenard was by her side.

Simon walked away.

Saddened that her son never thought to show her a like courtesy, she took the servant's arm and nodded her appreciation. The fatigue, briefly set aside, now returned, and she realized that every step she made required force of will.

As they turned toward the guest lodgings, Avelina hesitated to gather herself to the task and watched Sir Fulke talking with the tiny woman who held a crosier in her hand.

"How young to be a prioress," she remarked in a low voice, "and her manner is so grave. One might conclude that God has endowed her with wisdom far beyond her years."

Kenard followed his mistress' gaze. He nodded with solemnity.

Close to losing the battle against exhaustion, Avelina closed her eyes. Quickly she opened them as she felt herself falling into sleep.

Kenard gripped her arm.

The lady turned to look for Simon.

He was talking with Father Eliduc.

Perhaps the kind priest could succeed in directing her son onto a wiser path, she thought, something all others had failed to do. The boy had sought the company of Father Eliduc frequently during the journey, although Simon had never expressed more than a perfunctory faith. Just the other night, the priest had suggested to her that this visit to Tyndal might be beneficial to her son's soul.

"I shall pray for a miracle," she murmured, too tired to realize she had spoken aloud.

Bracing her with firmer grasp, Kenard nodded.

Yearning to find ease, Avelina now gestured to the lay brother that she was ready to follow him. Too exhausted to bear the additional burden of pride, she learned heavily on Kenard's arm.

In this way, lady and servant walked in silence and with heavy step to the guest quarters.

Chapter Four

A crowner and a hermit lay naked on the bank of a stream while the gracefully tumbling water flashed sparks in the sunlight. The priory mill served by its meandering course was not far, and the rhythmic thump of the great wooden wheel provided deep counterpoint to the higher pitched murmur of flowing water.

With an unabashed grunt of pleasure, Crowner Ralf stretched, his body wet from the recent swim in the nearby pond. "Have I been changed into a lizard, Brother?" he asked.

Brother Thomas, now better known as the hermit of Tyndal, kept his eyes closed against the blinding sun. "You must be a man, for I have never heard a reptile speak. Although Eden's serpent was eloquent enough, his descendants have long been rendered mute."

Ralf rolled over and propped his head on his hand as he studied the man he considered a friend despite their difference in vocation. "Nor have you changed at all yourself. I confess I cannot see any hermit's nature in you, although I never quite saw a monk either."

Thomas abruptly sat up, grabbed for his robe, and pulled the rough garment over his head.

Rubbing at his eyes, the crowner winced. "Forgive me. I intended no offense. Gytha must oft remind me that my blunt tongue wounds more than my sword ever could."

The frown on Thomas' forehead smoothed, and he turned to the crowner with a grin. "Gytha is cruel to reveal your unhappy secret. How did you survive as a soldier with such poor skills? Did you have a dog to bite where your sword could not?"

"There have been enough corpses to prove my competence. Methinks she meant my sword is so dulled from use that it could not cut the beard you've grown nor your length of hair." Sitting up, he scratched at his armpit. "Those at the hospital miss your gentle touch with the dying. I should have said that. My words were ill-chosen."

The monk raised an eyebrow. "Have you been to the priory then? I pray there has been no misdeed to trouble Tyndal's peace."

"Nay, unless my dear brother has brought it."

"Sir Fulke is at Tyndal?"

"I thought the boy from the inn brought you tidings along with food and drink?"

"He fears to intrude, or else I frighten him with my wild look." Thomas tried to run his hand through his shoulder-length auburn hair. His fingers caught in the tangles. "I suspect he hides until I leave the hut, then he sets the jug and basket at the door and runs away."

Ralf slammed his palm down on the ground with joy. "Perhaps I must visit you often so you will learn all the local tales!" Just as quickly, his expression darkened into a solemn one. "Unless my presence offends you. I have hesitated to come before now, knowing full well I am a wicked man and you have sworn yourself to a holy desert father's life."

"We are all sinful creatures, Ralf. You less than most." The monk tossed a small pebble into the running stream. "I am no different than I was when I comforted the sick at the hospital. As for becoming like a desert father, I can swear that no wild thing feeds me. Rather it is Signy from the inn who does so for the good of her soul. I am no more saintly than you, giving you no cause to avoid me. The sight of your face is ever welcome here."

"Then I do not understand why you sought this lonely place as a hermitage?"

"Did Gytha not counsel you against digging up a man's motives when no crime has been committed?"

The crowner's face flushed with embarrassment before realizing Thomas was jesting. "I have little experience of hermits. When I was a soldier, I did meet a few along the road. They may have offered me a dutiful hospitality, but there was evidence of honest glee when I left them in the morning."

"As you noted, no hermit is ever completely alone. In truth, Crowner, my stay here was always meant to be temporary. Our anchoress advised me to seek greater solitude if I wished to hear God's voice more clearly. Beyond those admissions, I shall confess nothing more to you." He smiled to temper his words, then wrapped his arms around his knees and looked in the direction of Tyndal. "Tell me more of your brother's strange visit. Surely he does not seek a monastic life."

Ralf spat. "One of the few things he and I share is contempt for our middle brother who glistens with fat after vowing himself to poverty."

Amused rather than offended by the remark, Thomas put his hand over his mouth to hide a smile.

"Nay, our new queen has mentioned she might undertake a pilgrimage in gratitude to God for bringing her and her lord safely home to England. Fulke, as sheriff here, volunteered to lead a party of those who must confirm that the route, fare, and accommodations are suited to royal needs. Tyndal Priory lies at the end of the journey."

"With Norwich so close, with a fine abbey and softer beds, I wonder that Queen Eleanor would choose to stay at our humble priory."

"My brother's very question. I suggested that Sister Anne's fame and her hospital may have caught the attention of our new king. Nor is it unreasonable to conclude that Prioress Eleanor's reputation for solving murders might be of interest to the queen."

"I concede the former to you. As for the latter, the queen might find it troubling that murder and our prioress are so often linked. If I were King Edward's wife, I would not greet with especial joy anyone who brings Death along as her frequent companion!"

"Granted. Tyndal Priory might not be the queen's first choice, should she ever wish to retire from the world and your prioress be its leader still."

"It does seem more likely that our lady queen wishes to visit the hospital." Thomas bent his head back as if his neck had stiffened. "Have the new guest quarters and stables been completed? They were being built when I left the priory grounds."

Ralf nodded.

"The chambers should be comfortable, albeit austere. Even though there is a need for such lodging, our prioress will not change this priory into a manor house for courtiers. As for the fare offered, whatever comes from Sister Matilda's kitchen could convert any queen into a Fontevraudine nun."

The crowner gnawed at the side of his middle finger.

"And the voices of our novice choir under Brother John would awe one of God's angels, let alone a king's wife."

"Aye."

"And knowing the passion with which you long for this, I am sure Sir Fulke will finally agree to join with you in becoming friars together."

Ralf nodded. Then he realized what the monk had just said. Horror paled his face.

"Forgive my jest. Why are you troubled? Something has distracted you." Thomas hesitated. "Is all well with your daughter?"

"Sibely thrives, and Gytha comes often enough to spoil her should my child lack any attention from this fond father or from the gentle maid who tends her."

Thomas nodded with relief. Although Ralf's dead wife had never won the crowner's heart, she had given him a child he adored. The monk was grateful no tragedy had struck the wee babe.

"It is Fulke's visit." Grabbing his clothes, the crowner tugged them on with angry impatience. "Methinks he plans another marriage for me." His voice was taut with fury.

"Are you so set against it? Having a mother of her own might be a wise thing for your daughter. However much Gytha loves her, she will surely marry, bear children of her own, and have less time for Sibely. The nurse may wed as well. She is a local lass and, with what you pay her, she must have lads preening like cocks at her door."

"Satan's tits!" Ralf snatched up a rock and hurled it at the closest tree. Bark exploded off the trunk from the force of the impact.

Awaiting an explanation for the outburst, Thomas said nothing.

"I did Fulke's bidding once," the crowner growled. "If I do take another wife, I shall wed as I choose."

Chapter Five

Sir Fulke paced like an anxious fox seeking refuge from a pack of hounds. Where were those lay brothers who swore they'd stable the horses, then return to take the party to the guest quarters? Although the men had appeared once to serve the Lady Avelina, they had long since vanished.

Now that the requisite words of courtesy had been spoken and graceful bows executed with that horde of religious gathered to greet the queen's party, Fulke was impatient to be freed from this company of courtiers, none of whom he liked. He had been traveling for much too long and itched from the dust that had bonded firmly with his sticky flesh. Today the hot ride had been made interminable because Baron Otes had insisted on retreating into the bushes for lengthy prayer.

"Or more likely relief of his leaden bowels," he muttered. Rubbing his neck, the sheriff winced. In addition to everything else, his skin was burned raw by the sun.

To further befoul his mood, Fulke had a proposal he must present to his youngest brother, a conversation he dreaded. Of the three brothers, Ralf was the contrary one, prone to resisting any reasonable plan and possessed of a tongue that was sharp and profane. The sheriff longed to complete the unpleasant task as quickly as possible. Although the queen's business with Tyndal Priory might be amicably settled in the time between Sext and dinner, the discussion with his youngest brother promised to sour Fulke's stomach for days.

Growing ever more disgusted with this long wait, he scrutinized the priory grounds. If the lay brothers did not return soon, he might seek out the fish ponds, strip, and wade around to cool his reddened flesh. If nothing else, the sight of his naked body splashing companionably with the evening meal might force either prior or prioress to find those errant lay brothers. He grinned with impudent pleasure.

Then he looked at the walls of the priory, darkly stained with stubborn moss, and lost even that brief joy. "The only things thriving in this place are rot and mold," he muttered to his sweating horse. "In this heat, the ponds have surely gone dry, and all fish must long be dead."

His eyes stung, his head ached, and his heart filled with hatred for this vile land. He had lost nothing by leaving behind the noxious fogs, plagues of biting insects, brutal storms, and pervasive mold. Since boyhood, he had hated the fens and the sea. His nights had often been filled with sweet dreams of escape.

Glaring at the earth beneath his feet, Fulke grudgingly acknowledged he was grateful Ralf had taken on the position of crowner here. While his brother handled all those trifling matters of local justice in this forsaken mud hole, Fulke was free to stay at court and further family interests. Ralf was not only tolerant of East Anglian winter mire and the thick summer air, he seemed to like it. A modicum of fond appreciation for this insolent brother slipped into Fulke's heart. It was just as quickly chased away.

After all, his rough brother was possessed of little subtlety, less tact, and was far better suited to examining rotting corpses and hunting down lawless men. Fulke might own the title of sheriff, but he cared nothing about assessed fines, unless the money came from his own coffers, or whether a man, other than one of his villeins, was murdered or died by accident. Why should he waste his talents on these matters when he could play the intricate political games at the king's court and thereby increase family land and wealth?

Unfortunately, the question reminded him of the matter he must discuss with prickly Ralf. He rubbed his eyes and groaned.

"You are troubled, my lord?"

Turning to see Father Eliduc nearby, Fulke swallowed a curse. The fellow made him uneasy.

The man in black smiled.

Could the creature read thoughts? Fulke instinctively shut his eyes to protect his soul. Maybe this man was no priest at all, but rather Satan's liegeman instead of God's. For an instant, the sheriff hoped that was the case and wondered if God would forgive him if he throttled Eliduc.

The priest's left eyebrow twitched upward.

Despite the heat, Fulke shivered and quickly replied, "I was only thinking about how we should proceed on this visit for the benefit of our queen." In silence he prayed that both words and tone were sufficiently bland to prevent any discomfiting interpretation.

The priest folded his hands and bowed his head.

Although the gesture was innocuous enough, the sheriff's throat went dry. He looked away. What was it about this man that made him want to flee? Fulke had met many other priests who served mighty Church lords, dressed in soft robes, and rode fine horses. This one was different. What was it? Inhaling deeply, he realized that, despite the hot journey, Father Eliduc did not even stink like a mortal man.

"Ah!"

Startled, Fulke gasped.

Eliduc nodded at something behind the sheriff. "Young Simon comes nigh." His tone was edged with warning.

Angry to be caught off-guard, the sheriff knew his face had flushed. Vulnerability in a man was a failing for which Fulke felt contempt. In himself, he despised it even more. Spinning around, he frowned at the approaching youth and snapped, "What problem do you have?"

"My mother begs a mercy of you, my lords. A frail woman, she has been wearied by the long journey and begs that the queen's business be delayed until tomorrow."

Although normally amenable to the needs of Eve's delicate daughters, the sheriff found this plea too much for his brittle patience and glared at the youth, willing him to tremble.

Simon glowered back.

Fulke clenched his teeth. Traitor's whelp! Surely King Edward's queen had other priests, nobles, and ladies who were capable of confirming proper lodging along the pilgrimage route. Why had he been cursed with the leadership of such an ill-assorted and ill-favored party, and why had Queen Eleanor even chosen to stop at this remote priory when Norwich was near enough? He bit back a spirited oath.

Father Eliduc smiled with benevolence at the young man. "Please assure your mother that we will wait on the morrow. I will come visit her soon for prayer and shall beg God to grant her a good night's rest. I am sure the priory fare will also help to renew her strength."

Simon nodded with due reverence at the priest's response and started to turn away. Suddenly he stopped and spat on the hoof of Fulke's horse. Without even a glance at the sheriff, he marched off with an arrogant swagger in the direction of the guest quarters.

The sheriff reached for his sword.

The priest laid a hand on his arm. "This is God's land, Sir Fulke. Remember Simon's youth and circumstances. Forgive, as He requires." Even if Eliduc's tone was soft, there was sharp iron in his meaning. Then he nodded to the sheriff and followed after Avelina's son.

Slamming his weapon back into its scabbard, Fulke tried to regain calm by repeating to himself that Simon could strut all he wanted. Nothing would change the young cur's lack of standing in the world despite his mother's best efforts. Were it not for Lady Avelina's pitiful living from those dower lands she had retained, he would not even have food to put into his impertinent mouth or clothes to cover his skinny nakedness.

Simon was fortunate his mother's family had wisely supported King Henry throughout the de Montfort rebellion. After the youth's father was slain at the earl's side in the battle at Evesham, the king had taken away all lands and the title, leaving Simon with nothing. The only inheritance passed on to the boy was the shame of a dishonorable sire, the curse of having Simon de Montfort for a godfather, and that traitor's name. The thought almost made Fulke smile.

These facts meant more to the sheriff than any demands for Christian charity. This once he would refrain from striking the lad's head with the flat of his sword for the insult of spitting on his horse. He might not be so charitable should Simon dare to defy him again.

Voices interrupted Fulke's thoughts and he looked up.

Two lay brothers walked toward him.

"At last you have come," Fulke said, making sure his annoyance was evident to the approaching men.

A louder voice grew more demanding.

The lay brothers abruptly changed direction and went to Baron Otes.

While the baron roared for assistance, his servant gestured frantically at the horse. The pitiful beast did look as if its legs were ready to buckle.

Nodding their understanding, the lay brothers eased Otes out of his saddle with deliberate care. Soon, the nobleman's feet were firmly settled on God's earth.

The horse snapped at his former rider. The gesture was indifferent and missed its mark by a foot.

Otes jumped away with impressive alacrity.

Had Fulke not been so exasperated, he might have laughed. "The animal should have bitten him," he fumed. "And if God were merciful, the wound would have festered. Satan could have had his company then and the horse my blessing."

As if he had overheard Fulke, the baron looked up, caught the sheriff's eye, and stared like a hawk hovering over a mouse.

Fulke willed himself to turn around and focus on the abhorrent moss covering the priory walls behind him. His heart filled with bitterness. Why had the Devil failed to lay claim to the baron's wicked soul? Or was God to blame for this delay?

He looked heavenward and hissed, "How can You allow the man to live? It would be unjust if one of his victims was hanged for taking revenge because of the baron's crimes."

Then terror struck him with an ague. Crossing himself, he wondered whether there was an ominous meaning in the baron's stare. Perhaps the man had decided it was now Fulke's turn for destruction.

Anger over the baron's profitable use of extortion was quickly extinguished by the waters of remorse. As Fulke well knew, it was his own fault for owning a secret this ruthless man could use against him.

Chapter Six

Eleanor was deeply troubled. Either the heat had chased away her reason or her heart did have cause to pound so.

Realizing she was panting with exertion, she slowed her determined rush along the path to the hospital and put a hand over her breast. As she took in a deep breath of hot air, the prioress willed her heart to a softer thudding. Then she abruptly halted. Looking across the priory grounds, familiar landmarks shimmered.

Were her eyes bewitched, or was she was going to faint? "You shall not," she commanded, and her body stiffened like a reprimanded soldier.

She changed direction and left the path, walking at a more moderate pace toward the monks' cemetery. A visit to the sick might not be wise until she had calmed sufficiently to think more of their needs than her own concerns. Just because Father Eliduc was an unexpected member of the queen's company, she should not feel such turmoil.

Of course she had cause to distrust him. After discovering how he had lied about the true nature of his visits to Brother Thomas, with piteous tales of the monk's dying kin, she grew outraged. It was such shameful abuse of her compassion.

She had seen the priest once thereafter and sent him on his way without the slightest tremor of unease. That day, her only emotion was unrepentant glee when she told Eliduc that her monk could not travel this time to care for some sick relative.

Brother Thomas had vowed to become the hermit of Tyndal and emulate a desert father because the weight of his sins had become unbearable. Today, the arrival of the priest had inexplicably frightened her.

Eleanor was not so naïve as to think she had ultimately chased him away after his last visit, nor was she so foolish as to conclude that this devious man was less skilled in clever ploys than she. She should not be shocked he had come back to Tyndal. Instead, she must ask the significance of his inclusion with these envoys from the queen. Perhaps the priest's influence was more extensive than she had imagined. If it extended to the new king and his consort, both she and her family must be wary.

As Eleanor pushed through the tangled grasses, she recalled she was not the only one to react with shock when the queen's envoys arrived. Prior Andrew had stumbled backward, when the members of the party dismounted to greet Tyndal's religious, and had even cried out.

Although he claimed to have stepped awkwardly, Eleanor noticed his eyes bulge and his face pale as if he had seen Satan himself. A man who fought at Evesham and survived a near-fatal wound would not respond like this to some lightly sprained ankle. The cause must be deeper. Terror seemed likely.

Unless a man's secrets posed some threat to her priory, Eleanor was inclined to leave them to the ears of confessors. Andrew might explain later and in private. She doubted it and suspected the reason for his lie was more than an attempt to conceal pain from a lame leg.

Was his reaction also caused by seeing Father Eliduc, or was it brought about by something else? Did Prior Andrew even know the man? She tried to recall if he had met the priest. While still a monk and porter at the gates of Tyndal, he had probably greeted Eliduc. It was odd that the prior had never mentioned this to her.

As she reflected more, there was one incident that seemed unusual. When Father Eliduc came to tell Brother Thomas that his father had died, just before the journey to Amesbury two years ago, Eleanor had offered him the hospitality of Prior

Andrew's quarters. Eliduc quickly refused, claiming another obligation required him to leave Tyndal that day. Since the hour was late and other accommodation some distance away, his excuse struck her as odd. He might have told the truth. Eleanor believed it more likely he had lied.

She would be wise to consider whether the two men did know each other and had cause to keep their acquaintance secret. As she thought more on this, she feared she might have to seek the truth behind Prior Andrew's outwardly simple lie today after all.

"May God have mercy on me," Eleanor murmured as a frightening idea struck her. "Surely the good prior is not another spy in my priory."

She had now arrived at the low stone boundary wall of the cemetery. Before entering, Eleanor banished her new worries about the loyalties of priors and the worldly schemes of priests. These were temporal matters, and she had a vow to honor, one made for the good of her immortal soul.

◇◇◇

The graves of Tyndal's monks were simple things, some gently rounded and others sunk into the earth. Few were marked, perhaps as a final act of humility, although those who had loved the dying found ways to remember where they were put in the earth. As the prioress continued on, she noted an apothecary rose, planted long before she had arrived to honor a monk whose name she had never learned.

Briefly she wondered how all the loved ones would recognize each other at the Resurrection. She had been taught that every one of the dead would rise aged thirty-three, reflecting Jesus' years on earth at the time of his crucifixion. "One of God's many miracles," she murmured and set the question aside.

For an instant she stood with eyes closed, savoring the tranquility of the moment. The grass was so green here. How quiet it was as well. Perhaps this peace was how God's earth honored the bodies it held in trust until the Day of Judgement. The thought was most certainly pleasing.

Since she had come in search of one particular burial place, she continued walking toward a corner near the far edge of the cemetery. There, under a shrub half-dead from the sea air, the grave lay. It was marked by a roughly rounded stone on which three words were chiseled in shallow, crude lettering.

Ora pro me.

In obedience to that supplication, Prioress Eleanor fell to her knees in the thick undergrowth, reverently folded her hands, and began to pray.

In the distance, mews cried out to each other, odd and amusing with their shrill, querulous ways. Insects buzzed and clicked in soothing rhythm close by. When her prayers were finally ended, Eleanor kept her eyes shut. A sighing breeze brushed against her cheeks.

"Ah, Prior Theobald," she whispered to the sunken grave in front of her. "After the term of my vow ends, I shall continue to pray for the relief of your soul. When I do so, I remember how quickly we forsake humility and charity, called a greater virtue than faith, and cling to sinful arrogance. How often have I assumed that I knew best? How often do any of us fail to beg for enlightenment before we condemn out of ignorance? Thus do we blind ourselves to our own wickedness by assuming we know better than God."

She opened her eyes and glanced to her left. Just outside the hallowed ground, so close against the wall that it might almost seem to beg for entry, lay another grave: small, unmarked, and covered with noxious weeds.

Brother Simeon was buried there, a tortured man in life whose cries from Hell she often thought she heard, especially when icy winds from the north pushed black storms across the sea.

Prayers for the damned were useless, as Eleanor well knew. Nonetheless, she did sometimes beg God to grant some small mercy to the dead monk. No matter how wicked Simeon had been, she found pity in her heart for the boy who had become such a man. Although God might ignore her pleas, her woman's soul felt better for having made them.

"Despite your failings," Eleanor said, turning her attention back to the grave of the man who had been prior when she first arrived, "you were humble enough about your sins. When you begged to be buried, face to the ground, outside the church with the common monks, many here were outraged. They cried out that a prior must be buried in the chapter house, on his back and prepared to rise with the virtuous on the Day of Judgement. Despite their roaring, I honored your plea with one difference. Although you may have been a weak man, your heart longed for God and was never cruel. For this reason, I ordered that your head must face the church altar. May my successor find me worthy of the same mercy when my soul flies to His judgement."

Her prayers finished, Eleanor leaned back on her heels and let her thoughts return to worldly problems.

The rumbling of the mill wheel now grew louder, drowning out melodic birdsong and humming insects. Even the grass looked more wilted in the summer heat than it had but a moment ago.

The prioress sighed, then gazed beyond the cemetery wall to where the new guest quarters had been constructed. At least she was confident all was well there. By now, the lay brothers should have curried the company's horses and would feed them when the beasts had cooled down from their long day's journey. The guests of rank had jugs of wine for refreshment. As for the company's armed escort, those men had been sent to lodge in the nearby village inn.

Signy, who inherited the business after her uncle died from a virulent winter fever, had continued his practice of providing good food and drink for reasonable cost. Although the young woman now draped herself in simple, dark robes to mourn her uncle's death, she could not hide her beauty. Even after the guards discovered that her virtue was as stunning as her face, Eleanor knew they would be far happier in Signy's care than they would be in any priory.

Calmer now, Eleanor stood and turned away from the grave of Prior Andrew's predecessor. "I have overreacted to the arrival of Father Eliduc," she firmly admonished herself. "Considering the rank of his lord, his inclusion in this mission should not have caused me either undue fear or surprise."

It was the rest of the company that merited more of her attention if her priory were to gain anything of value from this proposed visit. Rather than worry about one priest, she would be well-advised to recall what she knew or had observed about others, beginning with the leader of this group.

Sir Fulke had voiced all the right phrases when he greeted her, even if he seemed in bad temper, almost rude, and definitely impatient to get on with some matter or other. At least she had Ralf's word that his brother bore her no ill-will and would be vexed solely because he was too far from the king's side. "If God is merciful, and I am both brief and pithy," she said, "the sheriff should prove agreeable rather than petty over the comforts Tyndal has to offer."

As for Lady Avelina and her son, Eleanor had learned their history from her own father. When she saw the lady on arrival, the prioress felt much sympathy for her, although little for the pouting Simon. The woman's face had been grey with fatigue. Instead of showing filial concern, the young man had abandoned all care of his mother to her mute servant.

The prioress shuddered. Was his name *Kenard?* Something about the man made her uncomfortable. Many would conclude his muteness was an indication of God's condemnation. Although she did not always concur with common reasoning, he did remind her of some hellish cauldron, bubbling with tension. Maybe it was just his eyes, hooded like those of a bird of prey, which made her uneasy. Or was he truly cursed?

"In any case, the man servant is not my concern," she reminded herself, "nor is the thoughtless youth. It is Lady Avelina who will have the most questions about the queen's comfort in the priory."

Eleanor felt reasonably confident she could convince the lady that Tyndal was worthy. After all, Sister Matilda could cook almost anything to taste like manna, and Sister Ruth would make sure the beds felt as if they were stuffed with angel feathers.

Baron Otes was the last problem, and she doubted he cared much about anything here. In his eyes, she was only the leader of a minor priory with little enough income to interest such a courtier. Perhaps he had come on this journey simply to prove he had the king's favor. She hoped his presence did not mean he was using the time to extort something from another member of the party who held some sad secret. Her father has told her about this as well.

Continuing along the path, Eleanor noticed that the breeze coming from the sea had shifted. Inhaling, she felt a cool moistness, then saw the clouds growing thicker as they scudded across the sky. "All bodes well for showers," she murmured, "something that would bring some relief, however brief."

Her spirits began to lift, and she firmly resolved to banish all remaining fear of Father Eliduc. Perhaps he had come with some special demand involving Brother Thomas. Once again, she must refuse to be manipulated by whatever lies he had concocted.

With grim amusement, she imagined his expression when she told him that Brother Thomas remained a hermit and unable to attend the deathbed of any putative kin. Not even a priest would dare tear an unwilling hermit from his hut, although she suspected a man who served the Church's more secular interests might still attempt to do so. Were Eliduc to try, she would delight in describing the certain force of God's wrath should he persist.

Eleanor found herself looking forward to such an encounter.

Then she saw Brother Beorn coming down the path toward her, the lay brother's somber expression even darker than usual.

With fresh trepidation, she paused until he reached her side and then granted him the requested permission to speak.

"Baron Otes begs an audience, my lady," he said. "Shall I send for our sub-prioress to join you in your chambers?"

Chapter Seven

Ralf swatted through the cloud of midges swarming around his head as he walked the path along the stream. Whatever relief he had gained from the swim with Brother Thomas had quickly vanished. Even his sweat now failed to cool him.

"May Satan roast that infernal pig," he muttered.

A swineherd had claimed one of his sows was missing and insisted someone had stolen it. Although it was not part of a crowner's official duties, Ralf had agreed to hunt for the beast. After spending too long in the sun searching for that cloven-hoofed lump of lard, he finally found her, joyfully wallowing in a cool patch of mud. The curses Ralf directed at the swineherd might have been hellish enough to increase the day's heat.

He slapped his cheek. Glancing at his palm, he saw a smear of blood. "I'm at least swift enough," he said. "Had the damnable thing bitten my brother's flesh, it might have lived longer." Wiping his hand on his sleeve, he trudged on.

Ralf had never harbored much fraternal affection for his eldest brother, although he honored him as head of the family and was glad enough Fulke had been the one born first. The man was better suited than he to playing political chess games for worldly gain, an acknowledgment the crowner had no difficulty making.

"And he is usually more honest than our Odo," he conceded with some reluctance, then kicked at a rock in his way to compensate for the admission. Contempt for their middle brother was one of the few things Ralf and Fulke shared.

When it came to gratitude to the sheriff for arranging his appointment as crowner here, Ralf was of two minds. There was no question that he loved this land, and, before King Henry's death, Ralf had been allowed to perform his duties with little interference from Fulke, who was pleased not to have to soil his boots with East Anglian mud. After the old king died, the sheriff had begun to meddle, and Ralf was not happy with the change. So far he had been able to cope with it.

He hoped that situation would continue, although he had heard tales enough to trouble him. The new king, Edward, was intolerant of his father's lax ways in matters of the law. Of course Ralf agreed that corrupt sheriffs should be removed and the rule of law be honored. What he did not like was being told exactly how he should enforce the codes and the precise definition of justice.

Then his thoughts moved on to even less comfortable matters, and he grunted with the sharp pain the memory brought him. The time when his world had shattered and Tyndal village became unbearable had been relegated to dreams. Acknowledging that Fulke had ever shown compassion for him remained an arduous thing. Although he tried to convince himself that it was his sister-in-law alone who forced her husband to show kindness, Ralf was honest enough to admit gratitude was due Fulke even if he kept the moment both unspoken and brief.

"In truth, my cursed brother did take me in," the crowner growled. Then he spat out a few insects that had flown into his mouth. "His price may have been a land-rich and gloomy marriage, but I got my daughter from it." What he did not like to think on was that the cost of the babe had been her mother's life. "The lady deserved a far better husband than this rude man," he muttered, his heart aching with remorse as it always did when he thought about his dead wife.

Squeezing his eyes shut, he banished the memory even if he was unable to outlaw tears. He stopped, wiped his eyes with his sleeve, and realized he had reached the end of the path.

He was standing at the edge of that land he had gained from his brief marriage. Although mostly hidden from view, the house was not far and he could just see the rooftop above the brush. All this would be his daughter's one day, and he worked hard to make sure the land brought his beloved Sibely wealth enough by the time she finally reached marriageable age.

Or rather his bailiff and sergeant, Cuthbert, did. Unlike Ralf, that man was far happier farming and overseeing the construction of buildings than he ever was hunting miscreants, which was well enough as far as Ralf was concerned. Other than wayward sows, there were few real crimes to disturb the peace here, even though the reputation of Tyndal's hospital was attracting many strangers. Some violence was inevitable. Most of the time, Cuthbert could remain happy especially now he had married his beloved lass.

As for happiness, that emotion had been a rare guest in Ralf's heart before his daughter was born and taught him to laugh and even sing. The latter pleased only Sibely, but he cared not as long as his voice delighted her. Ralf fiercely cherished the time spent with his child. Was his newly discovered peace about to be destroyed by his accursed brother?

When Fulke sent word about this visit to the priory, he had hinted that he had another profitable marriage planned for his youngest brother. The arrival of the sheriff made the crowner feel like an apple about to be invaded by some ravenous worm.

Ralf clenched his fists. He would not agree to this union. He had paid his debt for any kindness his brother had given him. Head lowered, he stomped toward the house like some tormented bull, his humors shifting from choler to melancholy.

Then he heard a woman's laugh and looked up.

Gytha stood in the doorway, his daughter in her arms. Beside her, the maid was playing peek-a-boo with the child.

His mood brightened, and he ran the rest of the way to the house.

"My little beauty!" Ralf took Sibely into his arms and raised her up so she could touch the sky.

"Any higher and she'll need wings," Gytha teased.

"Da!" the child giggled and grabbed at her father's hair when he lowered her for a kiss.

"You have a guest within, Master Crowner," the maid said, her voice signifying reluctance at being the bearer of such news.

Ralf looked at Gytha.

"A man who claims to be your eldest brother. I did believe him for his face bore a likeness to yours, although I fear it also bore a most disagreeable expression," she said in a soft voice. "I brought him enough cider to mellow his ill humor and food as well. Nothing seemed to please him. I hope his arrival does not mean…"

"Trouble?" The crowner scowled. "Aye, I fear he usually brings it." Hugging his child, Ralf passed her back, with more unwillingness than usual, into the arms of Gytha.

His forehead deeply furrowed, he strode through the door.

Fulke sat on a bench with his feet off the floor. A bowl of small wood strawberries next to a fine cheese lay untouched on the table. He glared at his brother with evident disgust.

In the spirit of that greeting, Ralf scowled back.

"The whore is comely enough for a Saxon, brother, but I had hoped you'd choose a creature of better birth for your leman."

Flint could not have sparked fire quicker than the time it took for Ralf to wrap his hands around his brother's throat.

Fulke's eyes bulged with the need for air, and he impotently swung his fists in defense.

"You bawd!" Ralf roared. "She is Tostig's sister!"

"Remember Cain and Abel, Master Crowner," Gytha cried out from the doorway. "Might you not regret killing your brother—someday?"

He shoved Fulke onto the dirt floor, and then wiped his boots on the man as he lay gasping. "Aye, you have the right of it, Mistress Gytha. Were I to murder the badling, I would spend eternity with him in Hell instead of having some hope of Purgatory and a more peaceful torment."

"You show wisdom in that logic, good sir," she replied.

"He insulted you. I shall not tolerate it." Ralf folded his arms and watched his brother's cheeks fade from a shade much like that of ripe plums.

"For defending my honor, my lord, I am grateful to you. Remember that God does teach that truth will vanquish all of Satan's lies in time." Gytha smiled. "I have stayed overlong in visiting your daughter's maid and must return to Prioress Eleanor's service." With a mischievous wink, Gytha gave the crowner obeisance proper to their difference in rank and disappeared out the door.

Ralf knew he was grinning like a boy.

Fulke had pulled himself back onto the bench and was reaching for a mazer. "Assault on king's man. Arrest you," he croaked, rubbing uselessly at the muck on his robe left by his brother's foot. "Filth. Costly."

"Honest dirt. More honest than the night soil you roll in at court. As for arresting me, think again about the consequences. You claim that no rational man would ever live in this land. If you did not have me as your crowner, King Edward might insist you take up residence in Tyndal village in my stead." He looked into the jug and poured his brother some cider. "This is better drink than you deserve."

With a grimace, Fulke swallowed it and held out the mazer for more.

Ralf drew the jug back. "What did you say or do to Tostig's sister before I arrived?"

"Little enough."

"She is Prioress Eleanor's maid, you pocky boor. If you so much as brushed her robe…"

"A lay sister?" To his credit, Fulke paled.

"Nay, but she was a virgin before you came here."

"And remains so."

Ralf poured more into the cup and set the jug down. "Why did you come to trouble me?"

Fulke swallowed with a wince. "Your daughter needs a proper mother. I have a wife for you."

"To be more precise, you have hatched another plot involving land."

"Richer ground for farming and located in a place better suited to the raising of sheep. Even your befuddled wits must understand that wool is profitable."

"What advantage comes to you from this?"

He shrugged. "Did you care the last time I found a suitable wife for you?"

"You do naught unless you benefit. I later learned my wife's brother sided with you on a scheme that brought you both increased wealth."

"And did your marriage bring you nothing you value?" Fulke replied, brushing aside his brother's accusation with a sweep of his hand.

Ralf nodded readily enough as he gestured toward the sound of his daughter's voice outside.

"Your child, of course," Fulke said, "and this lovely bit of muck as well, near the village you so adore. All of which, I must remind you, reverts to your daughter and her husband when she comes of an age to marry. I hope you are making use of the income now to buy land for yourself."

"Any profit is used to improve my daughter's birthright from her mother. As for me, I earned enough spoils from my days as a mercenary to live on."

"Live like a wild boar, you mean. You need another wife with land who can bear sons, Ralf, or are your wits so addled that you have forgotten how a man is best served by seeding boys in fertile women?"

"Then do your duty, brother, and leave me alone."

"My wife has birthed many dead babes and now seems no longer able to bear. Odo has either truly chosen chastity or else hides his bastards. It seems God has cursed our family. Whatever I might prefer in this matter, our very survival lies in your loins. If it makes you happier, I would have chosen the matter to be otherwise."

Ralf looked away.

"I promise you she is a good woman. You and I may be ill-matched as brothers, but I have never abused you."

"Not since I grew tall enough to abuse you back." The crowner gazed at his hands. "Nay, the woman you had me wed was a better creature than I deserved. I do not doubt that this current one is much the same."

"Then you agree?" Fulke's eyes widened with delight.

"I refuse." Ralf stood up and walked to the door, closing it firmly.

"Surely you have not become besotted, once again, with Anne, the physician's daughter…"

"…who married John and took vows with him at Tyndal Priory? Nay." He leaned his back against the door.

"Then what objection could you possibly have for rejecting a profitable alliance which also brings your child a mother?"

"My reason is simple enough. When I agreed to your first marriage arrangement, I was indebted to you for finding me a place at court when I needed refuge. That debt has been repaid, and now I have no reason to agree to another of your schemes. Should I choose to marry again, I shall do as I please. If God wishes our family to thrive and grants sons of my body, they will come from a wife of my choosing."

"Not from here!" With a look of horror, Fulke gestured at the ground as if he expected a barely human creature to spring from the dust. "Surely you jest? You must have met someone suitable in Norwich," he added hopefully. "If so, let me speak with her family."

Ralf shook his head.

"You cannot wed beneath your rank. Third son though you may be, you are still my brother. Since I am head of this family, you are obligated to obey me, and I will not allow you to wed without my approval!"

"Think again, sweet brother. The little I inherited at our father's death, I gave over to you when I left England. What I own in my name alone, I earned from the sharpness of my sword, if not my wits. As for obligation, I wed once at your behest and you did profit well enough methinks. If there is anything owed between us, you are the debtor, not I."

Fulke fell silent and stared warily at the crowner. "What do you think I owe you, brother?"

"My silence," Ralf replied, his lips twisting into a thin smile.

Chapter Eight

"Sir Hugh saw our party off and sends his greetings, my lady."

With a gracious smile, Eleanor conveyed her appreciation of the baron's message, although she was surprised to hear her eldest brother had returned to court so quickly. Their father had included nothing about this when he last sent news, saying only that Hugh had safely arrived in England not long after the king.

The ruddy-faced Otes now turned his attention to the sub-prioress, honoring her with a flash of his widely spaced teeth. "And I had the pleasure of a brief word with your brother before I left the king's side."

Sister Ruth blushed.

Seeing her adversary turn bashful over a common civility amused Eleanor, although she acknowledged that this response was mildly sinful, unquestionably uncharitable, and ought to be dismissed with stern resolve. Her effort was not as swift as virtue required.

Now that formal courtesies had been observed, the prioress hoped to learn what profit the baron expected to gain from this meeting. She assumed she would not have to wait long to discover it.

"My lady, I am a man burdened with my sins."

An honest enough beginning, she noted in silence, for the baron had more than his share of faults. Inclining her head, she wisely kept her own counsel and politely suggested that all earthly creatures were flawed.

"I fear my soul shall be found unworthy when God calls me to Him."

Most likely the Devil, Eleanor thought, and then quickly moderated her unkindness with a firm reminder that God always forgave the truly repentant. Men often found their hearts filled with remorse for wicked deeds when they felt their souls striving to escape over-ripened flesh. Although she had no quarrel with this, she chose to be like the good sailor, who wisely suspects that coastal fog hides treacherous rocks, and remained wary of the man's expressed atonement.

"I came on this journey with a twofold purpose."

And so the circling of his real prey grows tighter, the prioress concluded with a nod of encouragement.

"When Queen Eleanor asked me to travel her proposed pilgrimage route, I agreed at once, knowing she values my opinion most highly." His sigh conveyed the immense responsibility such a regal appeal entailed. "When I first learned she had included a stay at Tyndal, I was quite perplexed until I did realize that this remote priory could be a proper destination for a pilgrim, even one of her rank."

There is less honey than sour wine in those phrases, the prioress thought.

"I began to hear talk of its saintly infirmarian and an anchoress as well. Now I have learned that you have a blessed hermit nearby."

Eleanor lowered her gaze, hoping to convey modesty while praying she could hide her anger at such thin courtesy and poor flattery. Not that more skillful praise would have fooled her, even though clever phrasing did entertain, but the baron had offended with his insufficiently veiled disdain. Even if she set her own pride aside, a prioress represented the Queen of Heaven in the Order of Fontevraud, and Eleanor would not so easily dismiss the insult to her office. She chose to counter the offence with a cautious and suitable response. Raising her head, she graced him a look of contrived benevolence to match his false smile.

He had misjudged more than the sharpness of her wits. Although King Edward and his queen favored other Orders, the king's ancestors had always looked fondly on their Angevin Order, and many were buried in the mother house of Fontevraud

Abbey. The king would be displeased should he learn of any insult given to one of its prioresses, and the baron might discover that his alleged status in court had diminished when he returned.

Baron Otes was a fool.

She patiently awaited the full revelation of his intent.

"With so many signs of holiness at Tyndal, I saw possible merit if I offered your priory some gift in return for the nuns' prayers after my death." He put a hand to his breast. "As you must know, I am a man whom God has favored with worldly riches."

Eleanor felt her interest quicken, then reined it in with caution. Without question, her priory suffered an ongoing need for income to feed the religious and care for the suffering as God demanded. Some in her position cared little what a gift cost in sin if it brought better wine to the priory table. Eleanor was not one of them. She believed some offerings came at a price incompatible with the demands of faith.

Nonetheless, she was also a practical woman and prepared to offer guarded appreciation. She waited for Otes to tell her all he expected in return for his proposed beneficence.

"In obedience to our Lord's command that we perform the charities encompassed in the Seven Comfortable Acts," he continued, "I thought to give this priory a bit of land. The income from it would provide enough to care for and feed some needy few, but I would also require that the nuns of the priory pray daily for my soul's swift release from Purgatory."

"You are most generous, my lord, and I do thank you for this offer. Most of our nuns are sequestered and spend hours in fervent prayer for souls. A gift of profitable land pays for the fare that sustains them. As for the poor, it is our duty to care for them, and your grant …"

"Of course, my lady, but another, who must remain anonymous, has also shown interest in this property and has sworn to put the needs of my soul before the feeding of the poor should the crops fail in any particular year." Once again, his hand went to his breast. "I fear my many sins demand priority."

Eleanor stiffened, then decided she could easily devise some plan to continue feeding the poor while also supporting the nuns needed to pray for this man's spotted soul. "I can promise that our prayers shall be equally devoted to shortening your time in Purgatory."

He bowed. "Might you also swear to offer pleas on my behalf in perpetuity to God? That provision was not included by the other interested party."

She agreed without hesitation.

Then he folded his arms, his eyes glittering

Eleanor was reminded of a snake, basking in the sun.

"There is one other matter which must be resolved before I grant title of this generous gift to Tyndal Priory."

Eleanor silently ran through the usual list of stipulations attached to bequests of this nature and knew she could accept most.

"You have given refuge to a traitor's kin."

Stunned, she was rendered speechless.

He stared at her, waiting for a gasp of horror. When his comment was greeted with continued silence, he scowled. "I fear that King Edward might misconstrue any gift I give you as my approval of such betrayal to kingship."

"I am quite ignorant of your meaning, my lord," Eleanor said at last. Although she knew she had concealed it, she was shocked by this accusation. Glancing at Sister Ruth's blank expression, she saw that the sub-prioress was just as unacquainted with the news as she. "What traitor's kin do you think we harbor?"

Otes looked appalled. "You do not know?"

Most certainly I do not, she thought. Then with great relief she realized that the baron must have heard false rumor about her prior.

Andrew, before he took vows, had fought in Simon de Montfort's army. When she first arrived as Tyndal's prioress, the monk had confessed this past to her, knowing her father had remained loyal to King Henry. As they were obliged to do under God's commandments, they forgave each other for any offenses committed by themselves or kin. Soon thereafter they had learned mutual respect. After Prior Theobald's death, she had prayed that Andrew would be elected to replace him.

"Surely you do not mean Prior Andrew," Eleanor replied at last. "He received a pardon after the battle at Evesham on condition he expiate his sins by entering a monastery, as he himself had ardently requested. Perhaps you had not learned that information."

Sister Ruth gasped.

The prioress bit back a groan. Although Sister Ruth would never spread rumors amongst the nuns, she'd not treat this knowledge with tact or compassion and would make sure Prior Andrew suffered her scorn. Eleanor regretted this had been revealed in her hearing. On the other hand, considering Sister Ruth's reverent attitude toward any of high rank, a reminder that the present king's uncle had pardoned Andrew might be sufficient to dull the woman's sharp tongue.

Eleanor grew ever more eager to conclude this increasingly unpleasant audience.

Baron Otes licked his lips as if savoring the taste of roasted venison. "Although Prior Andrew might have been forgiven, his elder brother was not, and it fell to me to execute him. For my loyal obedience to our anointed king, this prior of yours vowed to murder me."

An icy stillness filled the room like snowfall at the midnight hour.

This was news of which she most certainly did not have knowledge. Eleanor tucked her hands into her sleeves and gripped her arms with such ferocity that she feared she'd bruised herself. To give herself another moment to respond, she gave the baron a stern look.

"If that is the case, my lord, I must ask why you considered offering any gift at all to this priory."

"I believed that you would understand both the value of my gift and the need to rid your priory of a man who has shown disloyalty to a rightful king and has sworn to break one of God's commandments."

"And thus your gift is contingent upon my willingness to arrange the banishment of Prior Andrew from this house?" Eleanor began to smell something sharp in the air. Considering the day's heat, she might have concluded that the odor was honest sweat. She now suspected it was the stench of cruel arrogance emanating from the baron.

Otes nodded. "The land is very rich."

"Then I must refuse your most generous offer, my lord. Perhaps you were not told this: the man who issued the pardon was close kin to our King Edward. Soon after, Prior Andrew took vows and swore allegiance to God and all His commandments. Although he may have uttered menacing words after the execution of his brother, I see you before me many years later and in good health." Her smile was fleeting. "Since he has not acted on that threat and has long been a dutiful servant of God, I conclude he has regretted, confessed, and done penance for those heated words."

"He recognized me when I arrived, and his look belied such a conclusion."

"Have you seen him since?"

With evident reluctance Otes shook his head.

"I did not think so. After your arrival, he begged leave to retire to the monk's quarters so he could pray in the chapel." She shook her head. "You have given me no reason to doubt his continued devotion to those vows he willingly took long ago."

Otes started to speak and then seemed to think better of it.

The prioress rose.

Seeing the grim expression on her face, even the baron dared not argue that his requested audience had just concluded.

Chapter Nine

Brother Thomas reached up to lift the cloth-covered, woven basket off the hook above the door of his hut, then bent to retrieve the pottery jug of fresh ale. This daily offering of food and drink was meant to be anonymous. It might have been, had the gift been left by an adult more skilled in deception. When he saw little Nute disappear down the road, he knew the donor was Signy from the inn.

The woman's charity had never surprised him, for he had gotten to know her best at the time Martin the Cooper was poisoned. Her gifts of sustenance after Thomas entered this hut as a hermit were indicative of her frequent small graces. Many who suffered as she had turned inward and bitter. She had softened with kindness. Although he was thankful for her benevolence, he was more grateful she had found peace. He had grown fond of the new innkeeper.

Pushing open the door, Thomas stepped inside.

The hut was tiny, but it pleased him. Ivetta the Whore had lived here until her death during the last summer season. When he begged permission to spend some time in solitude, hoping to earn God's guidance in dealing with his own tormenting sins, he decided her former lodging would be most appropriate. That no one understood his choice mattered little to him. He knew the reason, and he was content to let others come to whatever conclusions they wished.

On first arrival here, he saw that the roof had collapsed and tall weeds were taking firm hold in the ground between the slanting walls. The hut had never been well-built, and he was grateful. Each morning he awoke, rejoicing in the prospect of strengthening the walls, restoring the roof, building a small altar, and finally crafting the rough bench and table where he ate.

In the spring, he had planted a small garden just outside his door. Some of the vegetables he ate himself. Most he gave to the needy. And to honor the desert fathers, whom he was determined to emulate for now, he had let his hair and beard grow wild. The sight of him did frighten young Nute. That was his only regret.

Thomas was unsure what this time alone had accomplished. He was not a man suited to long silence or the rejection of human companionship. Despite the Church's belief that there was much virtue in such a life, he dared to question the idea, his soul being a most contrary thing. Yet he was so wretched that he was willing to try almost anything once lest he miss what God wanted to teach him.

He had not been left completely alone, although he discouraged local visitors and sent the poor travelers he was obliged to shelter on their way as soon as was meet. Brother John came often to hear his confessions, and Thomas also urged him to return to the priory as quickly as courtesy and kindness allowed. The novice master might be compassionate, but Thomas hesitated to confess his specific agonies to him, as he had to other priests. No matter how dark Brother John believed his own sins to be, Thomas knew him to be a good man who suffered simpler lusts.

Only God could heal Thomas, and he was waiting for Him to explain why the act of sodomy was a grave sin while lying in arms of another man filled him with such peace and so much love. Although God might not have graced him with an answer, he believed He had not minded the question and would respond in time. Patience was a virtue the monk was trying to learn.

As he sat down on the bench and stared at the crude cross hung from a slim rafter over the altar, he could not suppress the bitterness that too often assaulted his heart. Squeezing his eyes shut, he put all his strength into fighting back. "Get thee behind me, Satan," he growled. "I know I am a flawed creature. Go trouble those who deem themselves otherwise."

The heavy darkness inched back, leaving Thomas exhausted from the struggle. Bending forward, he rested his head in his hands and wept.

When his sobs ended and Thomas sat up, questions began buzzing in his head like bees outside a hive. Was a hermit's life no longer the path he should be traveling? If not, what was he supposed to do next? Abandon this place, return to the priory, and again take up his work at the hospital?

At least that work had often given him solace, he thought. And he was growing ever more uneasy when others looked on him as some holy creature because he was a hermit. He shuddered. For a sinner to be called a saint was surely a travesty of all that was holy.

And why had Ralf chosen this day to visit? Perhaps the decision to do so had meant something. When Thomas took residence here, the crowner avoided him. A few months ago, Thomas might have even turned Ralf away. Today his old friend arrived at his hut, despite fearing that the monk would not welcome the sight of him, and Thomas had been filled with delight when he saw the crowner in the doorway. Walking down to the pond for a swim, they had talked together much as they were wont to do in the past.

Something had changed. God might be pointing out some new path for him to take. When next Brother John came to see him, Thomas would seek his advice in the matter. Signs from God were things with which the novice master had had much experience, and Thomas could ask his counsel without misgivings.

He had been musing too long and had not knelt to honor God since rising at dawn. "As penance, I shall delay my one meal until after the next Office." It was a small denial but would do until he decided on a worthier deed to offer in return for his negligence.

Lowering himself to the hard earth in front of the altar, he prepared to approach God with total humility. He pressed his cheek against the dirt, closed his eyes and ears to the world, and fell silent in reverent and hopeful anticipation.

A chill instantly filled him and he shivered, trying not to let rising fear suggest the meaning of this. Do not be anxious, he told himself, and then cautiously opened one eye.

A dark shadow extended over him, flowing from the doorway. He prayed that a cloud had only veiled the sun.

"I did not wish to interrupt your prayers, Brother."

Leaping to his feet, Thomas stared at the dark-robed figure standing in the entrance.

Father Eliduc gestured toward the bench inside. "May I?"

"Would I ever refuse you," the monk replied. "Please sit down. I confess I have neither good wine to offer as refreshment nor fine chalices from which to drink." His voice trembled, cravenly betraying his pounding heart.

Lightly running his fingertips over the rough boards of the bench, the priest replied with a modest upturn of his thin lips. "Out of respect for this hermitage, I shall stand."

Thomas walked to the table and uncovered the basket from the inn. He pulled out a loaf of bread and a sweating cheese with high odor. "There is this gift from the local inn."

Eliduc stared at the presented objects in the monk's hands before replying, "I am fasting."

It was rare that Thomas was able to discomfit this man and so he felt some joy. The pleasure was fleeting. He knew this visit did not bode well.

"Come, Brother, do not look so bleak. Is the sun not warm? Do the birds not sing with delight? Are you not free—to worship God in this hermitage?"

How cleverly this man reminds me of my past, the monk thought as the melancholy he had chased to the borders of his soul came thundering back with the force of destriers charging into battle. Shall I ever be free of him? Begrudgingly, he acknowledged he did owe Father Eliduc gratitude. It was this priest, and whomever he served, that had plucked Thomas from prison and kept him from rotting like the corpse of some rat.

"What a profound sigh! Oh, fear not, Brother. I have not come to wrest you from this tiny hut and drag you into the world." He fell silent, studying the monk for a moment that seems endless. "Dare you claim that I have ever summoned you when God's purpose did not demand it?" The priest's smile was as thin as the edge of a knife.

Thomas refused to reply.

Walking over to the simple altar, the priest studied the roughly made cross. It was constructed of two unevenly carved pieces of wood, bound together by rope. He inclined his head as if considering the workmanship and whether it suited its holy purpose.

Outside, a cart rumbled by, the wheels squeaking. Laughter from the men accompanying it balanced the heavy stillness between the two men in the hut.

"Why are you here?" Thomas shattered the hush first, conceding victory to the priest's stronger will.

Eliduc folded his hands into the sleeves of his soft robe and turned. "Queen Eleanor is planning a pilgrimage. Since she may stay at Tyndal, it is my duty to make sure the priory is prepared to uplift her spirit in godly ways and as she most ardently desires."

"Does our prioress know you are here?"

"Before the bells rang for the last Office, she and Prior Andrew greeted the entire party from court, of which I am but one humble member. Contrary to your suspicions, I did not fly over the priory walls, dropping venom from my jaws to poison the local wells, and land outside your hermitage."

Thomas dropped his gaze.

The priest glided closer until his body almost brushed against the monk. "You have grown rebellious, Thomas. Have you forgotten how you lay in a bed of your own excrement and were raped like some enemy woman?"

The monk covered his face and groaned.

Eliduc's breath was now hot on Thomas' cheek. "Do you not owe much for your freedom?"

"Shall that debt never be paid?" Thomas whispered. "If you think such servitude is freedom…"

"Would you have preferred to die with the weight of your vile sins dragging your soul down to Hell?"

"You lied to me! You swore I would burn at the stake for one act of sodomy, and I know of no man who has."

Eliduc stepped back, his eyes widening with surprise. "Lie? I think not, Brother. I presaged the truth. The year I offered you a path to atonement, many were proclaiming the day would come when sodomites would feel Hell's fire in their flesh before their souls were eternally damned. Sodomy is not merely a sin of the body, Thomas. It is a sign of heresy. Be grateful I gave you acts of cleansing penance before it was too late. It will not be long before the Church proclaims harsher measures against sodomites and all others who dare blaspheme against the only true faith. You would be wise to believe me when I say that King Edward agrees with this most heartily."

"You forget that my father…"

Raising his hand for silence, Eliduc continued. "Be advised, my son, to reflect with care on what I have told you. Before you point to any lineage or argue my conclusions, remember that you are a bastard and your father is now dead. Should the Church find you guilty of heretical sodomy, there is no man who would try to save you from burning. To do so would suggest his own soul was tainted. This warning is meant as a kindness, although you may not understand that now."

Thomas felt the world spin and he grabbed the edge of the table. Regaining his balance, his reason told him he should beg this man's forgiveness while his heart remained incapable of it.

"Let us make peace," Eliduc said. "Do we not both serve God?"

Do we? Thomas doubted it, and all he could do was nod agreement. He lacked both strength and words to dispute further.

Seeing the monk had conceded defeat, Eliduc stepped back. "As I said, Brother, I did not come to take you away from this place." His voice grew soft as if granting some mercy.

"You wish something of me. Am I also wrong in concluding that you would not have come if you had no demand?" Again

Thomas' voice trembled, and he was humiliated by such a betrayal of his weakness.

Eliduc clapped his hands once. "How perceptive!"

Thomas bit his lip hard at the mockery and tasted sour hate in his blood.

"You have indeed caught me out."

"Tell me what I must now do?" the monk hissed.

Father Eliduc shook his head and turned toward the door. After a brief hesitation, he looked back over his shoulder and gazed at the man he owned. "Methinks I need not even tell you. With your wondrous powers of reason and logic, you shall discover it yourself."

Then the man in black walked through the doorway and let the sun's warmth slip back inside.

Chapter Ten

Brother Beorn stood in awe.

The orange sun slipped toward the horizon, conceding all power to the night. Streaks of clouds, once vermillion tinged with gold, darkened. Birdsong grew hushed. Only the whine of biting things remained undiminished.

This daily surrender of God's light to the darkness of Satan's hours never ceased to amaze Brother Beorn. Had he been a man of less ardent faith, he might have questioned why this happened. Instead he accepted years ago that the message lay more in the recovery of light at dawn than any relinquishment of it at night. He often stopped to watch the event with both wonderment and reverence, and as he did each time, bowed his head with a briefly uttered prayer.

Had he pondered more on God's creations, he might have found many other contradictions to consider. Deciding the Church and its leaders were surely wiser than he, the lay brother had chosen to reject such diversions. For this reason, he was surprised to realize that, on the matter of the queen's party, he remained of two minds.

On one hand, he was delighted that King Edward's wife wished to show humble gratitude to God for the safe return from Outremer. A pilgrimage was unquestionably fitting, but he did not approve of the new guest quarters, however austere, because they were solely for the comfort of those serving secular lords.

Surely the priory could have found better use for what it had cost to build them. He could think of several other ways to honor the greater glory of God with extra coin, from thicker blankets for the dying to a bigger cross on the hospital chapel altar.

This quandary troubled him. He knew he must respect and accept any decision made by Prioress Eleanor, and he did so willingly most of the time. In this matter, he had little tolerance for secular foibles. No matter how many times he bid it be silent, his insubordinate spirit argued that Tyndal Priory would always be better served by a fine chalice to brighten worship than soft beds for the ease of wealthy bones, even queenly ones.

As he rounded the stables, he stopped to enjoy the snickering of contented horses. He was a countryman and four-legged creatures were dear to him. Although he knew they did not have souls, he had often to confess his lingering suspicion that many of them were more prefect creations than those allegedly made in His image. Never had he heard a cow blaspheme nor a sheep proclaim heresy. Goats, on the other hand, reeked of lust. He had doubts about goats.

He breathed in deeply, enjoying the smells of the earth, warmed by the sun. Dusk, so long delayed in this summer season, had fallen at last. He looked forward to prayers and the deep sleep of one who had labored hard for God and was blest with honest dreams.

As he walked on, he decided the day had been particularly joyful. The infirmarian, Sister Christina, had prayed with a young woman who came to the hospital with blinding headaches. Soon after, the sufferer had gone home to her husband and babes, cured by the grace of God. Many might praise the potions of Sister Anne while Brother Beorn believed the infirmarian was a saint. Herbs would do no good were it not for the blessings of Sister Christina.

Just then, angry shouts destroyed his tranquil thoughts.

Beorn stopped, staring into the darkness, horrified that such rage had invaded priory grounds.

Two men stood in the gloom near the guest quarters, their shadowy arms gesturing wildly as they argued.

The lay brother quickly covered his ears and hurried away.

He dared not interfere and had no wish to listen to their quarrel. If he tried to intercede, he might have been caught in a fight and tainted with the sin of violence. How dare they insult God's peace with their worldly argument and infect him with anger!

After gaining some distance from the scene, he was able to slow his pace and sooth his outrage by concluding that God would find a way to punish them. He would have dismissed this exchange of foul words if the matter had only been between two secular guests.

What troubled and frightened him was that one of the voices belonged to Prior Andrew.

Chapter Eleven

Thomas opened his eyes and stared at the pitched roof above his straw bed.

Dust motes drifted about in the fresh sunlight of the new day. From outside, he could hear the musical twittering of birds as they swooped to feast on the many summer insects. Before Father Eliduc's arrival yesterday, he would have risen with innocent delight, rejoicing in God's creations. This morning, despondency chained him to his mat.

"Why?" he groaned, unable to even face the altar of the invisible presence he served. "Have I not done this penance? Do I not honor my vows and seek atonement when I fail? Why must I suffer more than other men? Are their sins fewer? Surely the wickedness of some is even more loathsome!" He might have wept, but his melancholy was too great. Thomas turned over on his side, dug his fingers into the earth, and willed himself to lie utterly still.

As Anchoress Juliana once promised him, Thomas did learn, during these months as a hermit, that a little peace and the occasional revelation could be discovered in silence. Lying motionless and without thought, he felt an easing of the crushing weight on his heart and then enough strength to stand. Rising, he tightened the rope he wore around his robe and turned to face the altar.

Sunlight now warmed his back. The chirping birds sounded impatient, demanding that he get on with his day so their fowl-worthy labor might not be unduly disturbed by his traipsing about. Without giving voice to his prayers, he bowed his head for a few moments and then stepped out into the world.

A few feet from the hut, he hesitated, believing he had seen movement in the brush near the road. "Nute?" he called out.

There was no reply.

"You need not fear me. Ask your mistress, if you doubt it. She will confirm I am no monster and you have no cause to flee."

Once again, there was no response.

He was saddened that Nute hid from him, while understanding all too well why the orphan child was wary. When he was even younger than this boy, Thomas' own mother had died, and he had been left beset by dreadful fears, both in his waking hours and in his dreams.

"At least you have Signy to care for you, as I had my father's cook," he murmured. A woman with soft arms and a good heart could do much to soothe the inexpressible anguish of a child whose mother was buried in the earth.

Thomas shook off the thoughts. Since he was later in his rising, he suspected that the boy must have been waiting to see him depart before leaving the basket and jug. Not wanting to delay Nute any longer, the monk quickly turned toward the narrow path leading down to the pond.

The exercise of swimming should help rebalance his humors. Looking at the drying grass, he thought it a pity the earlier light rain had cooled the air so little.

Gently pushing branches aside on the descent, Thomas felt his spirits firmly brighten. Perhaps God did not hate him, he decided with renewed confidence. "Did you not test Job, a much beloved servant, far more than other mortals?" Then afraid he had been arrogant to suggest he might resemble that exemplary man of faith, he added, "Not that I am as good as he."

Considering the pain suffered by Job, faith and patience might not be the only lessons taught in the story. God could use unease, doubt, or even anguish like a cowherd did his goad to make a man change or question his direction if such were necessary. There was more than one similarity between himself and an ox, Thomas concluded. God might well have to goad him.

Pausing to stare through the tree tops with their halo of sunlight, the monk knew he must decide what he should do next. He could not continue to loudly spew questions at God without listening for the small voice whispering answers.

As he continued, wary of his footing on the steep path, he grew convinced that change was due. Enough signs were there. Not only did Ralf visit for the first time in months, but Father Eliduc had arrived in the priory. That coincidence of events caught his attention, even if he did not understand their precise significance. He vowed again to consult Brother John.

As often as he cursed Father Eliduc, his visits also meant adventures for Thomas, times he enjoyed. Although he had hated Tyndal Priory when he first arrived, he found friendship here, with Crowner Ralf and Sister Anne in particular, and some purpose comforting the sick at the hospital or in the village. Maybe he could finally find contentment as a monk in this Order of Fontevraud. Even serving a woman had taught him a little humility, and Thomas knew how easily a man fell into sinful pride. All these things must be taken into account in his choice.

For cert, he could not remain a hermit. He was no holy man. No longer could he tolerate visitors at his door, begging for his touch that they might be healed. Even though he sent them to Sister Anne and Sister Christina at the priory hospital, the look in their eyes as they gazed on him both horrified and brought him evil dreams.

"I am committing blasphemy by staying here," he whispered, then willed these thoughts aside as he reached the path's end.

The pond was just a few steps away, and he eagerly pulled his robe over his head. For just a moment, he shut his eyes and stood still, letting the sun warm his body before he plunged into the glinting water. His fear of Father Eliduc and all his other torments diminished.

Then he smelled an unsettling odor and opened his eyes. Clouds of hungry flies caught his attention. All newborn serenity faded when he saw the cause.

A twisted body lay under the bush to his left.

Thomas knew the man was dead.

Chapter Twelve

A large orange cat with round eyes the color of emeralds sat flicking his tail while Prioress Eleanor knelt at her prie-dieu.

She opened her eyes and looked down at the creature.

He began to purr.

"I know your ways, Arthur. Did you bring a rat, a bird, or something else to delight Gytha and terrify me?" Sighing, she picked the cat up, folded him into her arms, and rose. A dusting of bright fur settled on her dark robe.

"It was a rat, my lady," Gytha replied, walking through the door to the private chambers. "A fine one. Methinks Sister Matilda will be most pleased to hear of this."

Eleanor shuddered at the very thought but hugged the mighty hunter close. "I assume you have removed the gift?"

Gytha nodded and quickly disappeared. Someone was begging entrance at the door to the prioress' public rooms.

When she returned, the maid's face was pale. "Crowner Ralf begs a word, my lady."

"Your expression tells me to expect troubling news." She eased Arthur down onto her narrow bed where he quickly curled into a comfortable spot for a well-earned nap.

"A corpse has been found near the hermit's hut."

Eleanor's hand flew to her mouth. "Brother Thomas!"

A man's voice called out, "Fear not, my lady. He was the one to find the dead man on the stream bank below his hermitage."

Eleanor felt the sweat of fear begin to creep between her breasts. First terrified that her beloved monk had been slain, she now worried that her cry had betrayed her uncured passion for him. The prioress straightened and entered the public chambers with what she hoped was a somber demeanor.

Ralf expression grew sheepish when he saw her scowl. "Forgive my rudeness. When I overheard your concern, I wanted to assure you all was well. None of us wants ill to befall that good man."

"I thank you for the swift assurance that our hermit remains unharmed by evil men for he is truly beloved by those in both priory and village." Sighing with relief that she seemed not to have betrayed her secret, Eleanor gestured permission for Ralf to sit.

Gytha brought a jug of ale and platter of fruit for the table. Although many believed uncooked fruit to be unhealthy, she knew the crowner cared little for such common advice and preferred his fruit raw. He was also infamous for his appetite. The platter was piled high.

Ralf tried to catch the maid's eye.

She kept her back to him, then hurried away until she stood, head bowed, a suitable distance from the pair.

He turned to face the prioress. "I fear the corpse may have some connection to this priory."

"How so, good friend?"

"The man was not from the village or priory, at least neither Brother Thomas nor I recognized him, and his clothing suggested he was a man of wealth." He took a bite out of an apple, and half of it disappeared into his mouth. "Your monk suggested the man might have traveled to Tyndal, seeking cure for some ill. I said I would seek your help in identifying him."

Eleanor tilted her head with interest. "Did Brother Thomas think the man died of some illness or do you suspect violence as the cause?"

"His throat was cut, my lady."

Instinctively, Eleanor touched her own neck. "It is possible the poor wretch never reached Tyndal. If he did and was seen at the hospital, Brother Beorn is the most likely to recognize him.

He talks with those who seek ease and consolation here. Since it would be unseemly for me to do so, Prior Andrew shall accompany him, as representative of the priory, to look on the body."

"I am grateful, my lady. Any information will open or close paths of inquiry to follow and save time in the hunt for the one who did this."

"Can you tell how long the corpse may have lain there?"

"Brother Thomas found him this morning on the bank of the pond where he takes frequent exercise. Since I joined him there yesterday, when the sun was highest in the sky, I can confirm the absence of any corpse then."

"I assume neither of you recalls anything that might now be significant?" She smiled to show she meant the question in jest.

Ralf considered her query in earnest. "Nor smelled the stink, which would have developed quickly given the heat. That means the body wasn't lying hidden and the killer waiting to move it until after we left the pond."

Some found offence in the crowner's rough speech. Eleanor never did. She nodded in reply, having little patience herself with time-wasting circumlocutions.

"Fortunately, the morning rain was light. When we searched the bank today, we found much blood where the man had been killed, near the path to the hermitage and in the open. From there we saw drag marks to the bush where Brother Thomas found the body. Since the killer did not hide the corpse with more skill, or even bury it, I suspect he was in haste, or else had no reason to do more than briefly delay discovery." He shook his head. "No knife was found either."

"Did our hermit see any strangers along the road or nearby?"

"He said not. After we parted yesterday, he returned to his hut and never left it. The afternoon and evening were spent much as usual, he said. A little work in his garden. Prayers. Another visitor, besides me. One whom he swears would not commit such violence. He never even saw Nute come for the jug and basket, although he sometimes does not. The wee lad tries not to disturb him." He shrugged.

"What about strange noises at night? He observes the Offices and therefore lies in bed less than other men." Although she carefully phrased this, she knew Brother Thomas suffered sleepless hours when he was in the priory and was wont to pace the dark cloister garth, seeking relief.

"Lovers occasionally slip down the path to the pond, he said. He knows their whisperings and step. Beasts wander by as well, but he is familiar with the ways of wild things." Ralf was counting on his fingers. "Travelers seek refuge and avoid the roads at night. A party that did not would be numerous, armed, and loud enough to wake our monk." He hesitated, holding his thumb. "That was all, I think."

"I am not sure what I had hoped to accomplish with my questions and beg forgiveness for intruding in a matter where I have no cause." Eleanor fell silent as her grey eyes darkened with worry.

"Your questions lead me on the way to a more reasoned approach, and so I am grateful for your interest. Let us pray this man was a member of some lawless band passing by the village and was killed in a quarrel."

Crowner and prioress glanced at each other, neither of them for a moment believing that such a thing had happened.

"You are kind, and I have kept you from your work long enough." She gestured to Gytha. "The prior and lay brother will be summoned at once. I know they must see the body as soon as possible."

"Unnatural death is never welcome, my lady, but this one is especially ill-timed with the arrival of my brother and others from court yesterday." The last words were uttered in a tone akin to a dog's growl. "Methinks this death may cause some of them to grow uneasy."

"We shall calm any fears," she replied, her confident words hiding her own worry. She suspected the crowner was anxious about the reaction of his less-than-beloved sibling while she was more concerned with that of Father Eliduc. "I confess none will be pleased to find murder committed at the very gates of a priory where Queen Eleanor thought to stay."

Rising, the crowner bowed. "I spoke rashly. You cannot be blamed if men fight or die outside these walls. Please be assured that my brother, who has no quarrel with Tyndal, will do his best to calm all who came on the queen's behalf."

A brief smile twitched at the prioress' lips. "I do trust Sir Fulke shall argue that he keeps his county safe and no innocent need fear violence under his watch. The force with which he must present his case shall depend on the nature of this foulness. Come back with word as quickly as you can. Your brother must be told of this matter and soon enough."

"I hope to put a name to the corpse first," Ralf replied. "If I can assure my brother that the pursuit of justice is well in hand, he may not feel obliged to muddle my quest for the killer with ill-conceived interference and vain posing."

"Then I shall add my prayers to yours," Eleanor replied and summoned Gytha so she might instruct her on what was required to assist the crowner.

Chapter Thirteen

Father Eliduc walked along the path leading from the church. Glancing back at the dank stone building, he saw how thick moss blackened the glass of the window behind the altar. He stopped to glare at the offending growth. How reprehensible and inexcusable!

He also breathed a sigh of relief.

Earlier, when he had knelt inside for prayer, he noticed that the light in the chapel was inexplicably murky despite the intense summer sun outside. This dimness had distracted his worship and filled him with foreboding. Now he knew that God had not draped a cloud over the sun to signify ominous displeasure with mortals or to announce that the Day of Judgement had come. The darkness was due solely to improper care of the altar window.

Surely there was someone to perform the simple task of removing the foul moss. Was the priory so poor that a village man might not be found to clean the windows for the good of his soul and a pittance for his belly? Turning his eyes skyward, he muttered, "I should not expect competence in a place run by daughters of Eve." His expression suggested he was confident that God would concur.

Then he swiftly looked around. When he saw no one nearby, he closed his eyes and allowed himself just a moment to turn from the world and let his spirit drift in peace. Standing motionless, he listened to the birds sing, a sound so sweet his heart ached.

"I do miss the fine choirs of my lord's church," he sighed. Men's deep voices raised to honor God's glory uplifted his soul, something he often needed when his earthly work grew wearisome.

The instant passed. He opened his eyes.

Eliduc never allowed his soul self-indulgence for long.

As the priest's gaze dropped back to earth, he saw Lady Avelina's mute servant hurrying toward the guest quarters with something in hand. "Men say that one has been cursed by God for his part in assisting Simon's wicked father when the de Montfort faction captured King Henry at Lewes," he murmured, in part to himself and partially to God. "The old king may have been unwise in enriching his wife's foreign kin and choosing too many counselors amongst them, but he was anointed with holy oil at his coronation. God frowns when men fail to honor those whom He has blessed."

In contrast to any sins committed against the old king, Kenard had shown tender devotion to his mistress during the long journey here. Had the man not lost all voice, Eliduc wondered if he would be praised for his faithful service, not feared for his lack of speech.

For a moment, the priest pondered the scope of such loyalty which was both laudable and useful. Piously folding his hands, Eliduc bent his head as if in prayer while he continued to watch the servant until the man disappeared into the quarters.

In Eliduc's experience, common assumptions must often be discounted. The priest never cast inconvenient reality aside so he might continue to lie in the soft comfort of convention. He formed his own conclusions. Men who ignored exceptions to any general rule did not survive long in struggles for power.

His thin lips bent with subdued humor as he turned that logic from Kenard's situation to the oft bemoaned inadequacies of Eve's progeny, one of whom ruled here.

No matter what the Church preached about Eve's daughters, suppositions he himself willingly voiced in the company of his fellows, Eliduc knew there were women who did not suffer from the illogical minds and feeble resolve that were the common faults of their sex. One of those women who possessed a man's stout heart and a masculine mind was Prioress Eleanor.

Eliduc liked the Fontevraudine prioress and enjoyed jousting wits with her. Even though he had always been confident of his eventual triumph, he found her more of a challenge than most men and he did like a good contest. He was not so foolish as to imagine she might not hone her talents into more formidable skill over time. Her errors were youthful ones, born of inexperience.

If God granted the two of them a long life, the priest hoped to have many future contests with Baron Adam's youngest child. Despite Tyndal Priory's insignificant status, its leader was exceptional in birth and ability. Competent kings took note of such things, their queens often more so. What also delighted Eliduc was the possibility that he and this prioress might one day find themselves joined together to achieve some mutual purpose. After all, they both served God and the Church.

"In the meantime," he sighed wistfully, "this visit might be my last victory over her for some time." Before he left the priory, he planned to accomplish something of great significance to him and his own liege lord. Although the deed would be done almost before her eyes, he hoped she would not be aware of its value to him now or for some long time to come.

In return for her unwitting cooperation, he would leave her a gift. It would be one that both showed his appreciation and be of great worth to her. For this he knew she would suffer profound gratitude, and *suffer* she most certainly would. An honorable woman, she'd understand the debt she owed him and that she must repay the favor in the future. To that time, he definitely looked forward.

The sound of voices behind him caught his attention. Shading his eyes against the sun, he turned around.

Three men approached.

Eliduc recognized Prior Andrew. Accompanying him was a gaunt giant of a lay brother with an angry expression and a secular man who bore a strong resemblance to Sir Fulke. The priest concluded this must be the sheriff's younger brother.

Eliduc folded his hands, inclined his head with proper gravity, and waited for the men to come closer.

It was Crowner Ralf who spoke to the priest first. "You are from the queen's party?"

A lesser man might have taken offense at the brusque tone. Balancing the potential insult against other matters and concluding it was of little moment, Eliduc simply nodded assent. He knew the crowner's reputation for honesty and believed him cleverer than the elder Fulke.

"A dead man was found nearby," Prior Andrew said, his voice noticeably unsteady. "Brother Beorn and I wish to see if we recognize him as one who might have sought care at the hospital."

Eliduc's expression reflected surprise, quickly blended with caution. "This discovery has brought the crowner within the walls of a house dedicated to God's peace. Might I conclude the death was not natural?"

Ralf nodded concurrence, then his expression brightened with a wicked grin. "Perhaps he was one of the men who provided protection for you on the journey here, Father. Would you like to come with us? Although his throat was cut, he's not too bloody."

"Your brother might be the better choice to accompany you, Crowner."

Ralf snorted with contempt at Eliduc's quick response. Brother Thomas excepted, the crowner believed that most priests had strong stomachs for feasting on succulent meats, accompanied by better wine, and weak ones when confronted by mortal violence.

Crossing his arms, he continued to prick at the man. "A soul may hover, Father. Our hermit has tried to give it comfort. A familiar priest might be more effective in easing it toward God."

Eliduc thoughtfully nodded. "Since I was the one you first met, He must intend that I do as you have suggested. When the body is identified, there will be time enough for the sheriff and the king's law to take over."

He walked to the prior's side and gestured his willingness to continue on.

Ralf scowled. His expression betrayed just how deeply he disliked underestimating this priest.

As they started toward the mill and the path leading to Tyndal village, Eliduc's heart filled with joy. Dare he hope that this discovery meant God favored his cause?

Then he realized that the murder might have other meanings as well, implications that would bode ill for his hopes. He hurried on, his spirit subdued by caution.

Chapter Fourteen

The swelling corpse was covered by a writhing blanket of flies.

Prior Andrew's face paled to sea-green. Cupping his hand over his mouth, he rushed into the nearby shrubbery and retched painfully.

"He's been a soldier," Ralf muttered to Thomas, "and has seen both living and dead with far worse wounds than that over-ripe carcass."

Tilting his head in the direction of the dead man, the monk whispered, "Be prepared for greater amazement."

Father Eliduc was kneeling in the blood-tinged mire.

Ralf's eyes widened.

His robes pulled up around his thighs, the finely clothed priest was murmuring with fervency into an ear that would never again recognize human voice.

"I'll see to our prior," Brother Thomas said and disappeared into the bushes.

Ralf looked over at Brother Beorn who was standing several feet from the corpse. The lay brother remained motionless and silent, his eyes unblinking. The crowner could not decide if the man was stunned by the horror of this scene or had fallen into a trance.

Eliduc broke the silence with a disgusted grunt. Rising from the body, he looked with dismay at his filthy knees, then turned to Ralf. "God has granted your prayer for knowledge, Crowner." He pointed at the body. "This is the mortal flesh of Baron Otes, his soul most cruelly torn away and sent to God's hand."

Were I to take an oath on this, Ralf thought, I would swear that yon priest was more distraught over the mud on his knees than unhappy about the murder of one of his company.

Father Eliduc briefly studied the crowner's face, then scowled. "Without doubt, this is murder. Queen Eleanor will not be pleased to learn that she may not send any loyal servant here, lest some local felon kill him."

"More likely, someone in your party had a quarrel with this man and found the timing of the journey propitious," Ralf snapped.

Eliduc slowly raised an eyebrow. "Whom might you suspect, Crowner? Sir Fulke perhaps?"

Ralf reddened with fury.

The priest gestured toward Tyndal. "I only wish to point out how absurd your accusation is. If someone in the queen's party had cause to commit this foul deed, do you think he would wait until now? There was frequent opportunity for murder on the long journey, and flight would have been easier as well. Had the killer hidden his identity and followed us, he would have found the bustle of inns better suited to swift murder and safe escape. For these reasons, I counsel you to look closer to those dwelling nearby for the man who did this."

Although Ralf reluctantly conceded that the priest was right, he would not tell him so. He willed his temper to cool and turned to watch Brother Thomas assisting the prior down a slippery part of the embankment toward the pond.

Brother Beorn began to mumble something that sounded like a prayer, then covered his mouth as if fearful his words might be overheard.

With deepening frown, Ralf waited for the two men to approach.

"Forgive my weakness," Prior Andrew begged with evident embarrassment. "I have been fasting today."

"Might you have a name for this corpse?" Ralf asked.

Father Eliduc's expression remained impassive as if taking no offense when the crowner requested confirmation of the priest's word. Instead, he ripped a handful of tall grass up by the roots and began to scrape at the dirt on his knees.

Andrew nodded. "It is Baron Otes. I stood with Prioress Eleanor to greet the queen's party and remember him well."

Pausing, Eliduc glanced at the prior. "You seemed shocked to see him then," he remarked, and then returned to rubbing the drying mud with renewed vigor.

If anyone so pale could blanch further, Andrew succeeded.

The long silence amongst the men was broken only by the bubbling murmur of the stream on its way to serve the priory mill.

Eliduc tossed the muddied grass into the flowing water and carefully lowered his robe. "I may have construed shock for pain when you cried out," he continued, his tone devoid of any particular meaning. "You did step back awkwardly, and I feared you had injured yourself."

"Aye." Andrew's ambiguous response was barely audible.

Thomas gently touched his superior on the arm. "Methinks our prior needs to rest in the shade of my hut. The day is hot, and this baron's mutilated corpse stinks enough to trouble anyone, let alone one who has been fasting."

The crowner nodded. As he turned around to speak with the other two men, he saw Father Eliduc walking away.

The priest gestured to the dazed Beorn that they should return to the priory. Ignoring all courtesy, Eliduc had not sought permission to leave from the king's man, nor did he ask if the crowner had further questions.

Ralf said nothing. His lips twitched with amused satisfaction, knowing he had succeeded in insulting this arrogant priest. "Delighted to annoy you," he murmured as he watched the religious disappear.

Meanwhile, Thomas helped Prior Andrew climb the steep path, leaving the crowner alone with the rank corpse.

◇◇◇

Andrew grasped the empty mazer with such force his knuckles whitened.

Thomas poured more ale from the sweating jug. "I am curious to know why this priest joined you and the crowner on the way from Tyndal."

"His name is Father Eliduc," the prior whispered.

The monk almost confessed he knew this, then quickly thought the better of it. Instead, he sat down on the end of the rough bench and waited for what more this man, who rarely showed such unease, had to say.

Despite pressing his fingers against his eyes, the prior failed to stop the tears from rushing down his cheeks.

"Did you perchance know the dead man?" Thomas knew that fasting had never before caused his prior to weep.

"Aye, and have no cause to love him." Andrew raised his cup and emptied it in one gulp.

Thomas refilled it. "Whatever quarrel you may have had with the baron was surely long ago and before you took vows."

"Your loyalty and faith in me gladden my heart, Brother." Andrew reached out and touched Thomas' sleeve. "We both have lived long enough in the world to remember how the ways of men can bring mortal hearts pain and malignity."

Briefly grasping his prior's rough hand, the monk nodded. As for loyalty, Andrew earned that soon after Thomas' arrival. The prior who was then porter had noted the strong resemblance between the new monk and another man of high rank. Sensing Thomas' agitation, Andrew remarked that all men had secrets that could be left folded into the depths of the heart and never mentioned the matter again. From that day the monk knew this prior was a master craftsman in the art of compassion and quieting men's fears.

"You are aware I served Simon de Montfort and fought at Evesham before I entered this priory."

"That you told me not long after I arrived at Tyndal."

"And I informed Prioress Eleanor of my past as well, knowing her family had supported King Henry. Our lady forgave me with her usual grace."

"And you have rewarded her with loyal service ever since. Not only has God blessed this priory with a wise and compassionate prioress, He has given us a man of honor as its prior."

"What I did not tell her, for I saw no reason at the time, was that my beloved brother also fought with me at that battle."

Thomas raised an eyebrow, sipped his ale, and waited.

"He was killed." Andrew fell silent. Although he covered his face, the deep furrows in his brow betrayed the grief he suffered. "Death in a battle fought for honorable reasons should not…" His last words stumbled on the sharp pain of his sorrow, and he could speak no further.

"Many praiseworthy men fought for de Montfort and some believe he is a saint, claiming miracles at his tomb. It is well-known that King Edward himself showed much favor to the earl's cause until the end."

"It was not the cause that brought disgrace to my sibling." Straightening his back, Andrew wiped his cheeks, his face now scarlet with anger. "Dishonor was smeared on our family like ordure from a pig sty."

"And Baron Otes was involved?"

"More! He was the man responsible."

The monk poured more ale for them both.

Taking a deep breath, Andrew began talking as if the rush of words might heal him like the release of pus from a festering wound. "My brother and I were nearby when the Earl of Leicester fell. There I received the wound in my leg that still troubles me, and my brother staunched the blood flow, an act that saved my life. Had he not taken the time, he might have saved his own. Before he could escape, we were seized by Baron Otes' men."

"I thought you were captured by someone else."

"Nay, Brother, although it was the Earl of Cornwall who finally decided my fate and demanded mercy for many others who fought for de Montfort." He squeezed his eyes shut. "Had my brother been alive, I do not doubt we both would have received the same clemency."

"Continue, please. I shall not interrupt you again."

"There is little enough to tell. Baron Otes decided my wound would kill me soon enough, but he castrated my brother, as others had de Montfort, then stabbed him in the back to suggest he had been fleeing the battle out of cowardice. To further insult our family, the baron stuffed my brother's genitals into his mouth." Stretching his hands out as if begging God to banish the memory, Andrew wailed with indescribable agony.

Thomas grasped the man's hands, understanding one cause for his unhealed pain. "Do not blame yourself for what happened, Prior. You could have done nothing to save him."

"For the sin of not trying, I should have died unshriven."

"Your brother would have wanted you to live to pray for his soul."

"As I have each day since."

"Then you have served him far better than any hopeless attempt to save his life. You were too weak to succeed. For both of you to have been killed would have served no good purpose."

As his gulping sobs ended, Andrew ground his fist into the rough wood of the table. "There are brief moments when God grants my heart peace, Brother, and many more when I know the long penance before me." He bowed his head. "From this tale, you can understand why I have reason to hate the baron and might wickedly rejoice that someone murdered him."

"You did sicken at the sight of his cut throat which speaks more of horror than any joy," Thomas said with gentleness.

Andrew shrugged. "Father Eliduc did not reason so. When he suggested I cried out in shock at the sight of the baron in the queen's party, I asked myself if he had seen the dark spot in my soul."

This time it was Thomas who drank deeply of the ale and quickly refilled the mazer. "I doubt the priest knows anything of the history between you and the baron."

Yet he feared Andrew might be right. Eliduc knew much about men's sins and often used their secrets to make them do his bidding. That the priest never did this for personal gain made his intrigues no less terrifying to the victims.

"He smelled my fear," the prior said.

"Then quickly added he must have misinterpreted your cry. Surely all this priest meant to do was reproach our crowner for suggesting that the murderer hid in the queen's party." To shift the focus of their discussion away from Andrew, Thomas added, "I suspect the intent of his remarks was to prove how illogical the crowner was, not to make an accusation that would cast suspicion on you or on the integrity of our priory."

"Maybe you do have the right of it, Brother. As a priest, Father Eliduc would never impugn Tyndal, nor can I think of any reason for him to point an accusing finger at me. Although my kin own some land and a little wealth, they bear no title and have but small claim to one. Surely I am beneath the notice of a man who serves such a mighty lord of the Church."

Were they discussing any priest but this one, Thomas might agree. The monk could not quickly discount the possibility that the priest had reason to malign Tyndal Priory or slander its prior, nor could he see any value in doing either. Nothing the priest did could surprise him, however. Eliduc was as illusive as a wily trout in serving his lord's interests.

Yet Thomas knew that the Church was jealous of its authority over its vowed servants and fought like a she-bear with cubs against any claim of jurisdiction by secular law. It would be most unusual for a priest of Eliduc's rank to hint to a king's man that a prior might have motive for bloodshed or that any priory had been so lax as to harbor him.

"Surely Father Eliduc meant nothing ill," Thomas said at last. "Lest someone be foolish enough to suggest your guilt in this crime, you would be well-advised to tell your tale to Prioress Eleanor, if you have not already done so. Like me, she will know you are innocent of any violence. Learning how cruelly Baron Otes treated your brother will stiffen her resolve on your behalf."

"Should I tell Crowner Ralf as well?"

"Would you tell him?"

"He is an honest man. There is no reason to fear injustice from him."

"Remember that it is the duty of our prioress to determine how the matter must be handled, were you to be accused. You are not ruled by the king's law."

"I shall leave the decision about informing our crowner to Prioress Eleanor." Andrew rose. "You are a good man! In the past, I have confessed my hatred for the one who murdered my brother. Speaking with you has brought more peace to my heart." He smiled. "We miss you at the priory. Will you remain in this hut much longer?"

"I cannot say. God has not indicated that I am released from my vow."

"When He does, we shall welcome you back with joy." Andrew held out his hands to the hermit. "There is no need to accompany me. I have fully recovered my strength, and the priory grounds are close by. May God grant you peace, Brother."

Following his prior to the door, Thomas watched Andrew walk down the road until he disappeared around a bend in the direction of Tyndal.

Although he knew Prioress Eleanor had the right to decide if a king's man ought to hear Andrew's story, he feared Father Eliduc more than he dared admit to anyone. Ralf was a friend of Tyndal. The priest might not be, despite all the good reasons for believing he must. In case Eliduc planned to sacrifice the good prior in the pursuit of some unknown cause, Thomas was tempted to tell the crowner the prior's tale.

Realizing he was about to circumvent Prioress Eleanor, the monk shook his head. None of this was his responsibility, he reminded himself. His prioress was the leader of all religious at Tyndal. She alone had the authority to make decisions in this matter.

He shut his eyes and begged pardon for such overweening pride. After all, he was only a monk, one with no authority at all.

Suddenly he sensed more than heard a soft-footed approach. The hair on his neck stiffened. He spun around, wary of danger.

In the hazy light of the hot sun, a young man stood quite still near the hermitage door. He was as beautiful as one of God's angels.

Amazed by the handsome youth, Thomas was struck with uncommon lust.

The young man stepped toward him. "Are you the hermit of Tyndal?"

Thomas nodded.

"I beg a blessing," the youth said, then knelt at the hermit's feet.

"I will grant that wish," Thomas replied, his voice trembling, "although I am neither a holy man nor worthy of such obeisance." He reached out to pull the lad to his feet, then drew back, frightened by his overwhelming desire for the man. In a hoarse voice he asked, "What is your name?"

"Simon."

Chapter Fifteen

Prioress Eleanor faced the open window that looked out on her priory's extensive grounds. The weight on her heart stifled her as much as the summer heat. Pressing a fist against her breast, she prayed for masculine calm and the strength not to weep like the frail woman she was.

She turned around.

Prior Andrew's cheeks were wet with tears enough for them both.

"I did not know the circumstances of your brother's death," she said softly.

"I should have confessed it sooner."

"Although our families fought on different sides of the rebellion, you and I have vowed our allegiance to a far greater Lord than any earthly king." She hesitated and looked on her prior with compassion. "Upon joining the Order of Fontevraud, you swore you would follow a prioress' direction with the obedience any good son owes his mother. That vow you have honored in word and in the spirit of the command." She smiled with wry amusement. "That is more than most mortals accord any rule."

"Then I have doubly betrayed your confidence, my lady. I kept this part of my past hidden from you. In so doing, I may bring dishonor to this house." Andrew bowed his head. "I shall resign my position. A worthier man than I must serve as your prior."

Eleanor furtively ran her fingers under her eyes to make sure tears had not betrayed her feelings. "Before I make any decision on that plea, I must first ask a question, one to which I require an answer appropriate to your vows and dedication in God's service." She struggled to keep her voice steady. "Did you kill Baron Otes as you vowed on the battlefield of Evesham?"

Andrew did not hesitate. "I am innocent of his murder. That oath after my brother's death was made in the agony of grief and was fueled by the misery of my feverish body. Without hesitation I confess I hated the baron beyond all reason and even imagined the torture I wanted to inflict on him in retaliation. Since then, I have learned how empty revenge is. Every morning, upon rising, I recite God's commandments before I say my prayers. Thus am I reminded that He abominates murder, even for righteous vengeance."

"You show much wisdom, Prior. We all would be well-advised to follow your practice."

"Those kind words are more than this wretched man deserves."

Lest her trembling hands betray her distress, Eleanor tucked them into her sleeves and frowned. "As for your request to return to the life of a simple monk…" She stopped and waited for him to meet her gaze as she uttered her decision. "I cannot grant your wish. Remaining in your position, with all the burdens that brings, is not only your duty but shall be your penance."

"My lady…"

"Nor will I allow further debate on the subject." Her grey eyes darkened. "What happened to your brother was criminal, under God's law as well as the rules of combat, and his name shall be included from this day forth in the daily prayers of our nuns. I, too, shall beg God's mercy for him for as long as I remain on this earth."

"My gratitude is beyond mortal speech." He fell to his knees.

"You and your brother did support de Montfort, however."

"We fought for his principles, my lady, that all men have the right to just governance. War was waged solely to win a greater voice for Englishmen, not to remove King Henry from the throne. Had we believed the Earl of Leicester wanted to replace an anointed king, we would not have joined his cause."

"My father believed his ambition reached for the throne. Equally honorable men agreed with you and your brother. Whatever the truth of it, our new king also rode alongside the earl, with my eldest brother at Lord Edward's side, until both felt threatened by de Montfort's power."

"I have never been traitor to kingship," Andrew whispered, "and remain a true subject of our king."

"Rise, Prior. I never doubted your loyalty, but worldly allegiances are often changeable things. Men's reason and hearts are too flawed to follow without question. Only God's purpose is trustworthy for He alone is perfect." She sighed. "And Tyndal Priory belongs to God. Faithful though we may be to anointed kings, we have a higher allegiance and must be steadfast in following His direction. Unworthy though I may be, I am leader here and you are under my dominion. In the name of the Queen of Heaven, I require that you swear never again to hide anything from me which I ought to know."

He opened his mouth to speak. No words came forth. He nodded agreement.

Fearing for his weak leg, Eleanor gave him leave to sit in her presence. "You have proven yourself a good son to me. Your brother, by his unselfish act that saved your life, was equally devoted to the demands of kinship. In both of you, I see honorable men." She took a deep breath. "My father may have told me some tales of the baron, but I was unaware of the depths of his wickedness. You must tell me more of him. I have an obligation to the other envoys, our new queen, and our priory's reputation. Although Baron Otes was surely the victim of someone from outside Tyndal, he was our guest."

"I have never sought news of him since taking vows and finding my home here, my lady."

"Surely you remember something of his habits and character from the past."

The prior grasped his thigh and winced. "Muddied as my memory is with grief, some may doubt the truth of what I say. Others will swear they share my opinion. Like a hound, the baron was zealous in his hunt for any prey whose downfall would benefit him. Although the pursuit of worldly influence on behalf of family is expected and honorable, he lacked all restraint in his methods. With coin and threats he bought information that destroyed some and forced others to support him with acclamation far louder than he deserved."

"Surely not all his ploys worked."

"I point to his murder."

"That deed does suggest at least one failure," she replied, settling into her own chair. With one finger, she traced the deep carving on the arms and fell into troubled thought. "When he spoke with me, he did show deep concern for his soul's fate."

"The man I knew had little room in his heart for God."

"Perhaps he came belatedly to a fear of hellfire."

Andrew's expression betrayed a fleeting doubt before he nodded.

"He wished to leave land to the priory in exchange for prayers after his death."

"On arrival, he recognized me, as I did him. I doubt he would have given such a gift without demanding that I suffer in some way. Although fear of Hell may have finally crawled into his heart, a snail could traverse the earth's surface before that man ever gave a gift without expecting some worldly gain."

"You have the right of it," Eleanor said. "Without fees, wool, and fertile land for ample harvests, Tyndal cannot provide for our religious whose duty is to pray. Even though most gifts come with honorable requests, God does not countenance doing anything ignoble to keep a priory out of debt. I told the baron I must decline any gift that came with the price he asked."

Andrew lowered his eyes, and then looked up with evident horror. "When you refused him, did he not threaten reprisal?"

Eleanor took time to choose her words as she recalled the baron's suggestion that King Edward might grow angry with those who succored a man who had once drawn a sword against an anointed king. "I believe he was too surprised by my decision to come up with a suitable revenge," she said at last, hoping Andrew did not hear the lie in her voice.

Chapter Sixteen

"You're drunk." Ralf reached for the jug of ale.

"Had you any sense, you'd be too," Fulke replied, pulling the pitcher out of his brother's grasp. After staring inside with long and careful study, he tipped the last of the amber liquid into his mouth. "Is that all you have to offer me?" He slammed the thing down on the table, belching like a hog grunts over slops.

"'S Blood, Fulke! My daughter is asleep. If you frighten her, I'll skin your balls."

"Not before the Devil fries yours, little brother." His scowl wavered. "There was a time when you drank men under the table and swyved their wenches afterward. You're no saint."

"I've since become a husband and father."

"As have I, or at least I was a father until the babes died. My wife has long been barren. Of late, she has refused her bed to me. Seems the priest believes coupling without issue is no more than sinful lust. Now I seek relief…"

"God keep me from your tales of feeble gropings and pitiful couplings. I do not care."

Fulke raised his fist and bellowed outrage.

Ralf grabbed him by the wrist. "If you disturb Sibely," he hissed, "I swear I'll make sure you have nothing left between your legs to poke any woman."

"Cokenay," the sheriff growled, but his voice had dropped and his wrath quickly wilted. With his free hand, he gestured agreement.

The two men fell silent as they both listened for any sound of distress from the sleeping child.

All was quiet.

"More ale," Fulke whispered, "if you haven't any decent wine to serve your noble brother."

In response, Ralf pushed a platter of cold fowl and bread toward him, then relented and refilled the pitcher with ale. "Out of compassion for soulless beasts, you can stay the night. Were you to walk back to the priory, you'd pass out, be eaten by some wild creature, and poison the poor animal with your foul flesh." He gestured to a corner of the room. "There is straw enough there for a bed."

Fulke said nothing as he grasped the cup close to his chest. He was visibly shivering.

"I'll not geld you in your sleep," Ralf said, grabbing a handful of fowl from the platter. "You have my word."

Shaking his head, the sheriff noisily sucked his cup dry and reached for the jug.

With great deliberation, Ralf tore off bits of flesh from the wing and stuffed them into his mouth.

"I'm scared." Fulke's words were almost inaudible.

The crowner grinned.

"Not of you."

Ralf shrugged.

"I did not kill him."

"You had cause enough."

"I just affirmed my innocence."

"God was gracious and I never met the man in my short time at court. From tales I've heard of him, perhaps you should have slit his throat." Ralf tossed the denuded bird bones at the sheriff's feet. "As for questioning your honesty, you would question mine were our situations reversed. Tell me why I must conclude you are telling the truth."

"Be careful how you continue. If I hang, remember that Odo would get the land to use as he defines God's work, sweet brother. You would gain little except, perhaps, the responsibility of caring for my widow."

"You have been too long amongst devious men, Fulke. If I had longed for either title or inheritance, I could have killed you when we were boys and disguised the deed well enough as an accident. Why wait until now?"

Reaching across the table, Fulke clutched his brother's arm. "If you don't believe me, I will swear on any holy relic of your choosing! I did not kill Baron Otes, although you know well enough I might wish to."

Ralf looked down with disgust at the sheriff's hand. "Swear not. I think you'd lie to God Himself."

"Why do you hate me?" Fulke sat back. Even with his expression disguised by shadows, he looked defeated.

"You never gave me reason to love."

The older brother shook his head as if amazed.

"If you cannot recall the tauntings or the cruel jests when we were boys, then I have no wish, as a man, to remind you. As long as we stay far apart, Fulke, we shall remain peaceful enough brothers."

"We are kin."

"Saying that only means you want something from me."

"Find the man who killed Baron Otes, do so quickly, and keep all suspicion from ever falling on me."

"You are the sheriff of this land. I am only your lowly crowner and the brother for whom you show little respect."

"Did I not take you into my home when you fled this place? Did I not find you a woman with land?"

"It was your spouse who welcomed me with kindness in my grief. You greeted me once, then spoke only when it suited your purpose. As for the wife you gave me, she gifted me with a daughter who has brought the taste of honey back to my life. I cherish the child far more than the land."

"You owe me."

"As I have said already, I have repaid that debt."

Fulke leaned forward, his teeth clenched in fury.

Shoving his drunken brother backwards, Ralf filled his own mazer and drank deeply. "If you agree to a few simple conditions, I'll do as you ask."

The sheriff lowered his head.

Ralf walked over to the wall where his sword hung on a peg and returned with the weapon in hand. "As this represents the cross on which our Lord was crucified, I ask that you put your hand on the hilt and swear you will agree to my demands and never turn traitor to your word."

Fulke rested one palm on the hilt and grunted.

"Good." Laying the weapon down on the table, he turned back to his brother. "My conditions are simple. First, stay out of my way until the killer is found. Later, you can preen like a capon all you like and lie to your friends at court about how clever you were in trapping the murderer. I swear to support your tale if required. The last conditions are that you cease to plan any further marriage propositions for me and that you return to kneel at the king's feet, leaving me forever in peace."

Fulke did nod, but his head had grown too heavy to hold up. His eyes closed, and he slid off the bench onto the floor.

Ralf walked around the table and looked down at the man, dressed in robes of finely woven cloth, sprawled on an earthen floor. Did he believe Fulke's assertion of innocence in this murder? Whether or not he did, he knew he must confirm the truth either way and then decide what to do if his brother had lied.

The sheriff began to snore.

"God has cursed me with such brothers," the crowner muttered. Then he grabbed Fulke by the armpits and dragged him to a pile of straw where the head of the family could sleep off his drunken stupor.

Chapter Seventeen

The early morning light dancing on the pond did not bring the usual joy to Thomas. He was too weary to feel anything except the weight of fatigue, and his eyes burned as if dusted with grit.

Terrified by his reaction to his visitor last night, he had slept little. At least his flesh had calmed with the sleepless hours. He yawned.

With eyelids half closed, he looked over at Simon.

The young man was sitting on the bank, gazing at the stream flowing toward the priory mill, and peeling the bark off a broken limb.

Once admitted to the hermitage, Simon had eaten and drunk with fine appetite without expressing any appreciation for the hospitality. After kneeling at the small altar, he accepted the offer to take Thomas' bed, again with no thanks, and slept deeply all night. The monk lay down on his rough bench to endure the dark hours until dawn.

A discourteous heart belies the boy's beautiful face, Thomas said to himself. With relief, he realized Simon no longer tempted him. Now he grew impatient to send the lad on his way. "When you arrived, you told me you were in search of understanding, my son," he called out. "You have said nothing more of this longing since yesterday."

Simon ran his fingernail down the moist and tender wood, gouged a hole in it, and then tossed it aside.

"If I knew what troubles you, I could offer direction, if not answers." There was something about this visit that unsettled Thomas, apart from his brief lust and the intrusion on his solitude. If only his mind were not so dulled by lack of sleep. He could not grasp the reason.

"I thought holy men could read souls."

Even though the words were insolent, Thomas chose not to reply in kind. Despite Simon's tone, the furrows cutting into the youth's forehead did suggest honest concern. "If you seek a saint, you had best travel elsewhere" the monk said at last. "My sins stink like those of other men. Whatever advice I offer comes from mortal failure, not sanctity."

Simon looked oddly relieved. "I am grateful for those words," he said. "I feared my grave faults would horrify you."

"Cruelty does," the monk replied. "Little else."

Simon fell silent, picked up a rock, and skipped it across the flowing stream. "What is cruelty?" He did not look at Thomas as he spoke.

"What have you done to ask that question?"

He answered with a shrug.

"Lain with a woman against her will?" That suggestion was an easy enough presumption considering the boy's youth, the monk thought.

"You do understand a soul's secrets!" Simon picked up another rock, this time hurling it at a shrub from which an invisible bird chirped. "Your question does contain a false assertion. Women may claim they resist and thus remain innocent of what a man does, but Satan blinds them to the truth. It is their nature to seduce men into sinning. It is they who destroy our will to be virtuous and we who are unfairly abused."

"Some might agree with you, although that contention is flawed. Are there not laws against rape? The fact suggests some women may be forced into forbidden copulation by men."

Simon looked uneasy. "I have swyved virgins. Base-born wenches only. One did howl like a bitch afterward, claiming she had been unwilling. She lied."

"No matter the truth, your lust was sinful. Have you done penance?"

"I am here, am I not?"

Thomas struggled not to show his annoyance. My peace has been disrupted, he thought, shattered to no purpose. This ungracious creature suffers no agony of guilt. He has come solely for the sake of appearance. "Have you made retribution for all the maidenheads you have broken?" he snapped.

"None were virgins of rank." Simon tossed another rock. This one sank the moment it hit the water.

Clenching his fist over Simon's lack of concern for any injury he might have inflicted, Thomas longed to chastise the young man. Instead, he fell silent, wondering if he had been any more virtuous than this youth. Before he came to Tyndal Priory, he had cared little enough about the women with whom he had lain in London inns. Surely he dare not admonish when he had committed the same transgressions.

None of the women had been virgins, however, and he never forced the unwilling. Surrendering to lust might be sinful for both, but he had tried to give pleasure in return for the relief each woman gave him. When he suggested to a priest that he had done this out of gratitude, the man claimed his intended consideration had been perverted by the wickedness of the act itself.

Sin or not, he had meant to be kind. From the disregard too evident in Simon's tone, Thomas realized that the young man had not cared at all if the girls had bled without any joy.

Simon leapt to his feet, his hands stretched out in supplication. "Do you not understand? Women are like Eden's serpent, tempting me to suffer unbearably from lust. After my seed releases, I draw back from them in horror. I am befouled by their reptilian slime. I hear Satan laugh while I weep, knowing how these creatures have corrupted me."

"We are all born of woman," Thomas said, trying to calm him with reason. "Even our Lord."

Simon stiffened. "His mother was a virgin who conceived without sin."

"Your own mother…"

"There can be no comparison. I may show her honor, a son's duty, but the woman who bore me was cursed with Eve's pain and remains imbued with the imperfections of her sex."

Realizing that the defense of women, even based on the Virgin, would fail, Thomas turned to a more practical matter. "Must you father sons?"

"Only if my lands are restored," Simon replied, briefly telling his father's tale and the curse of his name. "My mother hopes to win back my title through service with Queen Eleanor. In this way, she proves the irrational nature of her sex. I see no probability of success." He spat. "No woman can restore a man's honor. He must do it himself or he is no man."

"Since you doubt you will ever recover what your father lost, then turn your back on worldly rank and vow yourself to God's service. If lust, even within marriage, offends you, find joy in the struggle for chastity."

"That was your path. Did lust trouble you so little that such a choice was easy? Were there no pleasures for you in the world at all?"

Thomas froze.

"I long for adventure," Simon continued without waiting for any answer. "If I had a horse and armor, I would leave this land." He raised his fist. "Fight for glory in tournaments." For a moment, he hesitated, and then his eyes brightened. "Go on crusade! I could serve God by killing infidels during the day and share tales of great deeds with other men at night. Might that not solve my difficulty? If I could find a man to pay for my needs, I would kill the ungodly on behalf of my benefactor's soul as well as my own."

Thomas was so amazed by this sudden turn from lust to killing that he was rendered speechless. Then he heard a sound on the path leading down from his hut, looked up, and breathed a sigh of relief. A friend was about to save him from what had become a most uncomfortable discussion.

"Crowner Ralf comes to join us," he said. "He is Sir Fulke's youngest brother and would have better advice than I on matters of war."

It was Simon's turn to look discomfited. "Methinks God has just whispered in my ear," he said, his voice rough with evident fear. He watched as the crowner pushed his way through thick branches. "Do not mention me, if you would be so kind. I cannot talk to the sheriff's brother now. God demands I pray by myself for awhile until He gives me leave to stop. Forgive me."

With those words, the youth ran like a terrified deer and disappeared into the brush edging the stream bank.

Chapter Eighteen

"Our meeting is fortunate." Father Eliduc bowed his head, his voice soft with unfeigned pleasure.

Eleanor smiled with less honest delight. Glancing in the direction of her chambers, she realized that time spent with her accounting rolls, a task not always pleasant, filled her heart with more joy than conversation with this priest. "How may I serve you?" She hoped any request would be minor.

"I have been praying for an opportunity to offer you assistance, my lady." A large fly buzzed past his nose. He swatted at it.

She would not call his manner exactly obsequious. He was far too clever for an obvious ploy, but she was ever wary of his motives, especially when his eyes narrowed like some creature prowling in the night. "You are most kind," she replied and assumed that he had some secret purpose.

"Since Baron Otes has been so cruelly slaughtered, I fear Sir Fulke will not be able to participate in the mission on which we were sent by Queen Eleanor." He inclined his head toward the guest quarters. "And Lady Avelina has not only been troubled by this murder, she has yet to recover her strength from the long journey."

The prioress nodded, letting silence linger between them.

Eliduc waited and watched as the stubborn fly attempted to land on him.

"I shall take assurances to her that both she and her son are quite safe within these walls." Eleanor grew uneasy. Did his words imply criticism?

He smirked. "Your comfort would be most welcome, my lady, although I did visit her yesterday when I returned from identifying the body." His hand shot out, grasped the fly, and squashed it.

Eleanor winced.

"She was long acquainted with the baron, and the violence of his death did trouble her." He bent to rub his hand clean on the grass. "The Church shall miss him most. He was quite generous, giving many gifts for the care of our least fortunate in exchange for prayers. Have you heard of his charitable reputation from other priories?"

"Not long after he arrived, he came to me with an offer of land as well." The moment she spoke the words, she knew she had been tricked into that proud reply. Although his scornful tone might have allowed her a remark in mild defense of Tyndal's status, her impulsive response was ill-considered. In silence, she promised God penance for her imprudence.

His expression brightened. "Then I must congratulate you on this fine gift which shall be used to the glory of God. May I ask where the land lies?" He lowered his eyes with shame. "Forgive me. I am suffering from the frailty of mortal curiosity."

Taking a deep breath, Eleanor hoped she might make amends with this next response. "The bequest was refused, albeit with much gratitude. Tyndal is a humble priory. I feared the offer was too great a gift for us." Although he would know this was a lie, courtesy demanded he not pursue the truth by questioning her further. Now she wondered where he might have been leading with this subject.

Clapping his hands together, Eliduc replied, "God will bless you, my lady, for that virtuous act."

Eleanor was unsure whether or not she should feel relief over his evident delight.

"Forgive me for the digression," he continued. "Instead of talking about the baron's death or his recent charity, I had meant to proffer modest advice since other members of the queen's party may not be able to do so."

"I am grateful for your concern." She dropped her gaze.

"I have had the pleasure of visiting your priory before, albeit on sad occasions, and have tasted the food prepared under Sister Matilda's skilled direction. Although a queen might feast on far finer cuisine than the simple fare meant for humble monks and nuns, I believe our noble lady will find your monastic meals suitable for one on pilgrimage as well as pleasing enough to her taste."

"Sister Matilda will be honored by your generous praise."

"If I may have your consent, I shall speak with Sister Matilda and offer a few modest suggestions. Our new queen comes from Castile, a far sunnier climate than England, and she is very fond, for instance, of quince, cherries, apples, and pears. I have even heard rumor that King Edward may order a garden of trees planted to provide some of her favored items."

Eleanor smiled in gratitude for this idea and said she would arrange for the requested consultation. Then she asked, "How do you find the guest quarters, Father?" Although she remained wary of him, his first recommendation was useful. Similar rumors about the queen's dietary preferences had reached her ears, including a fondness for olive oil, which the lady imported from Ponthieu.

"Austere, of course." Gnawing at his lower lip, he frowned thoughtfully. "She will bring tapestries to keep the drafts away. Having just arrived in England after sojourning in Outremer and other warmer lands, she will suffer dreadfully from the damp chill of our winter." He waited, watching for her reaction.

Although tempted to retort that she knew well enough to provide wood for fires to warm the queen, the prioress opted for a wiser silence. She nodded.

"Do not fear her displeasure, my lady." Eliduc's tone was surprisingly gentle. "There is enough room for her attendants, horses, and whatever she chooses to bring with her. This is a pilgrimage and some element of the ascetic is expected. I am confident you will supply all that is needed or expected."

"Should you find anything lacking, I beg you inform Sister Ruth so the defect may be put right."

"As you request, my lady. Your sub-prioress is most accommodating."

Had she just observed a fleeting smile? Eleanor raised an eyebrow.

"I have observed a few minor deficiencies, nothing that cannot be corrected quickly. I shall list them for you, and then for Sister Ruth, along with my recommendations for resolution."

Suppressing a chuckle, she imagined him, guttering torch in hand, prowling through the priory grounds at night in search of flaws. Perhaps he might soon have a plan for improvement of the fish ponds, she thought with brief derision. Then she chastised herself for lack of charity. Although he was devious and pernicious, she never doubted his competence at any set task. Since his current advice seemed offered in good faith, she should be grateful for advice based on greater experience than she owned.

"I must now ask about the entertainment planned to amuse our queen."

Eleanor was inclined to say that there were no jongleurs amongst her religious but restrained her tongue. "I was told her visit might be planned near the Christmas season," she said, keeping all hint of annoyance from her voice.

"Although I had hoped to dissuade her from traveling when the weather might be bitter with cold, she seemed determined to do so. Her desire to experience hardship on this pilgrimage is commendable."

"I thought a performance of the *Play of Daniel* might please her. It is commonly done during the Twelve Days."

"*Ludus Danielis*?" The priest's face expressed a rare astonishment. "The version from Beauvais or by Hilarius?"

"Brother John assures me that the one from Beauvais is superior."

He nodded before adding, "I fear the performance might be beyond the abilities of any choir here."

"Brother John performs miracles with his novice choir, which includes some boys whose voices are yet unbroken. In preparation for the event, they have already begun practice. Perhaps you have heard their sweet singing?"

Eliduc scowled. "On my way to join the monks for early prayer, I was astounded by loud roaring, followed by a surge of many boys racing from the chapel. Their laughter was quite irreverent. Seeing my confusion, one of the brothers said the lads took their lion imitation very seriously." He shuddered. "I did not seek any further explanation of such a strange remark."

"Brother John believes inclusion of the lion's den makes the horror of Daniel's unjust sentence and the eventual doom of the evil counselors more vivid. To accomplish that, he directs the novices to roar twice in the play. The boys practice the part often."

The priest's expression was a combination of great relief and mild disapproval. "Fortunately, I do not think that will terrify our queen, a woman who proved her courage in Outremer when her husband was stabbed," he said. "As I think more on this, I am unsure if she would take offense at the implied criticism in the play of an anointed king?" Eliduc's eyes widened as if afraid the prioress might agree.

"There is much praise for good kings in it. Darius is a man of his word and a just lord, as is King Edward. When he recognizes that evil men have taken advantage of his better nature, he demonstrates praiseworthy faith and says God shall save his friend and servant, Daniel. The play also shows a queen as both wise and prescient. I see no offense here." Eleanor was amused to see the priest exhale with evident relief.

Eliduc stiffened, embarrassed to have revealed a failing, and his expression grew solemn. "Very well, but I must see the full performance to make sure the quality is good enough for our lady's ears and nothing ill can be construed."

"I shall happily arrange it for you. Our novice master will be deeply honored if you approve the entertainment."

"Let me know when the choir is ready. I shall inform both Sir Fulke and Lady Avelina of our present discussion." He bowed and excused himself.

As he strode off, he exclaimed in undisguised delight: "*Ludus Danielis!*"

Eleanor had no idea Father Eliduc had such a weakness for music.

Chapter Nineteen

"When someone breaks God's commandment against murder," Signy said, "we all must aid the pursuit of justice." Although her voice was steady, her eyes narrowed as she looked up at the crowner.

"I am grateful you were willing to answer my questions." The innkeeper's suspicion pained Ralf. Nervously clearing his throat, he turned away and gazed around the busy inn.

The early hour meant few were drinking, but those wishing a quick start on the road, to or from Norwich, were breaking their fast and leaving to seek the other members of their party, their horses, or their wagons. Such bustle was a profitable noise and surely most pleasing in the ears of any innkeeper.

Perhaps that was why Signy's mouth gradually relaxed into a smile. "This time I have no fear you might want to hang me."

"That day was in the past and I never intended…"

"Hush, Ralf. For all your faults, and I have suffered from them, you are an honest man."

"Any pain I have given you distresses me beyond words. I am twice thankful that you deign to speak with me." He flushed. "I would not cast blame if you had refused."

"You did not hang me, Crowner. For that mercy, I am beholden to you. As for my other complaint, God demands forgiveness, even though He never said we must forget." Her expression was enigmatic. "In repenting my own multitude of sins, I am studying how to forgive yours."

A man far more comfortable with hard fists and sharp swords, Ralf was struck dumb when faced with what he considered saintly charity. Thus it happened that this third son of a Norman lord with noteworthy rank bent his knee to Signy, innkeeper and offspring of a landless freeman of Saxon birth.

"Merciful God!" Her face shocked into pallor, she grabbed at his arm. "Stand up before people think I have bewitched you. Neither my rank nor virtue is worthy of this."

Obeying with a sheepish look, he was grateful when a nearby commotion caught his attention.

A woman, whose stringy hair and pinched features suggested greater age than she might truly own, moved with evident pain on roughly made crutches toward the door. From outside, a man leaned into the inn and shouted that she must hurry. She stumbled, falling against a table from which she struggled to right herself.

A young boy rushed to her aid.

"Nute is a good lad," Ralf said, nodding in the boy's direction and happy he could so quickly change the subject.

"He and his sister were gifts to me from God." Signy looked equally relieved before she turned to watch Nute help the woman find her balance with the crutches.

"More likely they believe you are His blessing on them," he replied, his expression soft with respect. When Nute's parents died of the sweating sickness, soon after the death of Signy's uncle, she had taken in the child and his infant sister because they had no kin to care for them. This act was not the innkeeper's only charity, as Ralf had good reason to suspect. It was one of the few she openly admitted.

Signy ignored him and gestured to a man to bring ale for the crowner. "How may I help in this matter of murder?" Her tone announced that the sharp-witted owner of this inn had just supplanted the gentle saint.

"You are lodging the men who brought the queen's party to Tyndal Priory long after the bells for None. The murder occurred between their arrival and early this morning."

Gesturing with dismay, Signy's laugh was harsh. "And you think I should know if any of these guards disappeared long enough to kill?" Then she shrugged and gave the crowner a sympathetic look. "How many men did Prioress Eleanor say she had sent to me?"

He quoted a figure.

"I can easily confirm that is the number who came here. They did arrive together about the time you suggest. I counted the free beds; we stabled the horses and showed them where they might sleep. Since we also happen to have a group of goldsmiths with their families on pilgrimage to Norwich, a company of soldiers stands out." Briefly she flashed a mischievous smile. "Not that pilgrims always possess greater chastity and temperance than soldiers. They are simply more inclined to practice discretion with their sinning."

For just that instant, she became again the lively serving maid who had once shared his bed. Ralf grinned.

Signy turned so he could no longer see her face.

Fearing she had understood his thoughts, the crowner fell silent and hoped she would continue.

Suddenly, her attention was caught by a disturbance in a far corner of the inn. She called a man over, gave brief instructions, and seemed to forget Ralf was even there until the man gestured that he had settled the matter. Then she went on as if the conversation had never been interrupted.

"The queen's guards kept to themselves as I recall. They took their evening meal at that table." She pointed to a place just left of the door. "Drank profitably enough for the inn's benefit. Not too much to start fights or cause the pilgrims to complain. Were you to ask if any one of them went missing that night, I could not swear to it either way." She thought for a moment. "Surely the number gathered for supper must closely match those who arrived. If it would help, I could go over what the inn earned and see if that suggests how many of the soldiers ate here."

"Grateful as I am for the kind offer, I doubt the effort would point out a murderer. There is no way to connect a coin with the man who paid it," Ralf said. "They drank and ate. What did they do afterward?"

"Gambled. A few sought sleep. One tried to seduce a serving wench, but, knowing I do not tolerate any hint of whoring, she chose the pay I give over any babe with which he might have left her."

Ralf heard the trace of bitterness in her voice. Questions about Signy's own virtue had fluttered about in the past. After her uncle's death, when she became quite somber and forsook adornment in her dress as if she had been a grieving widow, rumors were finally silenced. Knowing he had a part in both the tales and the change in her, he saddened, yet he was happy the village now greeted her with respect, when she visited the stalls on market day, and that her business prospered.

Nute raced past the crowner and skidded to a stop in front of Signy, looking up at her without speaking.

She put an arm around him and hugged him close.

The orphan's eyes closed, but not before Ralf saw in them a child's longing to trust mixed with an equal fear of it.

"I saw your good deed, Nute," she whispered. "I am proud of you."

He hid his face in her robe.

Even though he wished otherwise, Ralf knew he must question the child. "Will it trouble Nute if I inquire about any knowledge he has of this matter?"

He regretted he had not asked Signy more privately and earlier. If she refused permission now, he would have to find another way of getting the information. A crowner might have the right to demand answers from whomever might have them. Ralf was also a father who did not want to frighten any child.

For a moment, she looked as if she might refuse his request, then she sat on the nearby bench and pulled the child into her lap. "Our crowner has some questions," she said to Nute, holding him tight, "and you have no cause to fear him. He is a good man. If you are uncertain about any answer, whisper it into my ear. I shall decide whether you must reply, stay silent, or should let me answer on your behalf."

From her glance Ralf knew just how zealously she would protect the boy. He nodded that he understood this well.

"Remember there is no excuse for hurtful lies or evasions. God honors those who speak the truth with courage and compassion." Signy ruffled Nute's hair.

Giving Ralf a wary look, the boy snuggled closer to the innkeeper.

The crowner cursed in silence. If he must do this, he hoped he caused no anguish.

"Ask your questions," Signy said, "but no harm shall come to my Nute."

Nute muttered something incomprehensible into her breast.

"Even if he is guilty of doing something wrong," she added, hugging the boy with fierce reassurance.

Ralf got down on his knees so his eyes were almost level with Nute's. The first question must be an easy one, he decided. "Our hermit is a terrifying sight and many fear him. Most do not have the courage to admit it." He waited for a moment to let the boy think about this. "Are you afraid of him?"

Nute nodded with vigor.

"Had I not known him as gentle Brother Thomas from the priory, before he moved into that hut, he would frighten me too with that long beard and wild red hair." Ralf winked companionably.

"And his hair does shine like fire in the sunlight." Signy added, her chin resting on top of Nute's head. "Many have been awestruck."

The crowner was not too sure how to interpret all she meant by those words. Then Nute rewarded him with a weak smile, and Ralf's thoughts returned to the problem of murder.

"Some boys tell wicked tales," he continued, "lies meant to foster terror because, out of false pride, they wish to hide their own, far greater dread." Ralf saw from Nute's expression that he had taken the right path here. "If you tell me what the stories were, I promise that those who lied to you will never know you told me."

"The hermit flies like a bat," Nute mumbled, "and captures in his claws those boys who have neither father nor mother. Then he bites them to death."

"Even were that true, which it is not, you would have nothing to fear." Despite his anger over the cruel teasing, Ralf forced a grin. "You have found a mother in Mistress Signy who has sworn to protect you and your sister against all evil."

Signy took the boy's chin in her hand and turned his face so he must look into her eyes. "Aye," she said, "and you heard me swear on a holy relic."

Nute wriggled in her lap until he could sit up, then he straighten his thin shoulders with manly purpose. "You speak the truth, Master Crowner! I watched the hermit. He never flew, morning or night, and he never tried to bite me although he surely knew I was hiding in the bushes near his door."

"He did that," Ralf replied, "and swore to me he would die before he let you come to any harm. Since you did not know that, you showed a man's courage to observe as you did, both day and night." He watched the boy flush with pleasure at the compliment. "And I think you were in those bushes the night before last, waiting to see if he flew after dusk."

"Aye." The voice now trembled.

"All night?" Ralf looked at Signy.

"He sometimes visits the hut where his parents died, and so I do not worry if he does not come to the inn for a night. He was absent at the time you mention, and I did not see him until late the next morning." She pressed her cheek against the top of Nute's head. "You are such a brave lad," she whispered.

"And what did you learn that night?" Ralf asked.

Reaching up, the boy pulled Signy's head down so he could whisper in her ear.

"You may tell the crowner all that, child. He will praise you for it." She winked at Ralf.

"The hermit did not leave his hut, and I fell asleep. When I awoke, I was very thirsty. The half moon was bright so I could see well enough to slide down the path to the stream below." He turned pale.

"And you saw some men?" Ralf hoped he wasn't suggesting answers to the boy.

"Aye. Two. They were standing by the pond."

"What more did you see or hear?"

"One turned to the other, asked where the man was that they were to meet, then shoved him to the ground. He laughed as he did it." Nute looked at Signy.

She nodded encouragement.

"The man who had fallen stood up and said something I did not hear. The one who had pushed him replied, 'Impossible' and backed away. The other rushed at him. They struggled, and the man who had laughed fell to the ground. The other bent over him, then ran away along the stream toward the priory."

"Could you describe the men?"

Nute squeezed his eyes shut for a moment. "One was very fat," he said. "One was thin."

Ralf waited.

The child said nothing more.

"Did you see their faces?"

The boy shook his head. Fear was painting his face an ashen shade.

"What did you do after the man ran away?"

"I waited, then crawled back up the path, and hid in the shrubbery."

Signy shook her head at Ralf.

He indicated he would not force the lad to say more about the murder. "And when did you come back to the inn?"

"I didn't think I could sleep, but I must have. I awoke when the hermit came out of his hut the next morning. He didn't fly then either. I slipped away after he went down the path."

"Good lad!" Ralf tousled the boy's hair. "You proved those wicked lads to be liars about our hermit, and you have helped me beyond measure!"

"Now go see if the soldiers are well served," Signy said. "You have earned a reward this day for all you have done. I shall ask the cook if she has some sweet to give you."

As he watched Nute run off, the crowner turned to the innkeeper. "Might he know more?" He kept his voice low.

"If he does, he is too frightened to speak of it. Let him be, and I shall find out if there is aught to learn. God has yet to heal his heart after his parents' death. That he should have seen a murder is unbearably cruel. Were God merciful, Ralf, He would let him forget this violence he has witnessed."

Chapter Twenty

The Office had ended. Nuns filed out to attend their tasks, whether prayer or less welcome work under the blistering sun.

Eleanor remained in the shadows of the chapel, hands clasped and neck bent. Her spirit seethed. Rarely had prayer failed to soothe or bring her much needed insight. Now was that uncommon occasion.

Every muscle and nerve tensed as she willed her mind to concentrate on those supplications she had promised to send to God. At the very least, she must pray that certain souls be granted an early release from Purgatory. The instant she completed each petition, her thoughts drifted away with mulish determination.

From the world outside, voices of men and women wafted through the hot air, their words muted and all meaning lost. Closer by, she could hear the novice choir singing one portion of a chorus from the *Play of Daniel* over and over again.

None of that was a distraction to her. A light scuffling sound nearer to hand was more difficult to overlook.

She opened her eyes.

A small, dark, and furry thing sped past her knees.

One of her cat's many feline progeny bounded after it.

Although she had no love for rodents, and found the many kittens a delight, she rather hoped this mouse would escape. After all, this was God's house and violent death had no place here.

She sat back on her heels, let her unclasped hands fall to rest on her knees, and surrendered to her failure. No matter how hard she tried, her prayers were as heavy as leaden tiles and would not rise heavenward. She'd not offer God any excuse for this inability to set worldly things aside even if one cause was not difficult to understand. She was troubled by murder.

The killing of one of the queen's men near the priory boded ill for future beneficence from either King Edward or his wife. When kings withdrew their favor, other men of rank followed their lead. Like any leader of a religious house, Eleanor depended on those small gifts of land, rents, or gold chalices to feed, clothe, and inspire her nuns and monks.

The prioress was not just concerned with the state of her accounting rolls or how brightly the priory plate glittered, she was angry that anyone would dare commit violence against a priory guest. Since all staying here were presumed to be under God's protection, the act was not only brutal but an affront to hospitality and an offense against God. Although Baron Otes had committed uncounted sins, the right to punish him belonged to God or the king. In this case, she believed the killer had encroached most on God's authority.

She gazed up at the window behind the altar. Dimmed by the moss outside, the light struggled to pass through the glass into the chapel. She had refused to order the growth scraped away. The weak glow reminded her and her religious that the human spirit must always strive to see light in the darkness of earthly sin. Now she needed the reminder more than ever to keep her seeking the elusive reason for this crime.

The first inquiry must establish whether an outlaw or someone from the village was the perpetrator. Since the body was found by the stream outside the priory, both were reasonable possibilities and would be thoroughly investigated by Crowner Ralf. She prayed that investigation would solve the crime.

She feared otherwise. To her mind, the most significant question lay in why Otes had left the guest quarters at all. He was not native to this region and, to the best of her knowledge, had neither kin nor allies in this part of England. Although he might have slipped out for an evening of whoring and drinking, Eleanor had strong doubts.

Otes was no longer young and had been giving lavish gifts to the Church. These efforts on behalf of his soul suggested he was either moved to repent his sins or, unable to satisfy favorite lusts with the ease of younger days, he had grown to fear the eternal consequences of past pleasures as each day brought him reminders of mortal decay.

Whether the baron was trying to bribe God to forget his sins or had learned He did love mended hearts, Otes' pattern of munificent gifts suggested a man who was now responding more to the rotten stench of Purgatory than the perfume of willing women.

She ran her fingertips over the rough stone on which she knelt. Whoring was probably not the baron's aim, yet she suspected he had left Tyndal to meet someone. With no reason to think that person was a local man, she concluded the killer was another member of the queen's party. If so, she was left with the question of why the meeting took place in that particular spot. The men might have met within the walls of the priory, unless the murderer did not want to add sacrilege to murder.

A sharp flapping of wings over her head disrupted her thoughts. Looking up, she saw that a bird had flown in and was perched high in the rafters. In due course, it would fly out again. In the meantime, she was glad it had found refuge from the heat. Although Sister Ruth complained that birds often drank holy water, the prioress had no quarrel with the creatures. God made them too, and she doubted He begrudged the sips of water.

The concept of refuge reminded her that the location of the crime was close to Brother Thomas' hermitage. And that made her think of Father Eliduc.

She asked herself if the priest had visited the hermit, hoping to lure him off for some task without her permission. That was an innocent thought compared to her second and more sinister one.

After visiting with her monk, Eliduc would have realized how remote the place was. If the priest had some quarrel with the baron, he might have lured him to the pond for private talk. If the two men then argued, the priest could have killed Otes.

A tiny voice within her quickly insisted that Eliduc would have done so only in self-defense. A louder one expressed doubt about that.

Eleanor shivered. Her logic was obviously flawed. She was equally certain there was a bit of truth in her suspicion.

The priest had shown interest in any gift of land that Otes might have offered Tyndal. As she thought more on her conversation with Eliduc, she remembered how relieved he had been when she said she had refused Otes' offer. That land might have been the cause for disagreement between the men, especially if it was rich enough.

One flaw in this reasoning was that she had spoken with the priest after the killing. If Eliduc was the perpetrator, he would not have been so pleased to discover the baron's death was not necessary after all.

"He is still a priest," she murmured, bowing her head with shame that she would even consider him likely to break a major Commandment.

On the other hand, all mortals were prone to sin, priests included. Despite being convent-raised, Eleanor had not been sent out to head a priory like some lamb to face wolves. Her aunt, who had raised her in Amesbury, made sure her young niece understood that tonsures, vows, and pretty phrases were not always matched by honest or even kind hearts.

She made a fist and pressed it into the stone until pain made her stop. Would she have even considered the priest a suspect if she did not have a quarrel with him over Brother Thomas?

"My logic is fouled by my own anger," she whispered. "Although his missions may have been to the Church's benefit, Father Eliduc deceived me when he came, with sorrowing demeanor, to take Brother Thomas away on pretense of family illness. I have not forgiven him for those lies."

Gritting her teeth, she reminded herself that she had been taught to be just even if the result was not to her liking. Aye, she hated the priest, even though God condemned that as a sin. The man was duplicitous, and she did have the right to complain of his treachery.

With significant effort she reversed her inclination to denounce. "Eliduc has done nothing on his own volition. The priest is only following the command of his own lord," she muttered.

Those words had a hollow sound. "And were a poor defense," she admitted to the surrounding silence. "Lies are unacceptable, but they are not the same as murder. I am still blinded by his deceptions."

With a bitter sigh, she stepped away from the easy conclusion that a man she loathed must be capable of homicide, even if her heart refused to reject the idea as quickly as a logical mind demanded.

From behind the altar, an orange and grey-speckled kitten emerged and boldly approached to sniff at the Prioress of Tyndal. She whispered that this act was an arrogant presumption of familiarity, then contradicted her stern rebuke by petting him. As he wandered off, Eleanor noticed with guarded relief that the creature held no mouse clenched in its teeth. Of course, he might well have eaten it in the shadows.

As she tried to quiet that inner voice stubbornly arguing for Eliduc's involvement in the violence, she knew that little was as straightforward as appearance suggested. "I do not know enough and have no actual reason to conclude Father Eliduc would slit a man's throat," she said to her willful heart.

In the silence of the chapel, she heard her heart reply that the priest might turn his head and let another do what he might not.

The fact remained that Eliduc acted only at the command of the man he served, someone who must be of high Church rank. The wily priest dressed simply, but his soft robes were finely made, his small gold cross skillfully crafted, and his grey horse notably well-bred. None of this spoke of a man in service to some poor lord. Surely such a mighty Church prince would never defile his own vows and order his servant to commit murder. The cost to both their souls was too great.

"And this piece of land must be of little value or the baron would not have offered it to my small priory. Should the gift be of more worth, a reasonable man would grasp that I might be agreeable to exchanging it for something just as useful to our needs here. Murder is far too extreme a solution for such a small problem." Clenching her teeth, she muttered with forced charity, "Therefore, the killer cannot be Father Eliduc. He would understand all this. Who else might have murdered the baron?"

Was it Sir Fulke? She had little direct knowledge of him since he stayed with the king's court and let Ralf handle all matters of wrongdoing in the county.

Her father, Baron Adam, had never said much about the sheriff except that he owned a fair cleverness and was reputed to suffer from no more than middling corruption. The crowner mentioned his eldest brother only with contempt, calling him a man who preferred comfort and prestige to catching thieves and keeping other lawless men far from Tyndal village. Between the two assessments, Eleanor concluded that Fulke might suffer a surfeit of ambition but shrink away from self-serving violence.

That assumption noted, many sheriffs were losing their positions as bribery and other unlawful deeds came to the king's attention. King Edward was swiftly eradicating fraudulent practices in the shrievalty, corruption his father had let run rampant. If Sir Fulke had committed transgressions in the pursuit of power and feared he might lose his rank and influence, could he be driven to extreme measures to save himself?

If Fulke had something damaging to hide, Eleanor also wondered if the crowner knew about it. Dare she ask Ralf if his brother hid a secret that might drive him to kill a man known for using knowledge of such things for his own gain?

Out of family loyalty, Ralf might lie, no matter how honest he was himself. On the other hand, the crowner had always honored his friendship with Eleanor. Forcing her friend to choose between two conflicting, yet equally compelling, loyalties was not something she wanted to do.

She had grown weary with these numerous complications and unanswered questions. No firm conclusions could be made without more information, nor could any clear path to the truth be seen.

The prioress stood, bowed her head, and begged God to pardon her inattention and negligence in prayer. If He willed it, she added, she would be grateful if He enlightened her in this matter of violent death. Being a frail mortal, she conceded that she would better attend her religious duties if she did not have this crime to distract her.

In the meantime, her promised visit to Lady Avelina was long overdue. Father Eliduc had said the lady was weakened by the hard journey and fearful because of Otes' murder. Providing hospitality demanded Eleanor also supply comfort and ease. Of course she must find out if the woman had need of Sister Anne's expertise.

"May God forgive me," Eleanor said, knowing full well what she also intended. She was not so oblivious to her failings that she did not recognize another, less benevolent motive in her concern for this woman.

She turned and walked out of the chapel into the harsh glare of the summer sun.

Chapter Twenty-one

The hot afternoon air lay heavily upon the earth. All birds had fallen silent, and even bees were no longer tempted by the lure of dazzling flowers. As the prioress walked with measured pace toward the guest quarters, she prayed that all mortal creatures had found relief and, for those unable to rest, there was shade in which to continue laboring.

Eleanor had no wish to join any in respite. Her mind now eagerly seeking ways to discover a killer, she no longer felt the heat.

As far as she knew, no one, including Father Eliduc, had asked Lady Avelina any questions about Baron Otes. Although God had judged the souls of both sexes to be equal, mortals believed Eve's daughters were cursed with feeble natures and weaker wit. Men did not often remember to query women, forgetting that powerless creatures survived by keeping their ears alert for sounds ignored by the more confident and their eyes vigilant for troubling details. It was possible Lady Avelina had noticed some small thing that might lead Crowner Ralf to Baron Otes' murderer. Eleanor was keen to find out.

As she neared the guest house, someone called out to her. She looked over her shoulder.

Brother Beorn hurried down the path toward her.

Eleanor waited, apprehension gnawing at her gut. Had there been another untoward death? Shading her eyes, she tried to interpret the concern darkening the man's brow as he approached. "Is all well?"

"My lady, I beg audience with you." Sweat poured down his lean cheeks. The air was sharp with his stink.

"Can this matter wait? I have learned Lady Avelina is unwell." He hesitated.

"When I return to my chambers, I shall send for you."

Although his face betrayed a hint of reluctance, he nodded. "I will pray for her recovery, my lady, and I am grateful you have agreed to hear me out. In truth, my concern may prove a small thing. I shall await your summons." With that, he bowed and turned away.

Bothered by the hesitation she had heard in his reply, she watched him walk back up the path. A good man, she thought, one who was always obedient and never troubled her with petty matters. This time, he had suggested the problem might be a minor issue, and surely murder superseded most common priory concerns.

She continued on to the guest house.

Eleanor knocked, noting with pleasure the finely crafted woodwork on this entrance to the recently completed quarters.

The man who opened the door neither spoke nor bowed in greeting. Instead, he stared at her and waited.

She stiffened at such lack of respect. This was Kenard, Lady Avelina's attendant, and the one whose hooded eyes unsettled her. It was a feature she had always found distasteful, for it brought to mind Eden's serpent. Now his haughtiness gave her reason to dislike the man even more. She glowered and said nothing.

He bowed.

"Is the Lady Avelina within and able to receive me? I have learned your mistress was much weakened by her arduous journey and wish to offer whatever comforts and healing power we own to hasten her return to health."

Gesturing for her to enter, the servant disappeared without uttering a single word.

Such unconscionably rude behavior from this servant must be worthy of rebuke. Her office should be honored even if she herself was not, Eleanor thought, and then reminded herself that she had been doing penance enough over the last year for her bristling pride.

She squeezed her eyes shut, willing her thoughts about the man to grow more charitable. She had been finding far too many reasons of late to argue that her office had suffered insult. Perhaps it was time to stop hiding the sin of pride behind that rightful claim.

The man returned and motioned in silence for her to follow him.

Bowing her head, she did as requested.

The room she entered was filled with shadows. Although the linen hangings around the bed had been pulled open to welcome both light and air, the windows were shuttered. Neither sun nor sea breeze could lighten the gloom or sweep away the stagnant odors common to mortal flesh.

Lady Avelina lay on the bed, her back supported by pillows and only a delicate silken quilt of checkerboard pattern covering her.

How frail she looks, Eleanor thought, then quickly decided that the pale shadows might have exaggerated the woman's infirmity.

"You show much charity in visiting me on this hot day. Please sit, and my servant will bring cool refreshment to revive you." Avelina pulled herself into a more upright position and pushed at her covering with peevish annoyance. "This heat sucks so hard at the body. Like enough to a ravenous babe. How could anyone have the strength left to walk or even stand?" Recognizing her tone as querulous and ill-mannered, Avelina tilted her head with shamefaced apology and gestured to a nearby chair.

Eleanor noticed it was set, convenient for conversation, near Avelina's bed, and a small table had been placed close to hand.

All had been readied for a guest's comfort. She eased herself onto the chair and smiled.

Now that she was closer to the woman, the prioress saw that Avelina's eyes were bright with wit, not fever. Perhaps the lady suffered only from the heat and fatigue of the journey, quite understandable for a woman of later years and heavier body. Indeed, her face had a reddish hue as if burned by the intense sun. How unfortunate that the lady had not been better protected on the long trip here.

Suddenly, out the corner of her eye, Eleanor saw something move and uttered a soft cry of alarm when a hand passed too close by her face.

It was only the servant who had reappeared with a bowl of dried fruit and a pottery jug, glistening with cool moisture even in the sallow light. Eyes half open, he glanced at her, his expression suggesting gratification over her reaction. Quickly, he set the items on the table and stepped back.

Eleanor shivered. Maybe this man was some malign spirit and no proper mortal at all.

He gestured at the pillows and waited for his lady to respond.

Avelina shook her head and dismissed him with words softly spoken.

His shoes scuffling in the lavender-strewn rushes, the man disappeared through the door.

The prioress was beginning to suspect a profound intimacy between servant and lady. Her reasons for concluding this were vague. Perhaps the cause was simply her dislike for Kenard and her disapproval that such a man would be treated with gentle courtesy when he had not offered the same to her.

As if reading the first of Eleanor's thoughts, Avelina sighed. "Kenard must do all for me while my maid is resting. The girl suffers ill health."

The prioress nodded. The swiftness with which this explanation was offered suggested the lady had too often made the same excuse. Although Eleanor did not witness any presumptuous look or gesture by the servant, she now realized there had been an ease between these two, most often seen in husband and wife long wedded.

The matter certainly did not concern her, although she did find it curious. Either the servant was in love with his mistress or else worshipped her far more than any mortal ought another. Whether or not the passion was returned, the prioress guessed Lady Avelina was both aware and countenanced it.

"Does your servant not speak at all?" Eleanor gestured in the direction the man had disappeared. As she did, she noticed the door was not quite closed.

"Not since the battle at Evesham. Kenard was my husband's servant and saw him killed. Since then, he has served me loyally and with competence but has not uttered a word." She bit slowly into a piece of dried fruit and chewed with the care of one suffering from sore teeth.

Eleanor gratefully sipped at her mazer of cool ale. "Sister Christina, our infirmarian, believes such afflictions are caused by a sickness in the soul. She has found a penance of fasting and a night of solitary, silent prayer helpful. If confession is needed, we have a priest who can interpret many hand gestures."

Avelina tugged at her quilt, then pushed it away as if undecided whether she was too hot or too cold. "Your offer is most kind…" Her words drifted into silence, and she pressed the edge of her hand just under her breast.

"I have heard many sad tales of those who were engaged in that battle," Eleanor said. "My father fought for King Henry but said there were brave men on both sides. As I think more on that, I believe Baron Otes was there too. Did you know him well?"

Avelina did not reply. She stared, eyes rounded as if she had just seen a vision.

Alarmed, the prioress rose.

"Do not trouble yourself, my lady. I suffer only from this heat," Avelina waved her hand. "I thank you for your suggestion. Perhaps Kenard has already learned of your nun's methods, although I shall certainly inform him of the treatment. Should he wish to seek the healing offered, I would give him leave to do so."

Eleanor hesitated. If the lady was unwell, perhaps she should not question her about the baron. Until she made up her mind, she opted for caution and changed the topic. "I understand your son accompanied you here."

Avelina laughed. "Simon did travel with me. Like most young men, he grew impatient with idleness once we arrived. He learned that a hermit lived near the priory and begged my permission to visit him. I sent him off."

"Then God has blessed you with a pious lad."

"The request was most unexpected, I fear. Until now, he has longed only to fight and perform brave deeds like some mythical knight so I hid my surprise and expressed pleasure over this sudden interest." She sighed. "In truth, I would be happy if he did find a calling to serve God."

"He is not your eldest then?" Eleanor struggled to remember if her father had mentioned how many children were in this family and failed to bring such details to mind.

"He is my only living son who faces an empty legacy. Surely you know that my lord was an early follower of de Montfort? The earl honored us by agreeing to be our son's godfather and for this reason my son is also named *Simon*. The honor turned bitter when my husband was declared a traitor after his death at Evesham. All his lands and title were forfeited to the crown, and so my boy has little inheritance and less honor."

The prioress grieved she had humiliated the lady by making her recount a tale that must bring her sorrow. Although the prioress never intended cruelty, she attempted to ease any pain by adding, "You now serve Queen Eleanor and must have her confidence for she sent you here on her behalf. Perhaps she will help your son recover what his father lost. Others in similar circumstances have won back their lands."

"I am honored to wait upon our king's lady wife and do so only because my kin were all loyal to the crown. Had my family not fought for King Henry, my son and I might have starved. The old king, at the urging of his brother, showed charity. I was allowed to keep a few manors to support us."

Eleanor was unable to read Avelina's expression, muted as it was by soft shadows, and wondered if it betrayed bitterness over the past or pride that she had gained favor despite her husband's unfortunate allegiance. "Your own fidelity is unquestioned," she said, bending forward with a gentle smile after deciding to emphasize the woman's trustworthiness.

Had Avelina's husband rejected de Montfort when the Lord Edward finally did, matters would have been quite different for this family. The new king himself had a history of flickering loyalties, and Eleanor's eldest brother, Sir Hugh, had followed his direction no matter which way Lord Edward had twisted and turned. Her brother suffered no ill and had even been knighted in Outremer by the king.

"How old is your son?" Eleanor shifted the subject away from these painful matters.

Apparently less discomfited by the unhappy topic than the prioress had thought, the Lady Avelina went on. "The boy was but a babe in arms at his sire's death and innocent of any treason," she said. "I have hoped Queen Eleanor would approach the king on my behalf and persuade him to restore both land and title even though I know the possibility is remote." She brightened. "So you can understand my happiness were Simon to declare that his soul longed to serve the Church." Pressing a hand to her heart, she added with greater enthusiasm, "And I think it most likely that our queen could convince King Edward to arrange some profitable living for my boy!"

"I shall pray for an honorable and just conclusion to this matter."

Avelina bowed her head with the required gratitude.

Eleanor sat back. Perhaps she would try again to raise the subject of Baron Otes, since the lady seemed content enough to talk about the past. "Evesham was a cruel battle, for cert. My own father suffered a horrible wound, as did Prior Andrew. Of those who accompanied you on this journey, I have heard that Baron Otes fought there as well, although not, I believe, Sir Fulke."

"Many on both sides did suffer." Avelina looked away. "Their names fade from memory over the years, except in the hearts of the survivors." She fell silent and picked at the quilt.

Eleanor slowly raised her mazer and sipped. What path should she now take? This time, Avelina had clearly avoided talking about the baron. Were she to pursue this subject, the prioress feared she might cause offence.

Like the Trinity, *three* was a sacred number, and so she decided to try a third time. If the lady showed annoyance, she would quickly turn to another subject. "The war brought a few to God," Eleanor said. "Prior Andrew took vows when he regained health, and I have heard Baron Otes was making gifts of land in exchange for prayers on behalf of his soul."

It was unclear whether the lady coughed or snorted with disdain. "So I have heard. A leper house in Yorkshire, I believe. Nor shall his sons suffer from these bequests. He will leave them prosperous enough."

At least Avelina had responded, and she did not seem upset over the land gifts as Father Eliduc had. Even if the mention of the baron's charitable donations had provoked her mild contempt, that reaction was no different than what many others had expressed.

Eleanor pressed on, hoping to learn something of interest if not of obvious value. "For all his charity, he died violently. I marvel at that and grieve as well."

Avelina stiffened. "His reputation may not have reached your ears at Tyndal Priory. He was not well-loved. The wonder may be that no one killed him long ago. I can only conclude he died now because of an accidental meeting with some brigand."

"How had he offended?" Eleanor crafted an innocent look.

Avelina matched her effort. "Do not men always find a cause over which to quarrel? We women are often left in ignorance of their reasons."

Nodding, Eleanor kept her tone light. "Were there arguments on the journey?"

"Considering some of the inns we stayed in," Avelina replied with equal levity, "I could not have heard a battle over the noise of animals and ruder men, let alone hot words between a pair of them. I know nothing of disagreements. During the day, we spoke little. What energy the heat left us was used to endure the long ride." She sat back and frowned.

Eleanor sensed there would be no further discussion of Otes. All this conversation had accomplished was to bring the prioress back to her first concern about any link between Father Eliduc and the land offered to Tyndal.

Otes had possibly offered the gift to several religious leaders to see which man offered his soul the best terms for escaping Purgatory. To Eleanor's mind, no land had such high value that possession of it was worth committing murder. Then she scolded herself for being a fool. Others would disagree about killing over a bit of fertile earth, and she had been wrong before in making similar conclusions.

So the priest again became a foremost suspect, and Eleanor found herself still uncomfortable with the conclusion. Eliduc might suffer from worldly ambition, but, for all his flaws, she did believe he feared God too much to utterly damn his soul.

There was far more to learn, and Eleanor suspected she must seek elsewhere for answers. In fact, Lady Avelina might not know much more that was pertinent. Even if she did, the prioress doubted she would dare question the lady more closely in this matter that rightfully belonged to the king's justice.

"Such earthly concerns!" the prioress said with proper dismay over her weakness in gossiping. "I came, not to speak of such sad matters, rather to offer some relief to you. I fear the journey here has unbalanced your humors."

"You have the right of it," Avelina responded. "I am no longer a young woman and long journeys require rest." She gestured to a small vial on a table nearby, next to which sat a mortar and pestle. "I do have a tonic which will revive me. When I am ready to sleep, Kenard prepares it. I usually awaken to find myself improved the next day. After so many days, the relief does take longer. My strength will return by tomorrow."

"If you or your servant need anything from our herb garden, Sister Anne is an experienced apothecary and can make whatever you might require."

Lady Avelina nodded. "Her reputation for skillful treatments has reached the court."

"If you would like her to visit and discuss your health, I will send her to you."

"I would be grateful for her opinion."

"Then she will await your summons, and I shall not fatigue you further." Eleanor rose. As she turned to leave, she recalled another matter she meant to mention. "Our novice and choir master had hoped to perform *The Play of Daniel* for the queen. Father Eliduc wishes to see it, and Brother John readies his choir for a performance. If you are well enough, I would be honored if you joined me in the nuns' gallery when this occurs. Although undue pride is a sin, I believe Brother John is most talented and that his choir sings like angels must. This enactment of the tale might both entertain and cheer your soul."

"I would be delighted!"

"Then I will let you know when it is to take place and send someone to accompany you to the chapel."

Assuring the lady she did not need Kenard to accompany her to the door, Eleanor left the guest quarters, relieved she did not have to see the troubling servant again.

She may have been disappointed with her failure to get the information she had hoped, but her visit did seem to raise Lady Avelina's spirits. The invitation to watch *The Play of Daniel* certainly pleased her. Whatever Eleanor did not accomplish, she had honored the commandment to practice charity.

Hurrying back to her chambers, the prioress remembered she had promised to call for Brother Beorn. If God is kind, she thought, the matter distressing him will be of minor consequence.

Chapter Twenty-two

Fulke knelt in the darkest part of the chapel and prayed. Even in these shadows, his head throbbed after that night of drinking.

If someone offered to chop off the offending part, he might have considered the proposition. Only the state of his soul would have stopped him, a concern that rarely troubled the sheriff except when he was reminded of death. Seeing Baron Otes' corpse was one of those painful moments.

"I have sinned," he muttered, dutifully herding guilt into his heart.

An insistent hiss of protest rose above the thundering inside his skull. Were his transgressions worse than others? Hadn't he been less corrupt than most in his situation? He had taken only one substantial bribe, looking the other way when a man paid far less into the king's treasury than was due.

Fulke had used that coin to buy a rich, ecclesiastic position for his brother, Odo. Since the money had gone to Church coffers, he deemed it only just that the ultimate beneficiary of the bribe count in his favor and that his deed be cleansed of any wrong.

Odo had also vowed to pray daily for his elder sibling's soul in gratitude for the gift. Since his middle brother spent more time lusting over his accounting rolls than he did bending his fat knees in prayer, Fulke had little confidence in the efficacy of that promise.

Even without Odo's infrequent intercessions with God, there must surely be less cause for apprehension now that the baron was dead. How would King Edward learn about that one act of corruption? Few had ever known what the sheriff had done, and they were unlikely to reveal the secret.

The man who had given him the bribe died long ago with neither wife nor sons surviving. Odo had gotten the position he craved and would never endanger his smooth wine, fat meat that crackled on the spit, and the soft pillow on which to kneel at his artfully carved prie-dieu. As for the crowner, his code of honor might be peculiar, but he did have one. Despite his errant ways, Ralf was loyal to family.

Fulke sat back on his heels and smiled up at the cross on the altar. He had nothing to fear. He was secure in his position as sheriff. The baron's death was fortunate. Countless men could now sleep easily, and many would bless the man who had killed Otes.

As for his soul's more common transgressions, Fulke also grew confident that God would not be too harsh. Muttering contrition for his drunkenness and whoring, the sheriff vowed he would seek the required penance once this unfortunate journey had ended. Briefly, he imagined his wife's oval face brightened with an approving smile.

His heart now beating so loud with its celebratory joy, Fulke belatedly became aware of another sound in the chapel: the whisper of soft shoes gliding across the stone floor.

The sheriff opened one eye and cautiously glanced to his right.

Father Eliduc moved toward the altar with the lightness of a spirit, his hands raised heavenward with reverence. Slowly he knelt, lowered his head, and began murmuring hushed prayers with a chanting cadence.

Fulke edged deeper into the shadows, inexplicably fearing the priest had seen him. There is no good reason to care if he had, the sheriff thought, and just as quickly hoped Eliduc had not recognized him.

Eliduc sighed between prayers.

Fulke shivered.

It was irrational to be frightened of this man of God. He could not be some imp in disguise, for no creature from Hell 'ever wore a cross around his neck. Although Satan was clever in the ways he used to deceive mortals, fallen angels did have their limits. Eliduc must be a true priest.

Maybe my soul is more troubled with sin when I am in the priest's presence, Fulke thought. The image of his wife returned, this time scowling. How often he had betrayed her with other women after he was refused her bed. "She is virtuous and kind," he murmured, swearing he would be a better husband.

He winced. He could not deceive God. Any vow he made to remain chaste was brittle and therefore he might well have good reason to avoid Eliduc's company if the man did read thoughts as the sheriff suspected. The more he thought on that, the stronger his sins began to stink like rotting fish.

Another, darker image came to him next. Might this priest, who wore such vibrant black, be Death's messenger? Cold sweat was now rolling down the sheriff's back. Otes was already dead. With Eliduc still here, Death might harvest other souls. And whose might they be?

Fulke clenched his chattering teeth. Such fears were foolish things, more suitable to old women and little children. Wasn't he a full-grown man?

Then a third possibility struck him, one that gave him far greater cause to panic. He covered his face and bent forward until his brow hit the stone floor.

What if Baron Otes had confided to Father Eliduc all he knew about the corruption that had occurred during the reign of the old king? Whether or not the knowledge was conveyed to the priest as a confession or the simple sharing of information by an uneasy soul, Fulke knew he remained in great danger despite the baron's death.

He took a deep breath and calmed himself. Otes only cared for his own advancement. Eliduc played for higher stakes in the struggles for power between the Church and kings. Whereas the baron pondered the value of each man's secrets as if they were gemstones he might want to purchase, Eliduc had no interest in the individual sin or man, caring only about the value of the aggregate. Even if Eliduc knew all the sheriff had done, the priest would find little of it useful to the Church. Fulke was not powerful enough, and surely Eliduc never dealt in trivial matters.

Yet there were others who might find benefit in minor secrets. If someone had overheard Otes talking to the priest, Fulke was not as safe as he had assumed.

Overwhelmed by uncertainty, he began to weep in self-pity. Since his father's death, the sheriff had devoted his life to increasing family prestige and wealth. The baron might be dead, but Fulke remained in danger of losing rank and all he had struggled to gain. Should the new king chose harsh measures to punish wrongdoers, he might also be stripped of his freedom or even his life.

After some time, Fulke's tears did cease. When he looked around, Father Eliduc had disappeared.

Had he only imagined the priest was here? God might have sent the man's image as a fearsome reminder to Fulke that his sins were many and grievous.

Once again the sheriff's teeth began to chatter as if he had been struck with an ague.

Chapter Twenty-three

"Why did you flee from Crowner Ralf?" Thomas shoved a roughly cut, wooden mazer of ale across the table toward Simon.

"I did not want to talk to him."

Although the youth covered his eyes with a weary gesture, Thomas suspected the act was feigned and meant to hide a forthcoming lie. He waited for it.

"The world and mortal men trouble me." Simon sighed. "Must I give any other reason for my flight?" He gave the monk a quick look, gauging the effect of his words.

Thomas raised an eyebrow.

"The wicked roar of men's sinful voices drowns out His direction."

Although the monk knew the young man must have come to the hermitage for some reason, he did not believe Simon was possessed by any sincere religious longing. Had Thomas seen any indication of a soul tormented over issues of faith, he would have sent Simon to the priory to speak with men better suited to advise him. Whatever troubled the youth, the monk also doubted the problem was the comparatively simple issue of unbearable lust.

In his years at Tyndal, Thomas had learned about a vast range of vices, some horrible, others touching in their innocence, and a few even amusing, albeit embarrassing to the sinner. There was little left to shock him, and he was growing impatient for Simon to get on with what he needed to confess. Thomas may have felt obliged to offer lodging to truth-seekers. Simon's annoying presence had begun to outweigh the value of the charity.

"I do not believe you want to hear God's voice." The monk softened his gruff tone by offering more ale.

Simon blinked and turned his head so his eyes did not meet the monk's. "I do seek counsel."

"That, I believe." Deciding to hurry the revelation, Thomas returned to the previously admitted problem, hoping that had been the first step in Simon's path to confessing his purpose. "Hesitate not to admit the full power of your lust. God knows all men struggle with desire, especially the young." As he watched the youth turn pale, he wondered if the cause of the young man's disquiet was truly this simple.

Thomas remembered what he had been like at Simon's age, a time of comparative innocence, yet one filled with fear of his own body. There were countless times he and Giles had confided their lust-filled dreams, the irresistible longing to pleasure themselves for relief, and how powerless they had felt to resist temptation. So driven were they by Satan's prickings that days went by when they seemed incapable of anything except copulating, sleeping, and eating enough to keep up their strength to satisfy the sexual craving.

"Like you," the monk said, "I was conceived in lust, born of woman, and suffer mortal failings. Be assured, however, that God understands this and does forgive the truly penitent."

Simon said nothing. A muscle twitched in his cheek, and he shut his eyes as if fearing they might betray something deeply hidden in his soul.

Thomas did not know which course he ought now to follow. Simon was of high enough birth to be named prior of some profitable house, should he choose God as his liege lord, and many of Thomas' fellow priory monks had discovered that His service cooled passions over time. Even he had found comfort if not tranquility at Tyndal, although his own lusts took a different shape and rape had rendered him practically impotent.

On the other hand, Simon could still marry and find relief with a wife for his rebellious genitals, if he had land or title enough to tempt fathers with too many daughters. Some followers of the Earl of Leicester had bought back the lands stripped away after the rebellion, although Thomas suspected Simon's mother possessed neither the coin nor the means to acquire it. Or Queen Eleanor might persuade the king to show mercy, return a small portion of the lands, and demand little or no payment. If she wanted to reward Simon's mother for faithful service at less cost to the royal coffers, the queen could also arrange a profitable marriage for the lad.

Whatever path Simon might pursue, he needed direction to protect him from his own bad judgement and keep him from seeding a babe in the wrong woman. His current situation was difficult enough. The youth did not need to destroy any hope for reconciliation with the new king because he did something ill-considered.

Simon sat ever so still.

Telling the lad that he should honor his mother's advice would do no good. Simon had already uttered contempt for feminine governance. Most religious would advise him to just exercise self-restraint and pray to dampen his obsession with lust, but Thomas recalled how quickly he and his friends had shoved aside such advice at the same age. It had taken prison, the loss of the man he had loved, and mocking impotence to learn that selfless deeds could numb the pain until he fell asleep and became vulnerable to dreams.

His mind raced. He must find a path for Simon to follow that would accomplish a beneficial result without the horrible suffering he had experienced. The idea must also be something the youth had not heard too often and already rejected. At least it must surprise him into considered thought.

The bench tipped over as Simon shoved away from the table and went to the altar. Bowing in reverence, he continued his silence as if he were deep in prayer.

Annoyance scraped like a persistent rat at Thomas' good intentions. Why did he suspect that everything Simon did was pretence? Shaking the thoughts away, he decided he must treat the youth's visit as sincere until he found good evidence that proved falsehood.

"Before I took vows," he said, "I swyved many women. I could not even tell you the number. Here at Tyndal Priory, I have experienced a miraculous transformation. In this Order of Fontevraud, we serve a woman who represents the Queen of Heaven on earth. As the beloved disciple was commanded at the foot of the cross, we obey and protect her. In doing so, I discovered I had lost all desire for a woman's mortal body."

Simon continued to face the altar. "I have heard many tales of you," he murmured.

Thomas froze in terror. What had the lad learned of him? Suddenly aware of a sharp pain, he looked down at his hands. He had clenched them until his nails dug into the palms. Opening one fist, he saw a small drop of blood emerging.

"Although your deeds have been done in modest silence, you are well-known amongst powerful men for your service on behalf of God's justice."

Swallowing ale to wash away the dryness of fear, the monk hoped he had command of his voice. "Methinks you are mistaken. I am of less significance in holy work than a dust mote." Rubbing off the sweat beading on his forehead, Thomas relaxed. At least Simon did not seem to know of the monk's time in prison or the cause. Then he wondered if he should worry that the young man knew about Thomas' work as a spy.

"I was told of your bravery in catching the man who murdered two others, one a monk, at Amesbury. Some credit your prioress for uncovering the perpetrators of sinful acts. They are fools. Women are but trifles, and not one would chase a killer up a steep roof. A single misstep could have sent you to your death. That was a man's deed!"

Thomas started to correct the story, for he most certainly had not chased anyone up a slippery roof. Then he thought the better of it. Believing the tale, the young man might reveal more of his concerns. He might even disclose his motive in mentioning this particular story, were he not interrupted. If some greater good was served, the monk decided God would surely forgive him for allowing an insignificant fallacy.

"I do wonder that you find any peace in a priory run by a woman and an Order with such an unusual rule." Simon shook his head and spun around to face the monk. "It may be my duty to serve my mother, for she gave birth to me. Now that she has denied me my rightful place as a man for too long, methinks it is against the natural order to obey her further."

"Forebear awhile longer. Queen Eleanor has shown confidence enough in your mother to send her on the journey here. She might yet persuade the queen to intervene with King Edward on your behalf. Should that happen and you regain anything of your father's estates, you can repay her diligence with honor and comfort in her aged years, as a man ought, if she does not remarry."

"Surely you cannot believe she will succeed!" Simon returned to the table, sat down, and began worrying the wood with his fingernail.

Thomas could not answer with any certainty, never having met Simon's mother or the queen. As for King Edward, the monk had seen him years ago. The young prince had been several years older and had no cause to pay heed to the many awe-struck and dusty boys surrounding him, especially one who was a bastard. All Thomas could remember was his height, that he was deft with a sword in practice bouts, and handsome, although he spoke with a lisp. None of that pointed to whether the new king might grant any plea brought by his wife on this lad's behalf.

"As I have already said, she cannot." Simon shrugged. "The lands have gone to men loyal to kingship, or else into the king's hand where the income helps fill his coffers. As for the title, some minor lord now boasts it, and he went with King Edward on his crusading pilgrimage to Outremer. I must remain the son of a traitor and am being kept from proving my manhood." Simon's tone was bitter.

Thomas nodded, stopping himself from responding to the youth's resentment. Although Simon's bristled cheeks might prove he had a man's body, his expression called to mind a petulant child.

"I have begged my mother to get me the loan of a horse and armor. With that, I would earn enough in tournaments to buy my own land and probably gain a knighthood. She refuses to ask for that boon of any at court, saying the surrender of hope would be dishonorable."

"If the likelihood of regaining your father's title and lands is so bleak, then you must earn trust by modest and responsible action. What have you done to prove yourself worthy to other men?"

A sheen of sweat broke out on Simon's forehead. "I spoke with one man who welcomed me to his table and heard my plea. He had been my father's friend and an early supporter of the Earl of Leicester. After Lord Edward escaped de Montfort's custody, by tiring his guards' horses and then fleeing on a rested beast, the man abandoned the earl for the king. Unlike my father, he saved his patrimony."

Thomas' look asked the question.

"His daughter was wanton! She lured me into a garden, tempted me beyond all reason, and then refused her body. I beat her for that wickedness and she screamed. Her mother found us and believed the creature's lies. I was cast into the street." Simon threw up his hands in outrage at the insult committed against him.

"No father would loan money to a landless youth who had just beaten his daughter, nor, out of loyalty, would any of the father's friends and kin. Surely you must understand why." Thomas was sorely tempted to forget his vows and pummel the lad himself on behalf of the girl and her father.

"So my mother has said, but men also understand how women lead us into sin. Priests remind us often enough of their wicked nature."

So much for that attempt to enlighten the lad about the ways of mortal fathers, Thomas thought. On the other hand, if Simon had a warrior's talent, he might find men with wealth and ambition who prized battle skills above any woman's honor, especially men who had not married and bred daughters they loved. "Do you know of any others who might take up your cause?"

Simon brightened and seemed about to speak. Then a frown dulled his look and he quickly turned away. "Most do fear giving any favor to a traitor's son, especially when the king has turned his back on several who fought on de Montfort's side." He sadly shook his head and gazed at the monk, waiting for him to respond.

Once again, Thomas caught himself suspecting that the expression of despair was calculated. "What of Baron Otes? There was time enough on this journey from court for either you or your mother to approach him. Or had he already refused?"

His face turning scarlet, Simon slammed his fist on the table. "He was an odious man, and I salute his killer!"

Thomas was shocked at the passionate response. With dismay he now remembered that Simon had not come to the hermitage until the morning after the baron was found dead.

Had he given shelter to a murderer?

Chapter Twenty-four

"Rise, Prior Andrew." Eleanor's voice was icy with controlled anger.

He tried, then stumbled, tears flowing down stubbled cheeks. His broken sobbing was painful to hear, as if some dull sword were ripping at his flesh.

She turned her back, refusing him the mercy of assistance and unwilling to let him see that she was as grieved as he. Raising her eyes to the ceiling, she waited until the sounds of his struggles to regain his balance had ceased. Slowly, she turned around, folded her hands, and waited in silence.

"I will accept whatever punishment you order, my lady. From this moment on, I bear no title and remain a simple monk who has deeply sinned against you." He bowed his head with respect and because he could not bear to look her in the eye.

Eleanor gestured for Gytha to approach. "We need wine," she murmured, then waited until the young woman had left before speaking further to Andrew. "There will be punishment, but not until God grants me the wisdom to make a just decision. In the meantime, I must know why I had to hear about your argument with Baron Oates from Brother Beorn. You swore to tell me all when we last spoke, and I can think of no reason why you did not mention this heated discussion then."

The prior opened his mouth to speak, then shook his head and began again to weep.

Gytha brought two pewter goblets with a pottery jug. As the maid poured the wine, Eleanor shuddered. For some reason, the bright red color reminded her of blood. Nodding for the young woman to retreat to her position by the chamber door, the prioress turned her attention back to the prior, her expression suggesting she had little patience left.

"I did not kill the man, my lady! I will swear to you on all that is holy."

"Did you not recently swear to tell me details even when you did not think them important? Surely you can understand my disinclination to readily believe you."

"I did argue with the baron, and, since murder is a sin when committed in the heart, I am guilty of wishing his death. I most certainly was blinded by hatred. He and I met by accident. When I first saw him, I turned to flee. He called after me, claiming I was no better than my traitorous brother. That alone caused me to hesitate and turn back. When he called me *coward*, Satan set fire to the dry tinder of my fury and I shouted curses on him."

"Did you strike him then? Or did you promise to meet him at a later time with intent to commit mayhem that resulted in death?"

"Neither of us laid a finger on the other, my lady, although our words were as sharp as swords."

"I also asked if you met him later."

"I did not. God, in His mercy, cooled my fury, and I was finally able to turn my back on the creature. As I retreated, he mocked me while I prayed for the courage of martyrs to walk away without retort." Andrew reached for the goblet and stared down at the wine. "He was walking on this earth when I left him, and I never saw him alive again."

"Where were you when you argued?"

"Near the guest quarters. Baron Otes was just leaving as I approached."

"Why had you gone there?" At least the prior's story was matching the details given by Brother Beorn.

"Father Eliduc had sent a message that he wanted to see me."

Her eyebrow shot up. "When did he summon you and who was sent? Was the request urgent? Did the messenger give the reason?"

The prior fell silent as if carefully gathering all the facts involved in the answer to each question. "One of the lay brothers, not Brother Beorn, found me. He said Father Eliduc had some problem with the accommodations and wished to speak with me about it. I would not say that his request included a plea for urgent response. Since these guests are from our queen, I did go immediately."

"And you had not spoken with the priest when you saw Baron Otes?"

"Nay. After the argument, I prayed for calmness in the chapel and did return to the guest quarters after I thought the baron had gone. I was not so possessed with evil that I failed to heed my duty to resolve Father Eliduc's concern."

Had gone? Eleanor's curiosity was sharpened by the phrase. She chose first to ask one more question before she pursued it. "Did you meet with Father Eliduc?"

"He told me the issue had been settled between the time he sent for me and my arrival."

Eleanor gestured for him to elaborate.

"He does not like ale and thought we had refused him wine with his meal. When I talked with him, he said the failure to bring the wine had been a misunderstanding and he was satisfied the error would not be repeated."

Although the story was consistent with what she knew of the priest, Eleanor wondered if there had been some plan to make sure the prior arrived in time to meet the man who had killed Andrew's brother. "And where did you go after that?"

"Back to the chapel for prayer, my lady. As you can see, I had much need for repentance."

"Were there witnesses?"

Andrew shook his head.

That lack of corroboration was most unfortunate. "At any time during your argument with the baron, did our guest say where he was going or even his purpose in so doing?"

He rubbed at his reddened eyes.

The silence was long. Eleanor remained patient.

"I think he went in the direction of the mill, although I cannot swear to it." He squeezed his lids shut. "Aye, he must have, for I now remember looking over my shoulder once in my retreat. He was walking along that path. I confess I had weakened again and longed to cast another curse in his direction." More tears slipped down his cheeks. "It seems my curses had already been sufficient to kill, is that not so? There was no virtue in my belated restraint."

"Drink the wine, Prior," Eleanor said. "It will help."

He lifted the goblet and gulped several times.

"Did he mention why he was out? Do you remember anything other than the insults he threw at you?"

"He did threaten me." Andrew gripped the goblet with such force that his knuckles turned white. "He claimed he could expel me from Tyndal in disgrace and that I would die along the road like the dog and traitor I was."

"How dare he say such a thing to you!" Feeling her face grow hot with anger, Eleanor was more outraged by the baron's presumption than her prior's previous omission of this detail. "As I told you, he did offer land to our priory and your expulsion was the price. He seemed to have forgotten that you were pardoned by the king and by God when you took vows. Now you are under His rule and mine. I would never trade my prior for land. I hope I have made myself quite clear."

"All the more reason to repent my grievous sins against you!"

"Hush." She poured him more wine and gestured at the goblet, an obvious suggestion that he drink. "Did he speak about this land, other than his ill-conceived assumption that he could bribe me?"

Andrew shook his head and sipped the wine.

"Again, I ask you to think carefully. Did he say anything at all that might suggest where he was going or if he was meeting anyone?"

Andrew silently thought about it, drank more wine, and thought a while longer. "God forgive me if I am wrong about this, my lady," he said, his words a little slurred. "He was in fine spirits about something, more than I can truly credit to his meeting with me. Now that I think more on it, he did boast that he was most blessed by God. Not only had he grown quite wealthy already, he claimed he was soon to increase his worth, if not his influence at court. Then he pointed to my rough-cut robes and said that God had clearly smiled more on him than on me." He pursed his lips and plucked at his sleeve. "Methinks that is when God took mercy on me and began to cool my rage. I am honored to serve Him and feel no shame for wearing this."

For the first time, Eleanor smiled. "You recall nothing else?" she asked gently.

Swaying a bit, he eased the goblet down on the table and pushed it further from the edge with studied resolve. "Nothing, I fear."

"Do you still swear, on God's sweet name, that you did neither kill Baron Otes nor have anything to do with the deed?"

"I swear it."

"Very well." Eleanor gestured that the audience was done. "While I seek God's guidance about any punishment you are due, I order you to temporarily turn over your duties as prior to whichever monk you deem most capable. Send him to me. When you explain this act, you will say you took a vow to seek solitude for prayer, spending a short time as an anchorite, if you will. Methinks you have need to take that vow and reflect on your sins. Is that not so?"

Andrew nodded.

"Then you will retreat to a small cell, which I will order readied for you, and that door shall be locked. Entrance will be permitted only to the lay brother I assign who will bring food and tend to your needs. Should you wish to speak with me, send that brother with the request for an audience. When I have decided on your penance, I shall order you brought to my chambers, again by that one lay brother alone."

Andrew knelt and begged her blessing.

As she watched him leave, she wondered if she truly believed him. Her heart cried out that he was an honorable man and

demanded her mind agree. Indeed, she hoped he was innocent.
She also knew he must remain in that solitary cell until this
murder was resolved.

It was always possible the killer might strike again, and, if
he did, there must be no doubt of her prior's innocence. Now
she must decide how much, if anything, to tell Crowner Ralf.

Gesturing to Gytha, she asked her to send for Brother Beorn.
Of all the lay brothers in the priory, he was the one she trusted
most. Although he was deeply troubled by the quarrel he had
witnessed between his religious superior and Baron Otes, he
would never treat the prior with discourtesy. Seeing Andrew
locked in that windowless room as hard penance for giving in
to the sin of wrath, Beorn would honor the prior even more.

As her maid rushed in obedience from the chambers, Eleanor
walked to the window and stared out at the priory walls. They
shimmered in the heat as if they had been crafted, not of stone
but of some flimsy cloth that now twisted in the slight breeze.
Even these works, so enduring to men's eyes and meant to house
God's servants, may prove impermanent, she thought.

Sighing, she shut her eyes and forced her mind to return to the
problems at hand. If only Brother Thomas had not left Tyndal to
become a hermit, then he might have become that monk chosen
by Andrew to act as temporary prior. Her sinful longings aside,
she had learned to value his insight, and, for reasons God would
surely condone, she deeply missed his company.

Chapter Twenty-five

Gytha tilted the jug and poured ale into round pottery cups.

Reaching for a ruddy apple from the platter, the crowner smiled with gratitude, his face red and sweating from the heat.

"What have you discovered about the killer?" Eleanor leaned back in her chair. Her voice was soft with hope.

"Nothing that would give a name to the man, although I think some possibilities may be discounted. I went first to Signy who said the inn housed the usual ardent pilgrims and assorted traveling merchants. Apparently they were a weary bunch and found their beds too early for any to be guilty of a quick murder after supper."

"For that, we must give thanks." Despite her worries, the prioress laughed at his phrasing and with some relief that Signy was willing to break her long silence with Ralf. Although Eleanor suspected their conversation had been awkward, she was pleased their festering quarrel showed signs of healing, even if it had taken another murder to bring that about.

"As for those village men most likely to make trouble, none are known for any greater violence than a fist fight after too much drink." Indicating he had several points to make, the crowner raised one finger. "The baron had not been here long enough to seduce a local woman into his bed so it is doubtful he was killed by a jealous husband or love-struck lad." He extended his ring finger. "Nor do I suspect that robbery was the intent. A bag of coin was attached to the corpse, and there were enough jeweled rings on the fingers to tempt most men of any rank." He waved three of his own, which, in contrast, were quite unadorned.

Stopping for a moment, Ralf thoughtfully stared at his fourth finger. "Oh, some mutterings about outlaws have been heard. That rumor I mistrust. If there are any such men in the area, they have managed to hide themselves well enough not to be seen before now. Why would they chance discovery by committing random murder without any gain at all?" He studied his thumb which remained folded into his palm.

"I have heard nothing on market day about real sightings or persistent rumors of lawless men, my lady." Gytha added bread and cheese to the offered food on the platter near the crowner's elbow. "At least not since the last snows melted."

"Although the idea is troubling for many reasons, we cannot ignore the possibility that the killer might be a member of the queen's party." Eleanor hesitated before adding, "What of the men who accompanied the courtiers on this journey?"

"According to Signy, they spent their evening gambling. To the best of her knowledge, no one left the inn."

Gytha frowned. "Signy could not watch everyone. Did any of those who serve food and drink notice…?"

"She asked them and later told me no one saw any of the men slipping away."

"Daylight lasts so long in this season that many seek bed before dusk. Signy and those serving at the inn must take time to rest. A man could leave and not be noticed, either during the busy time or after dark." Suddenly realizing she had been adding to a discussion she was supposed to ignore, Gytha turned red. "Forgive my intrusion, my lady!"

"You have just reminded me that we cannot dismiss the idea that anyone at the inn, whether he sought a bed early or not, might have left to meet the baron after dark." The prioress gestured permission for the maid to join in the conversation, then turned back to Ralf. "From what you have learned, this does not look like a random killing. Nothing was stolen, and no one has seen any brigands. I am unhappy we cannot rule out the possibility that some alleged pilgrim or merchant, staying at the inn, had a motive for killing, or that one of the escort might have had equal grounds for committing violence against the baron."

"I concur, but the pilgrims and merchants staying that night have since journeyed on. I fear we have no way of discovering which amongst them might have known the dead man." He tore off a large piece of bread, added cheese, and bit into it with marked pleasure.

"Most unfortunate. However, we might comfort ourselves by answering a question. How probable it is that an enemy of Baron Otes, disguised as pilgrim or merchant, would travel the far distance from court so that he might kill the baron on the banks of our particular stream?"

Ralf nodded.

"I am more inclined to suspect that something happened, either shortly before the party's arrival or just after, to rouse some member of the queen's party to commit murder. What is your thinking? Is it likely that a stranger would lodge at the inn, wait for the baron to arrive, and then ride off after killing him?"

"Your conclusion has merit," the crowner replied. "The route and length of the journey would give anyone many opportunities to kill and safely escape. The murderer did not have to wait until reaching Tyndal to do so." Ralf failed to add that it was Father Eliduc who had brought this to his attention earlier.

"As far as the escort is concerned, surely your brother would know all the men well enough. Have you asked Sir Fulke if any of them, or their families, had a dispute with Baron Otes?"

The crowner picked up his mazer, only to find it empty. He blinked.

"I will add water to the ale, should you want more." Gytha gave Ralf a mischievous grin before refilling his cup.

He muttered something incomprehensible and handed her the mazer.

Eleanor raised an eyebrow, sensing something between crowner and maid she had not noticed before. Although Gytha had often teased the crowner over the years, this instance had a different tone. Surely Ralf would never hurt Tostig's younger sister, and she knew the crowner to be honorable. She was probably imagining things, and, if not, Tostig would swiftly handle any problem.

Ralf cleared his throat, his expression suggesting discomfort at the prioress' steady gaze.

Eleanor's thoughts shifted back to murder. "I am sure you must have considered that question."

"I did ask the sheriff about the men," the crowner said. "Many at court have reason enough to despise the baron, but the guards were all too poor and too low in station to fall within his avaricious notice. The same was true of their kinsmen. The baron has long preferred to pursue the greater gain from the more prosperous ranks."

Eleanor sipped her ale thoughtfully. The dead man had chosen to torment Prior Andrew, a man who also could be thought beneath notice.

"One of the guards might have been hired by another who remains at court." Gytha lowered her eyes after glancing at her mistress.

"An observation worthy of careful consideration," the prioress replied, resting her chin on her hand.

"I did learn something else when I talked to Signy." Ralf tilted his head in the direction of the inn. "Nute was hiding in the bushes near Brother Thomas' hermitage the night of the murder and saw two men arguing near the stream."

Eleanor leaned forward. "Why did you not mention this before?"

"Because the lad recognized neither of them. When I asked for details, all he could say was that one was fat and the other not." The crowner shrugged.

Gytha looked relieved. "They were not local men if he could not identify either."

Eleanor wondered if *local* included the priory. Had Gytha heard about the quarrel between Otes and Andrew? Although

Brother Beorn was not one to gossip, she did not know if anyone else had witnessed the argument and failed to tell her, choosing to whisper the news about instead. Must she seek out these witnesses, question them, and demand prudence in their speech until this murder could be solved? The Prioress of Tyndal was not pleased with the possibility.

"More likely he could not see them well enough," Ralf said.

Gytha shook her head. "If he was able to determine that one was larger than the other, he might have been able to see enough to judge if they were from the village."

"Did he hear any of the argument?" Although Eleanor knew a child's word would have little weight against that of a man, she hoped Nute's story might at least help them find the killer. Getting the murderer to confess was a problem to worry about after capture.

Ralf thought for a moment. "He did say that the *fat one*, presumably the baron, asked the other where the man was that they were supposed to meet. An instant before the baron was killed, Nute did hear him exclaim 'Impossible'."

"Right away, as if there were a connection between word and deed?"

"I fear I did not pursue details. Signy thought Nute had endured enough questioning from me, and the boy was getting restless."

The prioress nodded. Considering the baron's reputation for greed, there was nothing surprising about the killer successfully luring him away from Tyndal with some promise of gain. The details of that bait might not be especially important, but she did wonder if there was any significance in the word uttered by Otes just before he was killed. Was it important that Nute remembered only that and nothing else? Or was it the only word spoken loud enough for him to hear?

"Is Nute still too frightened to give further details?" Eleanor hoped there might be far more to learn.

"Signy promised to draw them out, should the lad seem willing to talk more." Taking another large chunk of cheese from the platter, the crowner bit off a mouthful and chewed with the contentment reminiscent of some benign bull.

Eleanor decided she was exaggerating the importance of the coincidence between word and act. And, if there was more to learn from Nute, Signy would gently pursue the questioning, telling Ralf the result if there was anything of note.

As the crowner ate, she debated whether she should share one particular confidence with him. If she did, she was in danger of implicating Father Eliduc. If she did not, she might permit someone of secular rank to be ignored. Surely Ralf would honor the right of the Church to deal with him if the evidence did lead to the priest. She did not want a man subject to the king's law to escape justice.

When Baron Otes suggested a high ranking churchman was interested in the land grant, he might have lied. By suggesting this, his intent may have been to provoke in her an ambition to improve the wealth of her priory over that of others, a ploy that almost succeeded. If he had lied, the person hoping for this gift might be a man with a secular title. As long as Otes accomplished whatever he wanted, truthfulness did not matter. When it came to the question of murder, truth did.

"An odd thing happened just before the baron died," she said. "I am not sure if it has any relevance, but you should know of it."

His mouth too full to speak, Ralf nodded.

"Baron Otes came to me with an offer of land. He had some benefit to himself in mind, a price I did not wish to pay. He claimed the land was valuable. I did wonder if he had made the same offer elsewhere."

The crowner looked puzzled. "What did he want in exchange?"

"Unless it becomes necessary, I would rather not explain beyond saying he wanted reprisal against one for whom he felt some hatred."

"My lady, you must know I now suspect that man is one of your religious. Will you tell me if he had cause to kill the baron?"

"I believe the person to be innocent of any such crime, and I must be the arbiter here in Tyndal, as you well know." She softened her words with a smile. "Ralf, I would not let you continue hunting a killer if I thought I had the perpetrator under my rule."

Although he looked unhappy, he nodded agreement.

Eleanor was relieved. Not only had he respected her judgement on the matter, he had proven he would honor the Church's right to discipline its own wrongdoers.

"If Baron Otes tried to use that land as a bribe to someone else and failed, I have not heard any rumors. All that means nothing," the crowner said. "I am neither at court nor privy to such matters."

"I am aware of his reputation. He gained wealth primarily by threatening to reveal damaging secrets," Eleanor said. "That is why I thought his desire to actually pay for retribution was unusual."

"Perhaps he hoped to increase what he could get in return for the gift by playing one against another." He shifted on the stool with evident impatience.

"When he said another was interested, he avoided the mention of any name," she replied. All she wanted Ralf to do was pursue secular leads and so chose not to mention Eliduc's interest in the gift. Nor did she say that Otes had spoken of how much he hoped to gain for his soul with the grant, hinting that the leader of a prominent abbey might have been the other party.

The crowner grunted.

"I think you have better sources than I to discover who was wealthy enough to be interested in valuable land and able to offer Baron Otes enough in return, Ralf."

And should he find some link between Father Eliduc, or rather his liege lord, and the baron, the discovery would force kings and bishops to strive together for resolution and her own priory would remain safe from the power struggles of the mighty. The more she thought about it, the more she realized she had been very wise to refuse a gift that might well have been even more venomous than she had first believed.

His brow deeply furrowed, Ralf rose. "I will investigate further, my lady," he muttered, then quickly bowed and raced from the chambers.

Eleanor and her maid looked at each other with mild surprise. The crowner had left with uncharacteristic abruptness, without even his usual jest to Gytha or a promise to return after he got more information.

Considering the matter with more care, the prioress realized he had grown uneasy after the mention of what Otes had offered her. Might he have kept some secrets to himself, just as she had over the matter of her prior, the priest, and that land grant?

Chapter Twenty-six

As they strolled along the path from the chapel to the guest lodging, Eliduc stole a look at the Lady Avelina. Her expression was too sad for such a bright day. Stopping, he bent over a yellow wild flower, as if admiring its simple beauty. "Do you remain troubled in spirit?"

Her hands, modestly folded against her waist, began to twist and intertwine with nervous distress. "Although I should not be, the turmoil does continue."

Plucking the flower out of the ground, he straightened and continued to study the delicate color in the petals. "Simon is with the local hermit." He turned to look at her. "That he has stayed with the holy man this long, speaks well for your son. Methinks he wishes a better understanding of God's desires. Although his longing may be recently discovered, our Lord must be pleased."

"Is it sinful of me to doubt that my son has found a deeper faith?"

"I cannot imagine what other reason he would have to choose the hermit's company." Bringing the flower closer to his eyes, he touched one petal with the tip of a finger. Lacking moisture to sustain it in the heat, the flower was beginning to wilt. He frowned.

"He has always desired a warrior's life and never shown any inclination to serve God by taking vows."

"Saint Paul actively persecuted the faithful until he traveled the road to Damascus."

She paled. "I do not want my son to suffer such a hard revelation! A mother's heart never wants to see her child in pain."

"We all come to God by differing paths. Perhaps Simon has finally set aside childish things and become a man, as that same Saint Paul once said to the Corinthians."

Her forehead marked with anxiety, she walked on.

He tossed the flower aside and followed.

Avelina turned and waited for him to catch up. "He swears I shall never succeed in regaining his father's lands and title."

"Do you truly have any hope of it?" Eliduc shaded his eyes from the bright sun and looked over her shoulder to watch the lay brothers hoeing in the priory garden. From the chapel he heard the raucous banging on drums and winced, fearing it was practice for the advent of Darius the Mede in the liturgical drama. He had longed for delicately plucked harps and lightly rung finger cymbals. Subtlety was evidently beyond rustic novices, as he had dreaded from the start. He prayed he might endure this performance of *Daniel*.

"I thought I did until…" She shook her head and fell silent.

"As God's priest, you may speak freely with me, my lady." His teeth flashed white under the shadow cast by his hand. "I would never tell any man about the secrets confided in me."

"You have bestowed so much kindness on us, Father. I am grateful for the interest you have shown my poor lad as well as the time you have spent soothing my own weary soul."

With undeniable modesty, he bowed his head. "Such is the duty of God's servant."

"An obligation that you perform with a benevolence worthy of your calling." After a moment of hesitation, she continued. "My son is often imprudent and, I fear, did destroy the one possibility he had to regain at least some of his lands. A man of rank showed willingness to argue Simon's case before the king, then my son cruelly beat the man's daughter when she refused to lie with him. Although the father was absent when this happened, her mother was outraged and, I fear, will most certainly tell her husband of the act."

"Perhaps he might permit your son to marry his child."

"He had greater plans for her than union with a boy of unfortunate paternity, no wealth, and little standing at court." She shook her head. "Even this man never led me to believe that the king would return both title and all the land to my lad. Now Simon must remain poor, thanks not only to his father's injudicious acts but because he was foolish as well."

"Does Simon realize the gravity of his error in offending a man who might have supported his claims?"

Her smile twisted with bitterness. "He protests that he is cursed by the perfidy of women and even hates the rule of his own mother because I am Eve's daughter as well." Realizing she had failed to hide her frustration, she glanced at the priest to see how he responded to this indiscretion.

He met her eyes, his features transforming into an expression of sweet compassion.

"He longs to earn his fortune by jousting in tournaments," Avelina said.

"For that, he needs horse, armor..." Eliduc nodded encouragement for her to continue.

"All of which requires more than I can give him or borrow." She shifted her gaze so the priest could not see her eyes. "Recently, he suggested he has made contact with a man outside England who might help him with his ambitions."

Raising an eyebrow, the priest spoke in tones of innocent curiosity while probing for dark sins. "In France, perhaps? Or even Scotland?" There were de Montfort supporters in France, many of whom had escaped into exile with Countess Eleanor short months after the earl's death. And those cattle thieves to the north were always happy to trouble the English.

Avelina rested a hand over her throat. "France, I think. Are there not many tournaments there where Englishmen often go?"

"The events were prohibited in England while King Henry lived. Now that the Lord Edward is king, he has also failed to show them favor." He smiled. France suggested contact with those who plotted the king's death, or at least held little love for Edward in their hearts.

"Our lord king ignored his own father's prohibition often enough on this matter of tournaments." Her words were sharply spoken.

"Our new lord is no longer a prince. He must now be a king, my lady. Boys often take on their father's ways when they reach a man's estate."

Avelina cried out, her hand pressed hard against her heart.

"Are you ill, my lady? Shall I call for…?"

"It is no matter, gentle priest." She dropped her hand but her face remained pale. "I am well enough. I suffer only the sorrow of a mother who has birthed a child too much like his father in his willful ways."

"If I troubled you with some thoughtless remark, I beg pardon." His forehead creased with concern while his lips twitched into a fleeting smile.

She began to moan. Tears flowed down her cheeks which she did nothing to hide.

"I can promise you God's peace, if you will let Him into your heart," he murmured, stepping closer to encourage any confidence she might long to reveal.

Each word broken in two by sobs, she whispered, "Will He forgive treason?"

"Surely you have not done such a thing," he said, his tone a purr of comfort with no hint of condemnation.

"My son may have. Baron Otes visited me the evening before we arrived at this priory and claimed that Simon's name had been mentioned in the company of others who regret de Montfort's death. These *others* are men who plot to assassinate our new king because, they believe, he has turned his back on the principles of monarchial restraint for which the earl stood."

"Did you believe this story? The baron was not always correct about details or fully honest in his accusations." He waved a hand. "You son may have uttered little more than ill-advised words. Perhaps something about wishing his father had not been killed at Evesham so Simon would not be obliged to seek charity, or that his godfather showed him favor as a child. Innocent enough remarks by themselves, if Baron Otes did not tint them with a darker hue and suggest a deeper disaffection."

Avelina shook her head. "I did not have the courage to question the lad before he went to see the hermit. I pray you are right." Hope returned color to her cheeks. "My boy often says and does things without thinking, things that are truly of little note." Then the short-lived optimism faded. "Yet he hated the baron and was unwise in voicing his feelings. Might someone have overheard Simon and thought he had something to do with his death?"

"Your son is still a boy. Surely no one thinks him a threat. Was he not with you the night of the murder? He and I spoke some little while, then he said he intended to return to your side."

"In truth, I cannot confirm where he slept that night. In the morning, when I arose, he had left for the hermit's hut." All color fled Avelina's face. "Wasn't the baron found near that place? Did he not die just after we arrived here? Oh, I pray no one has thought to accuse Simon! I do fear for my son." She wrung her hands. "Child though he may be in my heart, he has the body of a man. That does not argue for his innocence if someone heard him speak ill of Baron Otes!"

Eliduc dismissed her fears with a smile. "I have heard no rumors about your son, either here or at the court. As for any accusation of murder, if others in this party had overheard Simon speak in anger against the baron, they would surely have accused the lad by now of the murder. Your son may own a man's body, but he speaks like a child as many know well enough. Nay, my lady, have no fear. Instead, go back to the chapel and pray for your son to find a true vocation serving God. With no hope of worldly wealth and a tendency to ill-conceived ideas, Simon might find safety and purpose serving the Church."

She nodded, the muscles in her face sagging with weariness.

This time he did not trouble himself to hide a satisfied smirk.

Chapter Twenty-seven

"I am your nearest kin, you lout!"

Ralf grabbed the seething Fulke by his robe and hauled him up from the bench. "I asked a simple question, dearest brother. Where were you the night Otes was killed? Answer it, or I shall assume you are either a greater knave than you sometimes act or else a fool."

The sheriff's face was a bright puce, although rage was not the only cause. From the number of empty pitchers on the table, it was evident he had drunk deeply. And then there was the serving wench who might have added color to his cheeks as well. When Ralf arrived, she had been wiggling with some enthusiasm on his brother's lap.

Releasing Fulke, the crowner reached for the nearest jug. Tipping it, he saw there was only a small amount of ale left and it was far from fresh. He dumped the few mouthfuls into his brother's cup, shoved it at Fulke, and raised a hand to demand a new pitcher.

With some surprise, he realized that the serving wench who had just been pleasuring Fulke had not fled when the brothers began to argue. She was standing, with sour expression and arms akimbo, near the sheriff's side.

Ralf waved her off to bring more drink. Although she was young and buxom enough, her sharp-angled face was deeply pitted. Either Fulke cared little about such things, as long as the woman would lie on her back, or he was too drunk to notice. Shrugging, the crowner decided his brother's choice of women was not his problem.

"What do you think I was doing that night?" Fulke swallowed the flat ale in one gulp, then stared at the cup as if it had insulted him.

Ralf shook his head.

"I was swyving that one." He gestured at the woman approaching with a jug of frothy ale.

"I hope Signy doesn't know of it," Ralf muttered.

The woman put the pitcher down with a thump and marched away.

Grimacing, the sheriff poured for himself. "Is Signy the inn's bawd?"

"How little you know your own shire. She owns this place and does not tolerate whoring."

"I left this land to your care because you begged to have it so, insolent cur. As long as you behave, I concern myself little about petty village matters." Fulke jerked his head in the direction of the vanished wench. "And this innkeeper of yours? If she does not allow a whore or two, she'll never make a profit of this inn. A bordel brings comfort to the weary traveler. Tell her to marry, breed, and let her husband take over the business."

Ralf folded his arms and said nothing.

Fulke gave him a lopsided leer. "Perhaps this Signy doesn't know what goes on here or else she winks at it with a hand behind her back to accept the slipped coin. In any case, the serving wench did meet me later in the stable, and she served me well and freely." He belched. "*Freely*, I repeat and you should note. I paid nothing to her or to this righteous innkeeper."

"Will the woman swear to that as well as how long she bounced you in the hay?"

"Surely you ask just to annoy me. As your eldest brother and head of our family, my word and my innocence are beyond question."

"So are the demands of justice, otherwise known as the king's law, in case you have forgotten the responsibilities inherent in your duties as *sheriff*." Ralf made a face. "Despite our differences, I long neither for your hanging nor that suspicion fall upon you. I do pray you are blameless. It would be a waste of good coin, bribing some hangman to grant you a faster death." He turned away for a moment, his brow furrowed. "Tell me the truth. If you did kill the man, I will do all I can to save you. As you said, we are kin, whether we wish it or not."

"I am innocent. How many times must I declare it? Would my oath mean more if I swore on my desire for heaven or on Odo's hope that he not go to Hell?"

Ralf laughed. "The latter." He again raised a hand and gestured for service. "You have drunk enough. It is time to put food in your belly."

Apparently, the woman under discussion had remained nearby with an eye on the men, for it was the same wench who returned. Promising to bring the best the inn had to offer, she ignored the crowner and flirted enough with Fulke that Ralf suspected they may well have spent the night together as his brother claimed. What surprised him more was the growing notion that the swyving might have, in fact, given the woman some joy. Inexplicably annoyed, he growled a specific request for stew.

The two men said little until the portions were brought, then slurped and chewed without speaking. They scraped the bowls clean of any remnants with fistfuls of coarse bread.

"Is that Signy?" Fulke bent his thumb at a woman easing her way through the crowd, stopping at the occasional table, and simply dressed in black.

Ralf nodded.

"My manhood might complain about how she runs the inn. My belly does not. The ale is good. So is the fare. And if it weren't for her mourning weeds, she'd be comely enough. Does she long for the priory or is there another reason for this wayward piety?"

"Leave her be," Ralf snarled. "She is a good woman."

Fulke raised an eyebrow, then snorted with glee. "Methinks she's the one who warms your bed, since the other lass isn't your leman."

The crowner brought his fist down on the table so hard, all vessels on the table bounced. "Another slur on an honorable woman and I will make sure you can do naught but suck your meals henceforth! Now tell me what you know of Otes. What is his relationship with the other members of the queen's party? You have surely heard enough rumors at court before this journey. And tell me if he had offered land to any of late, when, and the price. That question includes any deals you had or hoped to have with him."

Fulke groaned. "My bladder is too full to chatter on like some woman to amuse you. You demand much information."

"Go find a wall outside before you piss yourself."

As soon as Fulke had left the bench, Ralf called over the pock-marked wench. "Did my brother treat you gently enough the other night?" His smile suggested benign concern.

She stiffened. "What law have I broken that you should ask that of me?"

"None! I…"

"Then you'll get no answer. I'll not have you prating to the mistress, Crowner. She'd chase me from the inn if there were any accusation of whoring. And don't I have a babe to feed with no husband to hunt for faggots when autumn comes?"

"What a man and woman choose to do in some pile of hay on a summer eve is not my business. Since Sir Fulke is my brother, I am duty bound to make sure my kin treat all with just kindness. That is my sole concern."

She snorted. "Aren't you the right courteous knight? Straight out of some story of King Arthur, I swear, but I'm neither Queen Guinevere nor a fool." She tossed her head. "For your information, he did offer a pretty enough coin, and I refused. If you tell tales to Mistress Signy, make sure you pass that bit on as well."

"I swear not to pass anything on. I'm just surprised he wasn't too drunk to bed you."

"Although he did drink enough, Crowner, I served him for several hours." Folding her arms under her ample breasts, her expression softened. "Even if he did need help staggering to the stables, I've never known any other man, drunk or sober, who could stay rigid as a pole until the sun returned."

Ralf sat back with unmistakable surprise. "This time of year, darkness may be short-lived, but…! All night?"

She smirked.

Out of the corner of his eye, he saw Fulke returning. "Pleased to hear it." He grinned. "Now maybe another jug of ale, quickly served, would be in order." He touched her hand. The edge of a small coin briefly flashed between his fingers.

It disappeared in a trice, as did she.

"Getting her side of the story?" Fulke slid back onto the bench. "Why would a woman's word be more trustworthy than your brother's?"

Ralf chuckled. "I never knew you had such endurance in bed sports! She came to tell me that," he lied, then slapped the sheriff on the shoulder.

Fulke flushed with evident pleasure. "You wanted to know about Otes and the rest of us."

As the serving wench put down a jug, she added a platter of bread and cheese.

With a wink, Ralf handed over more coin.

"The baron has never demanded payment from me for his silence. Sometimes I suspected that my obvious fear was pleasure enough for him." He looked at his brother out of the corner of his eye.

Ralf knew how difficult it had been for Fulke to admit a weakness. Respecting his brother's pride, he said nothing.

"When you asked about acres, did you mean for sale, in trade for some favor, or as a free gift?"

"All."

"Baron Otes never spoke to me of such a thing. I have heard rumor that the baron promised to donate profitable land in his will to the man Father Eliduc serves. Since Otes had already given land to found a leper hospital, I assumed any other such gift to the Church was meant to buy more prayers for his mottled soul." He laughed. "Lest you think any of his get had a quarrel with his new-found piety, there was plenty left to satisfy his sons and his daughters' husbands."

"Otes was widowed, was he not?"

"To the grief of every pretty serving woman in his castle! And it is true that he banned the ones he deemed ugly. No bantlings, though. God showed mercy."

"If the land was profitable enough to bring joy to his lord's heart, Father Eliduc might grow fearful should the baron change his mind and offer the same land to another."

Fulke tore a handful of bread in half. "Methinks you have heard more than I about this matter." Taking a bite, he lifted his cup, then smiled at Ralf. "As we both learned from watching our Odo, a religious calling is no deterrent to avarice or violence."

"So Father Eliduc might have a motive for making sure Otes never changed his will." He scowled. "I do not like matters involving a struggle of authority between the Church and the king's justice. As sheriff, neither should you."

"Then we must pray he is as innocent as a priest should be, although I confess I neither like nor trust the man. He's as slippery as a trout, but I have no proof of any guilt."

"What of Lady Avelina and her son?"

"If they have deep secrets concealed, I have heard nothing of them. What more could be hidden? Their story is known well-enough. There can be little worse than being the widow and son of a dead traitor."

"Not all followers of de Montfort lost favor with our new king," Ralf said thoughtfully. "King Edward also knows the dangers involved should he seek retribution against them when so many claim miracles have been wrought at the earl's gravesite. He himself smiled on the man at one time, and there are many of all ranks that continue to believe the earl served the interests of every man while King Henry served only his own."

Fulke put his palm against his brother's mouth. "Do not speak treason!"

Ralf shoved the hand aside. "I report what I hear. As for treason, I am as loyal to this king as I was to the last. All I suggest is that Lady Avelina might have cause to hope her son's inheritance will be restored. Or did Baron Otes know something that would prevent that from happening?"

"Others may be returned to favor. Not this particular family. The father loudly and foolishly proclaimed that de Montfort should be king, not just an honored counselor. Some call it blasphemy that the earl raised a sword against God's anointed. Of those who stay silent, many shiver in fear. None dare speak up for declared traitors and few for their get. King Edward might forgive any who changed course, as he himself did. He will never pardon anyone who stubbornly fought against the very kingship he now owns. And Simon is much like his sire, imprudent in his ways and blinded by his passions. I do not think the boy is likely to breed trust in a king's heart, no matter how sweetly the mother begs."

Ralf stabbed at a hunk of cheese. "That matches what little I have seen of Simon. The boy troubles me, Fulke. He is now staying with Brother Thomas, a monk who is living as a hermit in the forest hut near the priory mill. Although I might believe the lad opened his eyes one morning, saw the horror of his sins, and fled to a man of God for guidance, I find it strange that he should run away at the very sight of me after Otes' corpse was found." He gnawed in silence. "Is there nothing more you can tell me about Simon and his mother?"

"Staying with a hermit nearby, you say?"

The crowner nodded. "Aye. Just above the pond where the baron was killed."

The sheriff thought for a moment, then shrugged. "I know nothing about the young fool other than the usual boyish swinking and maternal outrage when he can't keep his pintle in his braes. I heard rumor that he tried to breach the wrong girl recently, then struck her with his fists for refusing him. That news was silenced as well as might be."

"None of this explains why Simon hid from me when Brother Thomas and I spoke. Maybe Simon has another secret, apart from tearing maidenheads. I had best pay a visit to our good hermit and his recent guest." He rose.

Fulke glanced through the crowd, eager to catch the eye of his favored wench.

The crowner slammed his hand down on the sheriff's shoulder. "In the meantime, brother, take my advice and keep your own tarse strapped down tonight. If Signy discovers you riding one of her women in the stable, she might mistake you for a bull that needs some trimming."

Grinning with wicked delight at his horrified brother, Ralf walked away.

Chapter Twenty-eight

Thomas stared at the black sky above his hut. How vast it seemed and how insignificant he felt in comparison with God's heavens. He wanted to weep. His eyes remained dry and gritty as desert sand.

Glancing back inside, he could see the boy's dark shape, curled peacefully on the straw pallet. If he held his breath, he could hear a light snoring above the chirping of crickets in the night heat. Did he ever sleep so deeply at Simon's age? He must have. He could no longer recall.

As for his own rest, all sleep had fled. Tonight he had wrestled with the Prince of Darkness and survived. As he gazed into the infinite darkness of the sky, dotted with the flickering lights of candles carried by angels, he wondered which of them had truly won the bout. His body was weary beyond measure, and his spirit ached too much to admit any peace. Now melancholy ruled. Even if he could claim one victory, perhaps another if he was fortunate, he suspected Satan had bested him in some way he did not fully understand.

He had come to this hut for solitude, longing to hear God's direction in that silence. Tyndal's anchoress had discovered this behind the walls of her cell. All he ever heard was the roar of worldly praise from men who concluded he was possessed of greater holiness because of his choice. Although he denied the assumption, his words only fed the fire of their error. And in this way he had deceived, even though he had never so intended. He had befouled truth and himself with the delusion of sanctity.

After this night in particular, he knew he must leave the hermitage. He had lost all confidence in his ability to live without the comfort and support of his fellow religious. Perhaps that was what God had wanted him to learn despite knowing Thomas lacked a monk's faith and suffered his torturous longing for a man's love.

Had he learned anything else in this place? If so, he was blind to it. The only certainty was the realization that he must ask Prioress Eleanor for permission to return and perform whatever task she had for him. With patience, humility, and time, he might see more wisdom revealed with greater clarity.

Reaching down, he picked up the jug of ale he had brought outside. There was some left, and he inhaled the sharp scent before draining it all. He sighed and rubbed his face. At least he had not succumbed to lust when Simon embraced him and, in tears, begged for kisses. Thomas knew that was his clear victory. The rest remained questionable.

"Simon ached only for a miracle," Thomas muttered, "that his dead father would return to praise and advise him. He may own the features of a man, but his soul has a child's fat cheeks." So the monk had given soft words and chaste caresses. What he feared he had not done was give the lad wise direction. Indeed, he worried whether he himself had become complicit in treason.

What else could he have done except listen? He had heard the lad's tale as a priest hears confession. The lad may have longed to turn traitor against God's anointed king, but he had truly done little. Hadn't his mother suffered enough with her own husband's death? Must she lose her only son as well because he was more foolish than wicked?

And thus he had wrestled with the Devil a second time this night and tried to drag Simon from a sure and horrendous death as a traitor to a safer path. "Have I truly saved him or have I sent him along a road that may lead nowhere near God?"

"Are you talking to yourself, Brother?" a voice asked.

Thomas grew cold, despite the warm air, then realized the shadow standing a few feet away had the comfortable outline of a familiar crowner, not an imp.

"I did not mean to startle you," Ralf said, coming closer. "I brought a fresh pitcher of ale from the inn."

"My own company has grown tiresome. To enliven the hours, I have taken to arguing with myself, only to find I lose both sides of any debate."

"You're not meant for this hut. Go back to caring for the sick. They miss your soothing words."

Thomas smiled, grateful that the darkness kept his friend from reading anything more in his expression than humor.

"Have some ale." Ralf tilted his head toward the hut. "Where is Simon?"

Again, despite the heat, Thomas shivered and quickly drank from the jug. "He sleeps. Deeply, I think."

"When did he first come to you?"

The monk knew the question was not based in mere curiosity. "Just after the corpse was found, identified, and examined on site." His spirit instantly grew more cheerful, not with prayer but with the promise of a murder inquiry. Since he felt no guilt over this, he suspected the influence of evil and then wondered if God instead was actually pleased.

"You know he is the son of Lady Avelina and part of the group that traveled here on Queen Eleanor's behalf?"

"Aye, and he has also told me of his father's death at Evesham, the allegiance with de Montfort, and the loss of his inheritance."

The crowner chuckled, his white teeth a flash of brightness in the greying light that promised dawn. "To save time in this matter, I should have come to you first. What is your opinion of the boy?"

"He longs to be a man but has little understanding of what that means. For him, battles are full of glorious deeds, not cleaved skulls and festering wounds that send soldiers to Hell, screaming from their own agony and stench. Whether he will become worthy or a man with greater fondness for indulgence than charity is beyond my ability to foresee."

"Words like these make me suspect again you were something more than a soft-fingered clerk before you took vows, Brother."

The monk retreated into silence.

"Simon ran from me when I met you at the stream. Why?"

"He said he came here to seek God's wisdom. You and your brother remind him too much of the world. For this reason, he fled."

"Do you believe that tale?"

"A boy who thinks a knight's life is like some story from the adventures of Lancelot might well conclude that God's direction comes from another sinful mortal who lives alone in a whore's cottage. And it is possible such a lad would resent the intrusion of the world when he longed to escape any reminder of it." Catching the bitterness in his tone, he laughed as if he had intended to jest. "Let me reply to what I think you meant by asking such a question. I do not believe he killed the baron."

"Why?"

"As we both have described him, Simon is a boy. If he had slit the man's throat, his nostrils would no longer quiver as if the gates to Eden had just slammed shut and he still held the scent of the garden within him. Murder brands a man with the especial mark of Cain. That is not to say he might not have committed lesser sins, but I smell his mother's milk on him, even though I do not like the lad."

"Have you learned where he was when the baron was killed?"

"First he spent much time in conversation with Father Eliduc who counseled him on God's mercy and compassion. This moved him to attend his mother, a duty he admits neglecting often. The lady suffers dizziness and nausea, especially if she is fatigued, and she was unwell after the tiring journey here. When his mother fell asleep, his still troubled spirit drove him to the chapel, where he spent the remainder of the night in prayer. He claims it was there God showed him the path he must start to follow."

"I should have known that you would have questioned him."

The monk paused to take breath. "Although there were no witnesses to his actions after he left his mother, Ralf, I am inclined to believe his story for the reasons I have given."

"Like your prioress, Brother, I learned early after we first met to respect your conclusions."

"I, too, was troubled by his quick retreat when you appeared at the pond. As God knows well enough, I'm a flawed monk and sometimes doubt loud protestations of ardor in faith. Thus I question the depth of Simon's piety, even though I think he believes he is sincere. The latter may prove him innocent of killing Baron Otes. I do not think he has yet learned to cover insincerity with the tapestry of delusion."

"Was all of this learned in confession?"

"What I have just told you was not. Anything I did hear in formal confession must remain only in God's ears now."

"Would you tell me if he confessed to murder?"

"Had he admitted to killing the baron, I would have urged him to seek you out immediately."

Ralf took the jug and swallowed several deep draughts of cool ale.

"And if he refused to honor my plea, he would not be sleeping in my hut."

Laughing, the crowner handed over the jug. "Thank you, Brother. I may not quite dismiss him as a suspect, although I hear his snores and believe he would not be in your bed if you thought him a killer."

"Might it help if I told you more about what he and I discussed after his arrival?"

Ralf nodded.

"I told Simon he could find adventure enough serving God if he cannot win wealth and a knighthood with a borrowed lance and his mother fails to regain the lands taken from his dead sire. Tonight he grew more eager for God's service. This might suggest he feels greater inclination toward peace than violence."

"Indeed? Have you told him tales of your exploits in the service of Prioress Eleanor?"

Thomas shrugged. "He thinks little of Eve ruling Adam, and so our Order will not find him begging to serve it. Before he fell asleep, he did say that God had opened his eyes, and he could now see how glorious deeds were possible in the service of other Orders."

Ralf stood and stretched. "His high birth merits a horse. Maybe Father Eliduc will find the money to help the lad become a Hospitaller, Templar, or member of some other military Order. Considering the heritage of treason he got from his father, I fear that only his mother will weep if he goes to Outremer."

"Have you any other suspects besides Simon?" The monk held the nearly empty pitcher out to his friend.

Taking the proffered jug, the crowner drank before answering. "Although I bear little enough love for my eldest brother, he was elsewhere at the time of the killing."

"Risking his wrath, you confirmed this?" The monk grinned as he imagined the scene between the two men.

"And greatly enjoyed his discomfiture." Ralf lowered the pitcher. "Nor have I found any reason to suspect any of the armed escort, a sudden spate of outlaws in our area, or revengeful village folk. As for others, I doubt the Lady Avelina slit the man's throat. Women may kill, which we both have learned, and yet her age and ill health argue most strongly for her innocence. The deed required more strength than she possesses." He folded his arms as if bracing for a struggle. "Were I to point the finger of distrust at anyone else, it might be at Father Eliduc."

"I have a little knowledge of the man," Thomas said with care. "He is clever, and I think it unlikely he would commit rank violence if he could achieve the same ends by other means."

"Might he kill if he could only get what he wanted by so doing?"

Thomas shook his head. "I could not say for cert."

"Then I shall place him a step higher than Simon on my ladder of possible killers. And I am grateful you did not argue that no priest would murder."

"Just as there are king's men who are more lawless than those who hide in the forest out of fear they shall hang for their crimes, there are imps dressed as men of God."

"I know that well, Brother, for enough imps have called me *kin*." He groaned. "This should have been a simple murder. Sadly, my only success so far has been in finding the innocent."

"You have conferred with Prioress Eleanor?" Thomas decided to say nothing about Prior Andrew and his past history with the baron. By now, the prior had surely spoken with the prioress, and it would be her decision how best to handle the knowledge.

Ralf chuckled. "I have, and she did mention a possible connection between one of her religious and Baron Otes. She swore there was nothing in that tale which might lead to murder. Although I honor her authority within Tyndal, I confess curiosity. I don't suppose you know anything about the matter?"

"If I did, I would be bound by her decision, and that appears to be silence."

"I have kept you from honest rest long enough. Sleep, Brother! If God listens to the prayers of wicked crowners, He will send saints to appear in your dreams and order you back to the priory."

Reaching out, Thomas grasped his friend's shoulder. "Methinks God has already sent them," he said. "And I shall pray that He guide you soon to the discovery of the killer."

As the monk watched the crowner walk down the road until he was swallowed up by fading shadows, he wondered if Simon was truly guiltless of murder, as the lad had claimed. Although his heart insisted the youth had been truthful, his mind warily argued against the assumption. Dare anyone conclude that a man, dreaming of a king's murder, was too innocent to steal another's life?

Chapter Twenty-nine

Sitting in the nun's gallery that overlooked the nave of the church, Eleanor leaned forward to see who stood below, waiting for the drama to begin.

Father Eliduc was in conversation with Brother John. The priest was animated, chopping the air with his fist as if wielding a hammer. Although only an occasional word drifted upward, there was little doubt he was determined his opinion must be triumphant.

In contrast, the choir master's tonsured head remained bowed and, except for an infrequent nod, quite motionless.

If she could control her flaring temper in the presence of Father Eliduc and emulate the humility of Brother John, Eleanor suspected she might lull her adversary into complacency. In this way, she could possibly thwart him with far greater success than she had achieved so far. Considering how the priest had abused her trust, such force of will would be difficult. With clenched teeth, she vowed to practice that diffidence both monks and all women are taught. She was determined to win her battles with this man.

Now turning her attention to the others in the nave, she saw Crowner Ralf, arms folded and leaning against a pillar near the edge of the group. Surprised at his presence, she wondered what could possibly have drawn him to this event, a limited and unpolished performance intended solely to satisfy Eliduc that the final creation might be worthy of a queen's gentle edification.

Although Ralf was a good man, Eleanor was well aware he possessed only a common faith, and his appearance inside a church, apart from formal celebrations, was rare enough to be noted.

He might have come in his brother's stead. Sir Fulke had sent his regrets, pleading an unruly stomach. If recent rumors were true and he had honored the local inn with his presence last night, he probably suffered more from a sour head than belly. In any case, the prioress suspected the sheriff cared little more than his younger brother about liturgical drama. Any excuse to avoid suffering through it would suffice.

When both the Lady Avelina and Father Eliduc would be here, she did think it unnecessary to send Ralf as replacement. Putting a hand over her mouth to hide a grin, she imagined just how sharply Ralf would have raised that same question with his brother. Perhaps Sir Fulke had requested his presence as a way to torment him.

As she watched the crowner and his steady gaze, she began to comprehend that he had not come here to listen to the sweet voices of the novice choir. He was looking to discover a murderer, and the man he was staring at was the priest.

The realization gave her pause. He must have learned something that made him suspect Father Eliduc of either killing the baron or being implicated in some way. If the king's man now shared her distrust of the creature, she might have to reconsider whether the priest could be guilty of murder, although she hesitated doing so.

Her intuition continued to insist he had limits to his evil, a conclusion based less in reason than her woman's frail insight. As she thought more on this, she grew convinced her instinct was not so lacking in virile logic.

After all, Brother Thomas had served the priest, and, despite the monk's duplicity in concealing his fealty to another, he had proven to be diligent in her service. She had learned to respect his judgement. Even if she dare not trust her own opinion of him, there were others who shared it, like Sister Anne, who called the monk a good man. Even Sister Ruth had once commented favorably on his work with the sick and dying.

She rubbed her fist against the hard wood of the railing.

With so many praising him, Brother Thomas would be unlikely to agree to doing anything truly wicked. If a man like that had followed Father Eliduc's direction, the priest could not have taken Satan as his sole liege lord and must have some constraints on his wickedness.

Even if he had not slit the baron's throat, however, Eleanor was unable to say that he was not implicated somehow in the death. The extent of Eliduc's possible guilt remained unclear. The thought did little to dispel her uneasiness.

Sighing, Eleanor sat back in her chair, then realized she had been contemplating murder instead of entertaining her guest. Embarrassed, she turned to the Lady Avelina.

Even in the light shadows of the ill-lit gallery, the prioress could see the mottled skin of Avelina's cheeks and the dark circles under her eyes. At least Eleanor had ordered a chair brought for the lady to sit on. Others might stand, the prioress had told her, but Avelina's rank demanded the comfort even though Eleanor had actually provided it out of concern for the woman's fragile health. To allow the lady to save face, the prioress had also asked for her own chair.

"Can you see well enough from here?" Eleanor leaned closer to her guest.

"I can," Avelina said, her reply barely audible. The woman had shrunk so deeply into the chair that she seemed almost part of the wood itself.

How profound was this woman's fatigue? Had the heat and long journey strained her health so much or was she sickening? Eleanor stole a quick look over her shoulder to make certain that Sister Anne had arrived and was close by.

Surely, the lady would not have come if she had been unwell, the prioress concluded. The heat was certainly intense in this gallery, or perhaps Avelina's lethargy was due to boredom. Eleanor decided to see if a few details about what they were about to see would spark interest.

"We have had little time to improve the presentation. If God graces us, the pleasure with which Brother John has prepared the novice choir and the boys' enthusiasm may dim the imperfections. Our novice master himself will sing one of the parts. The role of Daniel went to a man who came to our hospital for healing and has remained to serve the priory both as recompense and penance. Our performance may be crude, compared to what the queen has seen elsewhere. May our zeal and dedication to God's teachings make up for the deficiencies, touch her heart, and allow her to smile on our efforts."

"Edward's queen is a pious lady. This pilgrimage was never intended to seek worldly amusements, and her heart will grow joyful in your company of God's servants." Sweat glistened on Avelina's forehead in the reflected light. "I know Father Eliduc expressed doubts that Tyndal Priory could entertain our queen. After he spoke with the novice master this morning about this *Play of Daniel*, he has grown quite enthusiastic." Avelina smiled. "I have rarely seen him so excited by anything. He reminds me of my son when he was a little boy and was given a toy trebuchet!"

Eleanor bowed her head, a gesture that suggested humility while hiding her delight in surprising her adversary. "With his joy, the good priest reminds us that God is always generous when simple hearts honor Him with well-intended offerings," she murmured, "even if they do lack worldly elegance." And, she prayed with some apprehension, may Brother John's art not disappoint this priest who bowed more to kings than he bent knees to God.

Avelina swallowed several times and then bent forward to gaze down into the nave. "Father Eliduc told me that this rendering of *Daniel* would not be as rustic as he feared."

The prioress nodded modestly in acceptance of the compliment. Concerning his work with the novice choir, Brother John was as self-effacing as his vocation demanded. Brother Thomas balanced this humility with high praise. Although she herself had little understanding of music, other than to take pleasure in the reverent joy it brought her spirit, she believed her monk knew far more about the subject. After all, he had heard the finest choirs in London churches before he took a monk's vows.

Suddenly her heart suffered a familiar ache. How she missed Brother Thomas. His absence had cooled her wretched longing to couple with him, but she also missed his wit and insight, pleasures that gave her a more chaste joy.

Curtailing further thoughts of the auburn-haired monk, she prayed that Eliduc would not be dissatisfied after he saw *Ludus Danielis* and quickly turned her attention back to the small group of men below.

Father Eliduc now stood alone. In the beam of dusty sunlight, his robe had taken on the hue of burned wood. All but the crowner kept their distance from the priest, and even Ralf stood several feet away.

How strange, Eleanor thought, and wondered if they had stepped back out of respect for the priest's status as envoy from the queen or whether they shared her almost primordial unease in the man's company. She shook the question away and studied the others who had come to watch this play.

There were lay brothers and monks, all to be expected, and several in secular dress as well. Although Eleanor recognized the religious, the others were unknown to her and thus not from the village. One man balanced on a crutch; another had a large poultice wrapped around the back of his neck. They must have walked from the priory hospital.

If the crippled and suffering could find the strength to come here, surely she could set aside her own troubling concerns. There was much to learn from this Daniel tale, Eleanor thought, and she should open her spirit to the lessons, rather than brood over murder, lust, and the whims of worldly creatures. Leaning back in her chair, she willed herself to relax and eagerly waited to see what Brother John had created.

No matter what Father Eliduc thought of it, Eleanor knew the performance would be special for the faithful in both Tyndal Priory and village. *The Play of Daniel* was a favorite, traditionally performed during the season of Christ's birth, but it had not been done here since Eleanor had become prioress. Although she had been told how much Brother John's choir delighted all several years ago, those novices had grown into men, their clear voices cracking, and the monks who sang in deeper tones had died. If Queen Eleanor was truly coming to Tyndal at the time announced, it was propitious that the choir master had again found that combination of voices he wanted to best portray the contrast between virtue and iniquity.

Quickly glancing around the nun's gallery, she decided there was not a better place for the queen to see the drama than here. Although it was now only used by the nuns on those rare occasions when the entire priory and village came together, the prioress believed that the location was a special favor to women.

When the monks performed the *Quem quaeritis* at Easter, the sound of their voices rose with especial power and resonated in her ears like the voices of angels, not mortals. When she had spoken of her experience with Prior Andrew, he confessed he might have felt like a real witness to the empty tomb with the Marys on Easter morning, but he had not heard the voices as she had.

The ringing of hand bells and the mellow tones of a recorder brought silence to those in the church.

A hooded monk walked out of a side chapel and stood, head bowed, in the center of the nave. Behind him, two youths appeared with a chair, placed it to the monk's right, and quickly disappeared.

"It is about to start," the prioress whispered.

Avelina moved to the edge of her chair, and Sister Anne slipped forward to stand behind her prioress.

The monk raised his head and began to speak, each word of his deep voice resounding with a cornet's clarity throughout the church.

"He tells the tale in our language," Avelina murmured.

"So that the meaning of the story may be understood by all, not just the religious who can follow the Latin in the choral songs," the prioress said. "See! Here comes the novice choir."

The high, bright voices of the young boys blended with the eager joy of the hand bells and the warmth of a recorder as the choir walked through the nave from the back of the church. Following behind were four monks, their deep voices lending both gravity and foreboding to the celebratory processional. Brother John, at the very end, carried a simple scepter to indicate he was meant to be King Belshazzar.

Avelina clasped her hands together as the novice master sat in the chair and waved his hand.

From the left chapel, two boys emerged, one raising a golden chalice and the other a glittering platter as they approached the king's throne. When they placed them on the ground at his feet, two deep-voiced singers rejoiced that the sacred vessels from Jerusalem's desecrated temple had become mere ornaments for the royal table.

Awestruck, Avelina looked at Eleanor.

"The plate belongs to the priory," the prioress whispered. Brother John had welcomed the offer to use them in the play, and they both hoped the items might finally be cleansed of their sad origin by performing this sacred role as vessels from Jerusalem's holiest site. They had been bought at the time when a former sub-prior had almost destroyed the priory with his greed for the flashing plate. That had also been a time when blood stained the cloister garth and Brother John had been accused of murder.

Suddenly the scene below froze in place. All song ceased. From the right chapel, two shadowy figures appeared and unfurled a banner that stretched behind the king's chair. On it were embroidered the words: *Mane, Thechel, Phares.*

Avelina gasped.

Recovering from the fright herself, Eleanor was delighted. She would congratulate Brother John on that chilling touch.

After the magi failed to interpret the meaning, the moment came that the prioress had been eager to see: the queen's processional and her speech to the king.

Accompanied by the choir, the tinkling of hand cymbals, and the softness of a harp, a young novice, his amice unfolded and draped over his head to represent a woman's veil, approached the king and began to sing in such sweet tones that Eleanor almost wept. Even if Queen Eleanor did not find favor in this, she knew God would.

Avelina leaned toward Eleanor. "Belshazzar's queen is finely portrayed! Our own noble lady should be delighted. Is it not a wife's duty, when her lord husband strays from virtue, to bring him back to the path of righteous acts?" Then she sat back, her hands folded prayerfully.

Overjoyed herself with the singing, Eleanor was pleased that the play had so far met with Avelina's approval. Even though she worried about Father Eliduc's final judgement, the performance seemed to be gaining strong support from this lady-in-waiting.

Two youths began to beat drums with an ominous cadence, then stopped. From the shadows, a harpist began to play as he led another king, Darius, to the king's chair. The choir began to sing the new king's praises, and when the monk playing Darius reached the chair, the two young men with drums chased Belshazzar into a side chapel. Hidden from view, Brother John loudly announced that he had been killed.

Avelina whispered, "And so all wives must learn to turn their lords from evil before it is too late."

As Eleanor bent to reply, the lady now clapped her hands together with delight. "Oh, how beautifully Daniel sings! Methinks he has the finest voice of all."

The prioress nodded and looked down at the man, now standing before the king. This was the one who had come here for healing and then stayed to offer his skills as repayment for the miracle of renewed health. Brother John had heard him singing in the fields as he tilled the earth with the lay brothers. Although the man had not taken vows, the novice master chose him as the perfect Daniel, liege man of God, because he could reach notes of unusual purity. If only Brother Thomas returned before *Daniel* was performed again. She knew how much joy he would receive from this man's voice.

"He must sing well for he is God's voice on earth," Eleanor quickly replied.

Once he was raised to high position, all knew that envy would bring Daniel and his grateful king down. The mood darkened as two monks, acting as the evil counselors, sang in high-pitched, nasal tones, of their plot to dupe the king and send Daniel to the lions.

Avelina slid back into her chair and groaned.

For just a moment, Eleanor feared the lady had become ill. She looked back at Sister Anne, but the nun shook her head. When the prioress leaned closer to Avelina, she realized the woman was so engrossed by the tale that she believed what she was watching was true. The sound of pain was nothing more. The performance was a success.

Only when Darius was fooled into signing a law that could be used against his beloved counselor, did Avelina frown and gesture for Eleanor to lend an ear. "I fear the queen might find that troubling," she said to the prioress. "Does it not suggest that an anointed king can err when he creates laws?"

"All mortals do err, but God knows the difference between honest mistakes and evil hearts," Eleanor whispered back. "This king is well-intentioned, and so God saves both Darius and Daniel as you will see. I doubt the queen would find offence in that."

And it was then that the lions roared from the left chapel.

Avelina muffled a scream.

Eleanor touched her gently on the arm. "We have no such beasts here, and Brother John did warn me that the boys especially love this part. They roar like lions with all their might."

Avelina gave her a very grateful smile.

The prioress hoped Brother John had offered the same reassurance to those below, although she had heard more than one man's voice express horror at the sound. With a brief prick of hope, she wondered if one of those voices belonged to Father Eliduc. Then she caught herself asking if the man even owned a mortal heart. She prayed she be forgiven that unkind thought, even though she also knew she had meant it.

"As you will hear," Eleanor whispered, "the lions turn quite meek when the door is slammed shut on Daniel in their den. Do be prepared for the time they next do roar. When they are given the wicked counselors, the boys have their finest moment as lions."

Daniel was led to a side chapel. A monk appeared behind him, in the white robe of God's angel, and raised his sword when the door was closed. The lions produced a fine imitation of loudly mewing kittens.

In the nave, Ralf and the man with the poultice applauded.

The moment Daniel was released and the malicious counselors were finally taken to the den, Avelina and Eleanor braced for the roar of delight from the eager lions.

When one of them screamed, however, Eleanor knew something had gone horribly wrong.

Chapter Thirty

The body of Kenard lay curled in a patch of shade outside the chapel door. An eager complement of flies circled and buzzed over the vomit, urine, and feces pooled around his corpse. As if taunting the dead man, an empty wineskin rested only a finger's breadth beyond the reach of his outstretched hand.

Eleanor ordered two lay brothers to move the horrified onlookers back. "Do not come near. No one may touch him except on my command."

Although the stench should have been enough to drive anyone away, the small crowd retreated with a collective sigh as if grateful she had thought to demand it.

Even Eliduc edged backward until checked by the stones of the chapel wall, his face revealing no less shock than other bystanders.

Ralf stood beside the prioress, his expression a mix of hope and anger as he stared at the priest.

The prioress searched the faces of those surrounding her. "Brother John?"

"I am here, my lady." The choir master was close to the chapel door, kneeling next to a chalk-faced novice. Keeping a hand on the boy's shoulder, he rose.

This lad must have discovered the corpse, she thought, and grieved that he had. Since her own mother died when Eleanor was six, she knew how soon children became acquainted with death and wished the knowledge came later. "Will you examine the body, Crowner? Although I would ask Brother John to help you, I think that boy needs the care of his novice master."

Nodding, Ralf bent closer to her ear. "I may have many reasons to respect your monk, my lady, but Sister Anne was the better apothecary when they had their shop as husband and wife in the world. Might you call on her to examine…?"

Eleanor whispered, "I had left her with Lady Avelina in the nun's gallery. The moment I recognized this man as the lady's servant, I sent for them both. If you will begin the inspection of the corpse, Sister Anne will be here shortly. Meanwhile, I must talk to the boy who discovered the dead man."

"Then I should be with you." Ralf glanced at the child clutching a hand bell to his chest as if it were a talisman that would banish the horror of what he had seen. "The lad is terrified," he said and shook his head with sadness.

"He must recover from the cruel shock of such a discovery. I will question him gently and report to you what he says. If further information is needed, might you speak with him later?"

Readily agreeing, the crowner walked away.

Eleanor signaled to Brother John that he should take the boy into the chapel. For a moment she watched as Ralf knelt by the corpse. Then she bowed her head and followed the novice master.

Inside, the dusty air was heavy with heat and pungent with the stink of fear.

The boy trembled as if a north wind had cut him with an icy lash. The novice master hugged him close. "Tell Prioress Eleanor what you saw, and that shall be the end of it," he said.

At least the boy was young enough to shiver without the added pain of a man's embarrassment, she thought, and prayed he would not suffer tormenting dreams. Glancing at the novice master, she saw he shared her fear and knew he would be kind.

"We were waiting for Brother John to give us the sign to roar, my lady. I was at the back, near the open door to the grounds, and heard a retching noise, then gurgling." The lad's voice cracked with remembered fright. "There was a dreadful reek."
He began to weep.

"He went to look, my lady," Brother John said, "and saw the man's body jerking as he died." Caressing the lad's head, he smiled down at him with evident pride. "Had he not shouted so loud to alert us, we might not have known about this."

"Well done, lad!" Eleanor raised an eyebrow, suggesting many unspoken questions.

"If I may?" The monk looked down at the novice, then tilted his head toward the nave.

"Of course," she replied.

Brother John led the child away.

When the monk returned, he was alone. "He just vomited. I sent him to the dormitory with a lay brother." He glanced back with evident concern.

"Although there are answers to seek, I shall not keep you long, Brother. The boy needs you by his side for comfort and prayer."

"What do you want to know, my lady? He told me little else."

"I am interested in details other than the death the boy witnessed. Do you know why Kenard was here, rather than with the others in the nave?"

"As I was going over a few of the parts with the choir before the performance, he approached me and asked a kindness. He begged permission to listen to our singing and to watch from the chapel. I saw no good reason to deny him, especially when he added that he was interested in the way some of the effects were created. He swore not to distract the boys, and, since he claimed to be the servant to the Lady Avelina, I agreed."

Eleanor gasped. "He *spoke*?"

"Aye."

"Clearly?"

"Plainly enough." The monk's brow furrowed with confusion.

"Then you have witnessed a miracle, Brother. That servant was mute."

Crossing himself, the monk looked thoughtful. "Most certainly he did speak, although his voice was hoarse." He hesitated. "I wonder that God would grant him the mercy of this cure only to let him die so soon after."

With relief she realized the novice master had not grasped that the death was possibly a murder. "We do not always know God's intentions," she said and quickly returned to her questions before he grew curious about matters she was not ready to discuss. "After you agreed to the man's plea, what did he do during the performance? You may have been in the nave for a brief time, acting the part of a wicked king. For the most part, you were in the chapel. I ask to better comprehend the cause of his death."

"There was nothing in his manner that suggested ill-health. His demeanor was most solemn. I assumed that was out of reverence for the story he was about to see enacted."

"Where did he stand? Did he speak to the choir?"

Shaking his head, John grew pensive. "He stood near the door, saying he did not want to be in our way. After the *Play of Daniel* began, I believe he spoke to no one."

"Only you, the men who sang the individual parts, and the novice choir were here?"

"That was all, and those are well-known to me."

Although the novice master's expression revealed that he now understood this death to be unnatural, Eleanor was grateful he had checked his curiosity. "No others, secular or religious, joined you in the chapel even briefly?"

"No one, and yet… This detail may mean nothing." John chewed on a finger. "He carried a wineskin with him. Now that I think more on it, one lad did ask him for a drink to moisten his throat before singing. The man refused, offering some jest in reply. I thought little of it all, but, when I took up my scepter to follow the choir into the church, he drained the contents like a man with a punishing thirst. I did fear he would become drunk. When I returned, he was sitting quietly by the door and hunched over as if praying. I forgot my concern and he said nothing more. We were too busy with our roles to pay him further heed."

Eleanor felt overwhelmed with surprises. Kenard had suddenly recovered his voice, if he had ever truly lost it. He had come to the chapel, wineskin in hand, like a Roman eager to be entertained by some pagan play. And he was far more interested in the details of the performance than most servants would be.

She pinched the bridge of her nose and hoped that the pain throbbing over her left eye did not herald one of her blinding headaches.

Although the servant had given a reason for wanting to watch from the chapel, and she agreed there had been no cause to deny him, she doubted he wanted to learn how boys roared to depict lions. There had to be another explanation for not joining the men in the nave. Was he a man who found tender boys sexually appealing? And why refuse to give a sip of wine to a young novice on a hot day? All but the most cruel or selfish would have granted the request gladly. How little she knew of this man. She was frustrated by too much ignorance.

"My lady?"

Feeling as if she had just been awakened from a deep sleep, she blinked and focused on Brother John's face.

His cheeks were pale with worry. "The boy…"

"Go to him, Brother. I have kept you too long, and he needs your gentle comfort. Should I have more questions, I will summon you."

When the monk ran off to tend his novice, Eleanor gritted her teeth, spun around, and went outside to see the corpse.

As the prioress emerged from the chapel, she saw Sister Anne bending over the body.

Touching first the neck and face of the corpse, the nun then knelt and sniffed at Kenard's hands and mouth. Next, she studied his wide-open eyes. "Is there anything left in that?" She pointed to the wineskin on the ground.

Ralf reached down for the object and shook it near his ear. "Little enough. Do you want the thing?"

The sub-infirmarian stood up, stretched as if her back ached, and nodded.

Out of the corner of her eye, Eleanor saw Father Eliduc standing close to Avelina. Had the prioress not seen this woman before, she might have concluded she was more aged than she was. Bent and trembling, Avelina clenched her hands. She reminded Eleanor of a prisoner, facing the gallows, who was belatedly begging God for forgiveness.

When the priest saw Eleanor, he whispered something to the lady and rushed to the prioress' side. "This is outrageous," he hissed. "While you were absent, that nun has been circling the corpse like a common whore seeking custom. When I protested, she claimed you had given permission! Had a bishop witnessed this, he would have been shocked and ordered severe penance."

"Forgive us, Father, but surely you would agree the circumstances are most unusual. We are not used to men dropping dead outside our chapels. Being but simple women, I fear the shock of this event has unsettled us, and we may have reacted in unseemly ways. Sister Anne is our sub-infirmarian and a trained apothecary, however, and I believe her guilty of nothing more than an ill-considered violation of modesty. I know the depth of her devotion to God and promise to counsel her." Eleanor hoped that calmed the man. She most certainly did not want to reveal how often she let Sister Anne assist the crowner in matters of murder.

His face flushing slightly, he stepped back. "In the turmoil of the moment, I did forget the reputation of your talented sub-infirmarian."

"I take responsibility for the failure to summon another to provide proper attendance in my absence. I was also alone here when we first discovered the body, a fault for which I shall demand a hard penance. You were both kind and wise to remind us that we must practice modesty and remember the spirit of our vows, even when we are forced to deal with worldly matters." She bowed her head, sensing the man was backing down from further outrage.

Eliduc cleared his throat. "Surely the corpse can be removed from these rude stares." He gestured at the small number remaining after the choir had been ordered back to their quarters. "The man was in the service of the Lady Avelina and owned a soul that belongs to God."

She gestured to Crowner Ralf and said in a loud voice "Have you further need to examine the corpse here? We would take the body to the chapel." Then she tilted her head at the priest.

Quickly, he glanced at Sister Anne who nodded consent. "I am done for the moment," he replied. "I do beg permission to consult later on the nature of this death. Perhaps with Brother John?" A grin teased the corner of his lips.

Father Eliduc walked back to the Lady Avelina.

"We must speak in private, my lady." Ralf watched the priest and kept his voice low.

Eleanor discreetly nodded agreement.

"Although I understand the need to move the body, I beg that it be placed where it can be guarded."

"We shall provide that protection," she murmured. "Brother Beorn will arrange to have it taken to the hospital chapel and assign responsible lay brothers to watch over it." Then the prioress added, raising her voice so it would be overheard by anyone standing nearby, "Brother John once owned an apothecary shop in Norwich. Although Sister Anne is also a talented healer, she is a woman. We shall honor your suggestion that he examine the body later this evening when he is finished with his duties as novice master."

"I am grateful," Ralf replied. "I have some other matters to attend to now…"

A commotion at the edge of the tiny circle of onlookers interrupted further discussion.

A woman pushed forward.

"Lady Avelina," Eliduc shouted, rushing to prevent her from moving closer to the corpse. "Return to your chambers, I beg of you! This is no place for you to…"

Ignoring him, she halted at side of the body, stared down at her dead servant, and began to moan.

Eleanor approached and laid a gentle hand on the woman's arm. "It is truly Kenard," she whispered. "I promise we shall find out how this happened. If there is any question of a violent death, the guilty will be brought to justice."

Continuing to stare at the body, Avelina nodded. When she finally wrenched her gaze away and looked at the prioress, her eyes were awash in tears, her face ashen.

"I will ask a lay sister to take you back to your chambers." Eleanor looked up to see that Sister Anne was already by her side. "And our sub-infirmarian will attend you as well. You must rest. She will make sure you are comfortable and have anything you need."

Avelina shuddered; her eyes rolled back; her knees buckled, and she slid to the ground in a faint.

Chapter Thirty-one

"Have you seen my brother?"

Awakening with a start, Thomas cried out, his dreams fleeing with all hope of remembrance.

"Forgive me!" Ralf stared down at the wide-eyed hermit whom he had assumed was only lost in thought.

"There is no reason to beg pardon, Crowner. Sinner that I am, I shut my eyes for a moment and fell asleep. I had meant to pray." He put his arms around his knees and shook his head free of the last remnants of sleep. "If you seek Sir Fulke, he has gone back to the priory."

"He was with you then?"

"Something has happened. Will you tell me the news?"

"Lady Avelina's servant, Kenard, was found dead outside the side chapel. Your sub-infirmarian suspects poison."

"And you think your brother had cause to murder."

Ralf squatted beside him. "I pray he has not."

"After you left him at the inn, Sir Fulke drank far too much and staggered to this hut, arriving not long after you yourself departed. Considering the profit from the number of pitchers he must have consumed, Signy could surely confirm his presence there." Thomas stood and looked inside the hut. "As for Simon, he has never left here. Unlike me, he is praying."

Saying nothing, the crowner jerked his head in the direction of the woods.

The monk bent to pick up the jug near the door and sniffed at the contents. "I fear the heat has turned this ale. If you are thirsty, we can go down to the stream."

In silence, the two friends walked down the steep path. Halfway to the pond, Ralf stopped. "I did not want Simon to hear what he should not."

"So I assumed," Thomas said with a brief smile. "Ask what you will, and tell me all you can." Leading the crowner off the path to a bit of shade, the monk eased himself into a sitting position on the ground.

"There is little enough known so far. Prioress Eleanor agreed to let Father Eliduc see the novice choir's presentation of the Daniel story, which she hoped might entertain the queen. Kenard was given permission by Brother John to watch it from the chapel. The servant slipped out the door toward the end of the performance and died. One of the novices found the body."

"Why does Sister Anne suspect poison?"

"He carried a wineskin, which he apparently drained quickly as if attacked by great thirst. She found suspicious leaf bits in his vomit and said she would examine them more carefully. There were no outward signs of injury." He shrugged. "Although God may have struck him down, I trust Annie's observations."

Nodding, Thomas said nothing about the crowner's failure to use the nun's formal title. Indeed, he was always touched by Ralf's deep affection for a woman he had known long before she had even married the man whom she later followed to Tyndal Priory.

"Why was Fulke here?"

The monk grinned. "You frightened him!" Then he grew more serious. "For all his faults, your brother longs to own a virtuous soul. When he pounded on the walls of my hut, I opened the door to a man so drunk he could barely stand, but I did not doubt that his supplication for wisdom was sincere."

"And so he kept you from your rest. I'll make sure he never bothers you again," Ralf growled.

"You must never speak to him of this. Show mercy, Ralf. He is worth that."

The crowner's shoulders sagged. "We have no love for each other, or little enough, and yet I neither hate him nor do I want him to be a suspect in murder."

"If there is any possibility that poison was slipped into Kenard's wineskin last night or up to the time he died, your brother is innocent. You stayed with him at the inn, and surely Signy or others will confirm how long he remained there. While he was here, we talked, wept, and prayed. When Nute came with food and drink from the inn, the sheriff sent him to Prioress Eleanor, explaining he could not meet with her this day."

"When I did not see him in the church, I assumed he had suffered too much from drink," Ralf muttered. "And you also swear that Simon was with you the entire time?"

Thomas stiffened. "He is innocent as well."

"I confess I had hoped he was guilty of one or the other murder."

"It seems he is not."

"You sound confident. What have you learned?"

Rising, Thomas stretched. His eyes were red from lack of sleep. "You and Signy succeeded in convincing Nute that I am no imp, eager to devour little boys."

The crowner looked puzzled over the significance of this.

"The child approached with caution this morning, perhaps reassured by the sight of Sir Fulke. Once here, he relaxed when I did not fly at him, claws extended." The monk grinned. "When your brother sent him to Prioress Eleanor, Nute whispered that Signy had told him he must confess something to me. I walked with him a short distance along the road."

Ralf struck the ground with his fist. "He has remembered something more about the murder he witnessed!"

The monk raised an eyebrow. "You will know best if this detail is meaningful. Nute said that the man, who met with Baron Otes the night he was murdered, owned a shadow of short stature with wide shoulders. His voice was hoarse."

For a moment, the crowner considered this. "When I first talked to him about what he had seen, he said only that he saw two men, one fat and the other lean. The first was obviously the baron." He frowned. "The description of the killer does not fit my brother. Although his shoulders are broad enough, he is of my height and has a voice like a rutting bull."

"Nor Simon either. He is thin, tall, and spoke with clarity the morning he arrived here."

"Father Eliduc?"

"He is short. The descriptions of the shoulders and voice do not match. Those arms never lifted a sword, and his voice has the endurance of any man who preaches."

"A short man might stretch in moonlight or shoulders grow with adjacent shadows. Large men rarely shrink."

"Agreed, but I do not think the priest is the one you seek. Although the baron was fat, he would have been more than a match for a man as small as Father Eliduc. I think we must look for a stronger killer."

"Prior Andrew?"

"Why name that good soul?"

"Your prioress said one priory inhabitant had cause to hate the baron. As I told you, she refused to name him. Since then, I have heard rumors that your prior has had himself shut up in a cell to serve penance for sin."

"If he has done so and the same person killed the baron and Kenard, Prior Andrew is innocent."

"As I most certainly hope. I must confirm that the prior remains locked away with no opportunity to leave the cell." Ralf picked up a stick and ran it through the earth like a small plow. "Why did no one send for me when Nute remembered this detail?"

Thomas smiled. "He admires you, Crowner, and longs for you to think well of him. When he told Signy that he was afraid you would call him a worthless creature for not recalling all he saw at first, she advised him to tell me and I would convey the message."

"Signy cannot believe I would be so cruel with the boy." Ralf looked hurt. "She knows I understood he might summon up further details later."

"She does. By having Nute talk to me, she also hoped he would finally lose his fear of the terrifying Hermit of Tyndal.

That was her motive in handling this as she did. You must admit she achieved what she wanted. Did you not get the information quickly enough?"

The crowner nodded, then forced the stick deeper into the earth. It snapped, and he frowned with continued unhappiness.

Two birds argued in the trees overhead. Below them, a fish leapt out of the stream for an insect, then splashed back into the water.

Thomas shifted his weight. "Are you sure one man murdered both the baron and the servant?"

Ralf blinked, then swatted at a persistent fly. "Why do you ask?"

"The baron had his throat slit. The servant was poisoned. The first at night. The next in broad daylight. One victim is a man of rank, the other a servant. Two different methods. Two different times. Two different…" He fell silent and squinted at the treetops as if looking for guidance.

"You seek consistency where there need not be any."

"Both required planning." Thomas shook his head. "These crimes were not committed because a man was in the wrong place at an unfortunate time like some wealthy merchant meeting with a band of outlaws as he traveled through a forest. There is reason hiding behind each act. The logical link between them eludes me."

"This killer is surely a courtier, monk, and men like that love intrigue and clever plotting."

"Courtiers are still men, and men follow patterns." He pulled at his beard as if the hair annoyed him. "We know Baron Otes had many enemies. How had Kenard offended?"

The crowner grunted, then fell silent.

Thomas watched Ralf walk away and down the road toward the priory. "Weary," he whispered. Every muscle in his body felt unbearably leaden with fatigue. Leaning against the wall of the hut, he went limp and let the weight of his body pull him to the ground.

"Perhaps it will rain later," he said as he stared at the promising cloud wisps that were stretching white fingers across the sky. At least summer rains cooled a man's body for a short while, even if they left the air heavy with damp afterward.

Turning his head, he looked into the hut and saw that Simon remained stretched out on the floor in front of the altar. As a monk, he should be overjoyed he had been able to convert the young man from bedding women and playing in tournaments to serving God. Instead, he feared he had created a monster, more likely to be a better servant of the Prince of Darkness than he had been as some thoughtless youth.

He had meant well by telling Simon how he had striven, in the service of his Order and prioress, to discover God's more perfect justice and how worldly sins should be treated under it. In doing so, he had hoped to teach the youth compassion, charity, and a way to find peace.

Instead, he had seen the lad's eyes begin to glow with sharp fire, and, when the youth threw himself on the floor in front of the altar and began to twist, buck, and moan, Thomas knew he was not witnessing holy ecstasy. The act might look godly. It stank of evil.

Had Sir Fulke not arrived when he did, the monk feared he would have fled the hut and run until he collapsed from exhaustion. If some wild and ravenous creature had come upon him then, he might have prayed for a quick descent to Hell and blessed the beast for killing him.

Mercifully, the sheriff's grief had calmed him. With growing compassion, he learned how deeply this man loved a wife whom he called *good*, but whose health now prevented her from welcoming him to her bed. Although Thomas knew that Fulke's tears must taste more of ale than salt, he had believed his sorrow and took pains to soothe him. The monk had not found a way to heal himself, but his heart understood how deeply both body and soul ached when lust could not find comfort in permitted love. Even if his own wounds might still bleed, he had learned the right words to console other men.

So he had sent Sir Fulke on his way back to the priory with knees as sore as his head from long prayer and much guidance. Perhaps the sheriff would return home a kinder husband and a better man.

Then, as the sound of Simon chanting incomprehensible prayers grew louder, Thomas begged God to keep the monster he had created out of good intentions from wreaking havoc on the world.

Chapter Thirty-two

Eleanor settled into her chair, gripped her staff of office, and begged God for wisdom. Quickly glancing to her right, she took comfort in knowing Sister Anne stood close by. At least she had had time to confer with her before this meeting, and the company of her dearest friend never failed to give her courage.

Not that she minded discussing matters with Ralf, but she must treat that eldest brother, standing next to the crowner, with care. Sir Fulke, for all his evident disinterest in local crime, was highly enough placed at court to cause problems for her, Ralf, and even her own family if he was sufficiently offended.

"Kenard's body rests safely in the hospital chapel," she began. "There the corpse has been more carefully examined in the presence of Crowner Ralf." She nodded at Fulke. "I hope this has met with your approval, my lord sheriff."

"It has." Fulke stood, legs slightly apart and arms folded.

Although the sheriff had reminded her earlier of some bright-feathered rooster, today he resembled a more bedraggled fowl. What had kept him awake all night was probably ale and not a fox. She hoped this had not made him more contrary.

Eleanor turned to Ralf. "What have you learned from your study of the corpse, Crowner?" Or rather what has our sub-infirmarian found, she amended in silence, and was grateful that he respected Sister Anne's knowledge enough not only to listen but seek her advice.

"There were no signs of violence on his body, nor any other indication of struggle. His skin was mottled with red patches. His pupils were enlarged. He had vomited and had also drooled a great deal, staining his clothes. This suggests poison. Although the wineskin nearby was almost empty, there was enough left to find bits of leaves in it. The vomit contained the same. All this suggests Kenard drank wine mixed with a lethal dose of leaves from a plant called Lily of the Valley." Out of the corner of his eye, he looked at Anne.

She lowered her head in subtle concurrence.

"Adequately done," Fulke growled.

Ralf's face colored, although his tightened jaw suggested a successful effort to control his temper.

"Both you and Brother John were trained apothecaries before taking vows," Eleanor said to Anne, crafting her phrasing with care to suggest that John had been present at the examination of the corpse. In fact, he had been with his novices. "Based on that experience, what can be learned about this plant?" The prioress hoped she was also ambiguous enough to avoid the sin of bearing false witness.

"Brother John and I agree on this, my lady." Anne now bowed her head in the direction of the sheriff. "It is a most dangerous plant, especially the leaves. Death occurs very quickly if mixed with a liquid and drunk."

"Would someone be able to taste it and become suspicious?" Fulke grimaced.

"The flavor is much like that of wild garlic often used in soups."

"That might be noticed in wine," Eleanor said.

"Am I correct is assuming that this is a poison not well known by most?" Ralf eyed his brother.

Fulke glared back.

The sub-infirmarian ignored them both. "Lily of the Valley has medicinal use as well. The proper dosage requires training if death is to be avoided."

"Curative?" Eleanor straightened. "What treatments?"

"Many believe it improves memory, strengthens the heart, soothes eyes, and even cures headaches." Anne smiled at the prioress. "I prefer feverfew for the last since that herb is not lethal."

"I am grateful!" Eleanor leaned back in her chair. "Let us now consider the deaths, the first being Baron Otes. Since our crowner has found no evidence that he was killed by lawless men or other local felons, we are obliged to look to members of the queen's party for the man's enemy." The prioress turned to Fulke.

His face reddened, and he quickly bowed his head without offering either comment or protest.

"And enough men did hate the baron," Ralf said.

"Well noted, Crowner. Do we know of any reason why Kenard, a servant, should have been poisoned?"

"No," he said. "Nor do we know if there are two killers amongst the courtiers or just one."

Fulke opened his mouth to speak.

His brother ignored him. "While the servant's body was being removed, I did seek out Brother Thomas."

The sheriff began to cough.

"I wanted to know what visitors he had that night and whether they were with him long enough to prove innocent of murder. Simon was the only one, and he is most certainly without guilt." He fell silent as he looked at Fulke, then turned back to the prioress. "Since I have learned to respect the good hermit's observations, I stayed to talk over the details of the deaths with him. He is troubled by the differences between the two and fears there may be two killers. He says that the facts of each crime suggest no unifying logic or pattern."

Eleanor considered this. "Although I would never dismiss whatever he has to say, I am not sure I agree with his concern."

"We know little about Kenard's past or any connection with Baron Otes that might suggest a reason for his murder, my lady," Ralf said. "It is possible he saw the baron's killer or was somehow involved in that first death, reasons enough for a murderer to kill him also."

"Then we must question the one person here who knows him best." Falling silent, the prioress looked around briefly. "The Lady Avelina." Before anyone could speak, she continued, "Although she is the queen's lady, she is still a woman…" Carefully, Eleanor left the rest of the statement unspoken.

No one said a word.

Fulke blinked. "A woman should talk with her first," he said. "It is more seemly."

Grateful that the man had fulfilled her hope, Eleanor quickly asserted the authority to make the one investigation she deemed most important to do herself. "Then I shall go to her immediately and take Sister Anne with me. The lady's fragile health has been violently assaulted by this shocking death of her servant. We must offer what succor we can. Such is our duty as God's servants." She began to rise.

"That would be wise as well as charitable," Fulke snapped, his face quite scarlet. "Queen Eleanor will not be pleased if her own lady were to die in this priory as well as Baron Otes, her lord's man."

It was the prioress' turn to glow with rising fury.

The atmosphere in the room grew foul with tension. "I do not think we should suggest that Tyndal Priory bears any blame in these deaths," Ralf said, his tone apprehensive.

"We are casting everyone in the queen's party into the shadow of suspicion," Fulke growled. "Have we considered whether or not someone in this priory had cause to hate the baron?"

"Becalm yourself, brother! You act as if you yourself were a suspect, which you are not."

Fulke deflated like a burst bubble. "I did not mean to offend," he muttered with an abashed look. "I beg forgiveness, my lady."

Eleanor's face quickly recovered its usual hue. "Of course you did not, my lord, and your concern is justified. One of my religious confessed to me, soon after the baron's body was found, that his family had been at odds with the murdered man. After swearing innocence of the death, he begged to be locked away in a cell until he had served penance for any uncharitable thoughts."

"A penance which has continued," Ralf added. "His cell is without windows, and the door is locked from outside." He bowed to Eleanor.

"And I hold the key," the prioress added. "All this was confirmed just before we met in my chambers. If there is but one killer, as I believe, then my monk has been proven innocent. If there are two…" She spread her hands. "He remains under my jurisdiction to examine, find innocent, or punish if guilty."

"I never meant to question your authority on behalf of the Church, my lady." Fulke nervously cleared his throat. "I withdraw my concerns about the innocence of all here. You have satisfied any doubts I might have had." Then he turned to the crowner. "We must ask when and where Kenard acquired the full wineskin. Anyone could have easily slipped the poison into his drink. The poisoner could have been any man and done the deed anywhere."

Ralf's expression darkened as if he suspected his brother had continued to suggest that someone in the priory was guilty.

"There is so much that is unknown regarding the servant, his habits and his companions." Eleanor tried to calm the evident strife between the two brothers by distracting them with questions. "Was the poison added before he came to the chapel? Why did he drink the wine so quickly? Had he been given something to increase his thirst?"

"Who?" Fulke shouted in evident frustration.

"Guards. Other servants." Ralf pointed at his brother "How much time did Kenard spend with yours?"

"How dare you suggest that any man in my service would commit murder?" Fulke roared.

"I meant nothing by that. Maybe Kenard swyved some woman at the inn, and he so offended her that she sought revenge by putting lily leaves in his drink," the crowner replied with an evil grin. "Shall I talk to the innkeeper about her wenches?"

Fulke stepped toward his brother.

Ralf raised a fist.

Eleanor lifted her staff and brought it down with a crash.

The two men jumped back.

"We have delayed long enough," the prioress said. "Should we not each depart on our separate ways to question anyone that might have knowledge of the motive for Kenard's death?"

"My brother and I shall interrogate the servants who attend the queen's courtiers, as well as those who escorted all here," Ralf said, glowering at Fulke. "And we shall do so, acknowledging that we are here only with your permission and by swearing that we will abjure any violence in seeking answers. My lord sheriff and I both honor the sanctity of this priory."

Fulke snorted, then remembered the prioress and flushed with embarrassment. He nodded concurrence.

"Permission is granted, but I shall speak with the Lady Avelina and will question her female servants as well." Rising, she indicated the audience was finally over.

Both men bowed and left the chambers. As he approached the door, Ralf looked over his shoulder and raised a questioning eyebrow.

Eleanor smiled to reassure him all was well.

Watching the door to her public chambers swing shut, she wondered if she should have shared the information about Kenard, a man allegedly mute who had suddenly found voice enough to ask permission of Brother John to stay in the chapel and watch the play.

Fulke might well know whether or not the servant could speak on occasion, although Lady Avelina had claimed he had not uttered a word since Evesham. Under the circumstances, Eleanor feared that the sheriff would have said one way or the other.

The tension between Fulke and Ralf was evident today. Instead of considering facts with objectivity or conceding any merit in the other's ideas, they had exhibited anger and inflexibility. For this reason, she feared this bit of information about Kenard could just as easily have caused further controversy between them, rather than generating helpful debate.

Once again, she missed Brother Thomas. Were she given the choice now, she would have endured the pain of desire in exchange for his insights. At least Ralf had spoken with him, and, the more she thought on the monk's observation, the more she wondered if he might be right.

She turned to Sister Anne, and the two women conferred about what they must do next. Either or both of the two men might learn something helpful. In the meantime, Eleanor could talk with Lady Avelina, as she very much wanted to do, and Sister Anne, with her expertise with poisons, would be with her to assist.

As the two friends left for the guest quarters, the prioress shivered. Details were slowly forming a logical pattern, and she began to see just how wrong she might have been.

Chapter Thirty-three

Father Eliduc was accustomed to death, but this particular one caused a flutter of distress. Closing his eyes, he mumbled a prayer over Kenard's corpse, then quickly leaned backward. The overripe stench of decay was pungent in the heavy heat.

He rose. Forcefully exhaling the reek of corruption that had invaded his nostrils, the priest nodded at the lay brother, standing watch by the body, and hastened to the chapel door. Once outside, in the bright sun and fresh sea breeze, he gulped air like a man who had just escaped drowning.

Kenard might have died by violence, not disease, but there was something hovering around the corpse that reminded Eliduc of a malevolent and contagious miasma. Were further prayers needed, he would let other priests expose themselves to whatever evil drifted in the shadows there. He had done his duty.

Now he hurried on, gaining needed distance from such loathsome decay. The farther he got from the chapel, the lighter his spirit felt.

This latest fatality might have been convenient. It had not been required. A better conclusion would have allowed the man to give his confession and not go directly to Hell. In Eliduc's opinion, Kenard was not truly wicked. He was a man who still deserved a good death.

As the priest passed the low-walled cemetery, his gaze took in the many overgrown and sunken patches of older graves, mixed with the newer, rounded mounds of naked earth. How many lying there had been aware enough of all their vile sins before death, he wondered. Perhaps some had begged forgiveness for too little and found themselves condemned to interminable, unimaginable suffering because of their paltry confessions. Kenard might have been one of those even if a priest had been at his side. The thought eased Eliduc's heart into a more trifling grief.

Once beyond the boundaries of the cemetery, he slowed his pace and now ambled along the path to the mill. Although he had no purpose for going in that direction, the path was long and gave him time to think.

Not that he was a meditative man by habit. He left ponderous debate to those inclined to philosophy, but he did pride himself on pursuing his lord's best interests with precise attention to detail. He also took care never to do anything that might be discovered and reflect badly on the Church.

He was a man of deep faith, or else he would not have taken vows. He also knew he would never be granted sainthood, his skills being more suited to worldly matters. Let no one disparage the value of such talents, he thought. Clever manipulations and plotting were crucial if the Church were to vanquish its enemies.

Who dared forget how the faithful suffered the plight of the powerless before the Emperor Constantine was converted? Secular powers were often owned by the Prince of Darkness, and the Church must retain worldly power to keep its people safe until the Apocalypse. To that end, he had dedicated his life, and, when he took his last breath, he would die knowing he had served his God well.

Yet he grieved over the loss of Kenard's soul to Satan. As for Baron Otes, he might have felt a similar sorrow had the man not tried to cheat the Church. The baron had behaved in a duplicitous manner when he threatened to go back on a promise made to Eliduc's lord about very profitable lands. Some might argue that Tyndal, as a priory, was just as worthy a recipient. Eliduc found that argument specious. He knew which beneficiary would make better use of the profits for the betterment of Church interests in a choice between his lord and Prioress Eleanor.

He snorted.

Nonetheless, he had done his duty as a priest when he knelt in the mud to whisper to a soul that might have remained close to its fleshy corpse. That he did so with disgust and reluctance was something he might confess in due course, but priests were flawed mortals and surely he would be given light penance. He had tried harder with Kenard's spirit, but both souls were now in God's hands, facing judgement and no longer his particular concern. A few sequestered nuns somewhere would at least offer prayers for the baron's soul. He would find a monk to remember Kenard.

Sighing, he walked on.

When coins were required to learn secrets, Eliduc paid. When the plots of both wicked and useful mortals must be learned, he never hesitated to press his ear to thin walls. During this journey on the queen's behalf, he had concluded that the flaws and weakness of others would drag them down to inevitable disaster. All he had to do was step aside and let it happen.

His choice had been wise. Not only was the originally promised land saved for his lord, but Eliduc had kept his own hands unsullied.

The priest blinked. He had passed the mill and was now at the gate that opened onto the road which led to the hermit's hut and the village farther on.

Eliduc had not intended to visit Brother Thomas just now, preferring to wait until a time closer to departure from the priory. As he thought more on it, he concluded it might be the right moment to claim young Simon after all. The monk had surely accomplished all Eliduc knew he would. To leave the youth there longer than absolutely necessary might not be wise.

"And knowing the skills of Prioress Eleanor in ferreting out murderers," he said aloud, "I believe the hour of our departure from here will arrive most swiftly."

With those words, he unlatched the gate and hastened toward the hermitage. Had anyone been nearby, they would have heard this dark-robed man softly humming a chorus from *The Play of Daniel.*

Chapter Thirty-four

The Lady Avelina sat bolt upright in the chair, her face in shadow. Although a timid light did creep through the shuttered window, it remained a pallid glow as if uncertain whether or not clarity was welcome.

"I have been waiting for you, Prioress Eleanor."

"I beg pardon for the delay. Your servant's death required…"

"I am guilty."

Eleanor stepped back, struck dumb by the blunt confession. Had she expected this, she would not have asked Sister Anne to wait outside the room until called. She regretted not having her friend's reaction to this unexpected statement. Unsure exactly how to respond, the prioress chose to say nothing.

"Where is my son?"

"He has been with the hermit outside the priory since soon after you arrived."

"Has anyone accused him of involvement in this crime?"

Eleanor felt her body tremble with nervous uncertainty and was grateful the lady could not see her lack of composure in the faded light. Taking a deep breath, she willed herself to calm and to listen carefully, less to what was said than how it was spoken. "Crowner Ralf confirmed he has not left the hermitage, or, if he did, Simon's absences have been too short to travel to the priory and return."

Avelina laughed, the sound more akin to the screech of a knife against a whetstone than any merriment.

"There is no doubt that your son is innocent in the death of your servant, and so you have no cause to shield him."

"The death of Baron Otes remains unsolved."

Eleanor stepped closer, hoping to better read the woman's expression. "If the person who killed the baron also killed Kenard, then your son is innocent of the former since he is most certainly blameless of the latter."

Uttering a soft groan, Avelina pressed her hand against her breast. Even in the muted light, Eleanor could see sweat glistening on her face.

"Are you unwell, my lady?"

"A mild indisposition. I ate something that disagreed with me. It will soon pass."

"Sister Anne waits just outside the door. Shall I send for her?"

"You are kind, but I need her not." The lady smiled, and then bit her lips as if the effort exceeded her strength. "Let us return to the subject of murder. Is that not why you came?"

Indeed it was, but Eleanor now regretted she had not spoken with Brother Thomas before coming to see Lady Avelina. Once she understood how blinded she had been by the land gift, she realized that two killers might be involved. Her reasons for changing her mind could also be wrong. She had rushed to this meeting ill-prepared.

And now something else troubled her, although the cause was elusive. She had little time to ponder it and was growing anxious to get to the truth of this matter. "Why did you claim guilt?" she asked, choosing to be as direct as this woman had been with her admission.

Avelina bowed her head. "The evening we arrived here, Baron Otes begged a private audience with me. I was well acquainted with his reputation as a man who collected secrets to his benefit." Her eyes narrowed as she glanced up at the prioress. "What did I have to fear? The widow of a known traitor has nothing left to hide." She fell silent as the words required for further explanation refused to be spoken.

Hearing the bitterness in her tone, Eleanor wondered if the woman had any tears left to weep. She nodded sympathetically.

"Although I could not imagine what the baron wanted from me, I decided to grant the man's wish. It is often wiser, I have found, not to remain in ignorance when it comes to the ways of wicked men." She rubbed nervously at her eyes.

"Had you any fears or suspicions of what he came to discuss?"

Avelina shook her head. "How clearly does a mother ever see the true nature of her beloved son? How can a dutiful wife ever judge her lord husband?"

Eleanor answered with care and, she hoped, compassion. "Mothers and wives may see the flaw but love the man in spite of it. When a man pledges loyalty to another mortal, his unbending fealty may be honorable although his judgement may be in error. Sons are often much like their sires."

Avelina's eyes betrayed her surprise. "You are kind! I doubted that Baron Otes could have discovered some horrible secret related to my dead husband. Ghosts cannot surpass the crime of treason, and God is the final judge of blasphemy." She began to gasp as if the summer air had become too thick to breath.

Eleanor moved closer to the woman. "Are you sure you are well?"

"It is only my sorrow you observe. I beg you to let me finish!"

The prioress stepped back.

"As you noted, my son is much like his father, both in his longing to serve a lord well and his inability to recognize which one is strong enough to survive any fray." She coughed. "Will you swear to me that what I tell you shall remain in confidence?"

"I cannot, unless Simon is innocent of both murder and treason." Eleanor shuddered at the implications of what the woman had just told her. All she really needed to know was who killed two men, not necessarily the details of why. "I shall be frank with you," she said. "Two souls have been sent to God unshriven. Although Baron Otes was a cruel man, his killer had no right to execute him in that manner. Our Lord has said that only those without sin should ever cast stones. God alone has that prerogative. As for your servant, I know nothing of him, virtues or vices, but the same applies to him. For the sake of proper justice, I seek the murderer."

"I am grateful for your honesty," Avelina said. "I shall only say that my son has been unwise in his choice of men to support his ambitions, and Baron Otes came to inform me of Simon's entanglements. Even though I should not have been surprised, the shock was quite hard to bear."

Then the boy's foot had at least slipped into treason's quicksand. If she was to learn the names of murderers, Eleanor knew she must step away from the further unveiling of Simon's crimes. She knew she was too close to the discovery for any distraction. "What did he demand for his silence?"

"Oh, he wanted more than a small price for keeping that secret!" Avelina looked around as if fearing an unseen presence. "He offered to help my son regain some of his lands, although not the title. As recompense for his efforts, he demanded half what he had recovered for Simon or else the value of it in coin."

Eleanor winced. "Were the remaining lands adequate to support your son?"

"Not as his birth deserved, and I have little enough to add when I die."

"What did he say he would do if you refused the offer?"

"He swore to tell the king the names of the men who demanded Simon's support in return for funds to pay for horse and armor."

"So I must conclude your son was in peril of his life." Had the dimming light cast the lady's face in greater shadow or had her cheeks turned sickly grey?

Avelina nodded.

"Were you alone when the baron spoke with you?"

"Except for Kenard. Since he was both mute and a servant, the baron found him only an object of mockery."

Now Eleanor grew confident that Brother Thomas had been right, at least in principle. There were two who were complicit in these crimes, and she knew she must proceed with care. "Did you tell Simon of this discussion?"

"As a woman, I may be imprudent. As a mother, I am not so foolish as to tell a boy, already condemned for unwise behavior, of matters that might cause him to act with even greater rashness." She covered her eyes.

Eleanor suspected that the image of what might have been her son's fate was too much to bear.

"After the baron left, I confess I showed a woman's weakness and railed against the baron, tearing at my hair and begging God to smite the man for his greed and lack of pity."

"Whose ears heard you?" Eleanor asked softly.

"Kenard's."

"And he took pity."

Avelina looked away.

For a moment, the prioress said nothing, hoping the lady would continue her tale. Instead, the woman stared at the ceiling in silence. Her breathing was labored.

"Have you need of your potion?" Eleanor whispered. When she looked at the table where the vial had once sat, she saw only the mortar and pestle. That was the detail which had troubled her. The implications grieved her.

Avelina shook her head. "Only Kenard knew how to make it."

"Sister Anne might…"

"You do not need to summon her."

Although the woman's appearance concerned her, Eleanor knew from the lady's tone that she would not win any debate on this matter. Instead, she hastened the discussion. "You confess guilt in the baron's murder, but I do not think you capable of cutting his throat."

"You think not?" Avelina laughed and tapped a hand against her breast. "Unlike this weak and errant child of Eve, you have never brought forth a man's babe in agony and blood, and then put the wee suckling to your breast. Methinks a child drinks, not milk, but the heart's blood from his mother. When he is wounded, it is she who bleeds the most."

Eleanor knew silence was wisest.

"Like the old King Henry, when the saintly Becket offended him, I bewailed the curse laid on my son, a babe when his father fell in battle, and asked God to mercifully lift it from my lad. My prayers were answered. The baron was killed. It was I who caused another to commit murder."

"By the man who was your husband's servant, saw him killed at Evesham, and fell mute with grief. How did you learn of Kenard's deed, my lady?"

Turning her face away, Avelina pressed her hands against her cheeks and groaned. "The day after. He came to me and spoke for the first time, claiming God had restored his speech when he lured the baron to a death the man had long deserved. I can still hear the rasp of his voice." She whimpered like a sleeper longing to awaken from an evil dream. "He believed the deed could not have been evil if God had granted this miracle of giving him back his voice." With piteous expression, she looked at the prioress. "Can that be true?"

How could it be? Yet Eleanor had heard many incomprehensible tales of men and women who had been cured of grave afflictions in strange ways. Perhaps God had shown favor to this former servant when he killed a very wicked man. She doubted it. "Have you confided any of this to a priest?"

"I have told Father Eliduc of my son's indiscretion, although I said nothing of Kenard's deed."

Eleanor recoiled. She prayed the man would keep the confidence, although she still feared he might find some use for this knowledge. On the other hand, Simon had sought the counsel of Brother Thomas with Eliduc's urging. The priest may have hoped to save the youth. If Prior Andrew's past could be forgiven in exchange for his dedication to God, then Simon should be given the same opportunity to cleanse his sins with penance and service. She tried to silence her persistent suspicions.

"I understand why you take responsibility for the murder," Eleanor finally said, "but it was Kenard who did the deed and the blood remains on his hands." She did understand why Avelina believed she bore guilt in this, and, in truth, the prioress agreed with her.

"Kenard was an honorable man! He might have wielded the knife, but the deed that brought about the murder was my foolish moaning as well as my son's poor judgement. Yet my lad cannot be condemned. He is a child in so many ways. I, as his mother, ought to have been wiser. I take full blame."

"Kenard did far more than even the most loyal of servants."

"I thank you for not accusing me of unlawful lust, although I heard that meaning in your tone. He was my husband's servant and chose to serve me out of love for him. He and I never shared a bed. What we did share was love for Simon, as my husband's only son."

"I must ask how your loyal servant died."

"I bear the guilt of that sin as well. He never would have committed self-murder if…" She began to cough.

Eleanor reached for a pitcher on the table near Avelina's chair and poured watered ale into a cup. "Please drink this. It will revive you."

Her face quite scarlet, Avelina gulped the drink and set the cup down.

Then the prioress took the lady's hand and stroked it as if it were that of a sorrowing child. "Sister Anne is within call," she reminded her.

Shaking her head, the woman continued. "Were he arrested as a suspect in the baron's murder, Kenard planned to claim that he had done the deed out of revenge for my husband's death. He swore he would hang and not reveal Simon's secret. If tortured, however, he was terrified, since he had recovered his speech, that he might confess to killing the baron to protect the boy."

"He took your potion with him to the chapel. It was made from Lily of the Valley, was it not?"

"A physician believed it might help slow my racing heart, and he showed Kenard how to make it safely." She began to sob. "I saw that the vial kept by my bed was missing. Aye, I feared he had taken it. More than that, I did nothing to seek him out and stop him." Then Avelina threw back her head and screamed. "Have I not done all I could for my son? Could any mother have done more? I let a good man go to Hell because I, too, feared he might reveal my boy's wickedness under duress. I let Kenard commit self-murder!"

Eleanor put her arms around the woman and held her close. "He did choose to die within sight of the altar," she whispered. "By doing so, God surely knew he had not given his soul completely to Satan." Although she was uncertain whether this would ameliorate the sin of self-murder, she felt that comfort was paramount at the moment.

For a moment, Avelina clutched the prioress and wailed piteously, "May God forgive me!" Again and again, she repeated the plea.

As Eleanor bent to murmur more solace into the lady's ears, Avelina's body stiffened. Her eyes widened as if she had just seen the Devil fly through the window.

Eleanor straightened and stared at her face.

"Bring Sister Anne," Avelina gasped, her face chalk-white with terror.

Eleanor ran to the door, calling out for the sub-infirmarian to hurry.

Entering quickly, Sister Anne rushed to kneel by the stricken woman. First, she felt her neck and then pressed her ear to Avelina's chest.

"Her heart has stopped," the nun said, looking up at the prioress.

"Grief did break it," Eleanor whispered, then closed her eyes and wept.

Chapter Thirty-five

Dust swirled as men carried baggage to load on carts. Horses, impatient to leave, pawed the ground and twitched their tails to chase off annoying flies. The dry air was thick with heat, but nothing was quite as arid as Simon's eyes.

Eleanor studied the young man for any small sign of grief. Did his lip just quiver or had she imagined it? "I shall pray for your mother's soul," she said at last, determined to be charitable. After all, the lad must be eager to leave this place where his mother had died, and, once away, he would surely allow himself to express sorrow.

He smiled. The implied emotion did not extend beyond his lips.

"We shall bury her here, as you asked."

"Facing the chapel so she will be ready to look on God's terrible face when the trumpet announces the Day of Judgement." Simon's tone made clear he believed the prioress had been incapable of comprehending his request the first time he had made it, necessitating a stern repetition to enforce understanding.

Eleanor nodded, willing her flaring temper to subside. Out of the corner of her eye, she saw Father Eliduc approach. At least he would be leaving as well. For such kindness, she thanked God, and, with the promise of imminent calm, she greeted the priest with courtesy.

He bowed. "The days here have brought great sadness to this young man," Eliduc said, his tone grave, "although God often brings us trials for good reason."

Had the comment not come from this particular priest, Eleanor might have readily agreed. Instead, she feared his remark hinted at some ominous portent. At times she wondered if the two of them even worshiped the same God, for hers spoke of peace and justice while his seemed ever to howl with anger and vengeance like winter storm winds.

"Simon now wishes to take vows and serve God as his liege lord." The priest put a hand on the young man's shoulder and gripped it possessively.

Eleanor failed to see any joy reflected in the young man's expression. Instead, she detected a glittering light in his eyes, as if flames flickered in his soul. She trembled. This was not the gaze of someone imbued with tranquility.

"I shall fight God's enemies," Simon said, unblinking, "and bring the firestorm of His wrath to any who seek to thwart His true purpose."

"And I shall pray that He grants you true wisdom," Eleanor replied softly. Glancing at the dark-clad priest, then back at Simon, she had the fleeting impression she had just met two of the four horsemen of the Apocalypse.

The priest smiled down at the lad, his thin lips taut with restrained glee. "Go, now, and see that all your mother's belongings have been placed in the cart. We shall leave soon." He watched as the young man walked away.

"May he find peace," Eleanor murmured, then realized she had, perhaps unwisely, spoken aloud.

Turning back to her, Eliduc's face had a pained look. "He has found purpose, my lady."

She glanced heavenward, expecting to see dark clouds racing to hide the sunlight.

The sky was quite blue.

"We may thank Brother Thomas for that," the man continued. "During Simon's stay at the hermitage, the good monk was able to persuade him to turn his zeal for combat on behalf of an earthly lord into a more righteous passion."

The prioress modestly bowed her head and managed to disguise her conflicting thoughts about this news.

Eliduc sighed. "I know Brother Thomas has oft served you well, my lady. Indeed, he has also come to the aid of his family when they most needed him. Like a dutiful son, I might almost say."

"I pray no one has fallen ill of late." Eleanor instantly regretted expressing the sarcasm she felt.

Eliduc's eyes closed like those of a cat who has just fed on some unlucky prey. "A hermit should never be called from his hut, my lady, although I know his intent to remain there has always been a temporary choice."

Surely she had never told him this, because she hoped he would conclude that the monk would remain in his hermitage until death. Who, then, had reported the truth to Father Eliduc? Was it Brother Thomas himself or, she asked herself once again, did she have an unknown spy amongst her religious?

"That is no longer of consequence, for God is ever merciful, and the hermit's family remains in good health. In fact, I am optimistic that His blessing on them shall continue, and Brother Thomas need not be called forth by me again from his service to God in this priory." With a most munificent look, he bowed.

Eleanor knew she was staring at the priest, but she let the sound of those words echo several times in her mind before she dared respond. "Then we shall not see you in the future, Father Eliduc?"

"Although my visits here were always darkened by the sad news I brought, I found your hospitality worthy of what our dear Lord required as one of the Seven Comfortable Acts." A wistful look darted across his face. "The vessel in which it was served might have been properly humble for a priory, but your wine was a worthy descendant of that served at Cana."

Just this once Eleanor knew he had spoken with sincerity.

"I regret I shall probably not return to Tyndal, my lady." He briefly shut his eyes. "Any yet none of us can ever predict what

God has planned for us. As you see, I was chosen to accompany others sent by our queen on this journey." He smiled. "We may well meet again, and I pray that we shall, for I have always found our meetings most agreeable."

In reply, Eleanor mumbled something incomprehensible which she hoped suggested courtesy. Most certainly, she did not dare speak her true thoughts. Thinking more on this, she suspected that bluntness might actually amuse rather than offend the man. He was a strange enough creature that the obvious assumptions might not apply.

"Until that day, I wish you God's grace, my lady," Eliduc said, "and pray that Brother Thomas will soon complete his penance and return here. That would surely bring pleasure to the hearts..." The priest held her gaze for a long moment. "... of all who have mourned his absence." He then bowed abruptly and quickly took his leave.

Shutting her eyes, Eleanor begged God grant her the mercy of never seeing the priest again.

Ralf glared at his brother.

Fulke gazed longingly at his saddled horse.

The horse flicked its ears, successfully dislodging a flying irritant.

"We are quite clear on this? I shall suffer no more from your marital plotting on my behalf," the crowner growled.

Fulke continued to stare at his horse, then nodded once.

"Ah, sweet brother, do not look so glum. Have I not proven myself to be a loyal kinsman when I made sure there could be no doubt of your innocence in these recent, unhappy matters?"

Fulke frowned.

"Have I ever spoken a word about your past, might one say, *misdeeds*?" Then he leaned forward and whispered, "Nor shall I say anything to your virtuous wife about a certain local wench, although I praise you for seeking the wisdom of a holy hermit for those..."

"I need a male heir."

"That is in God's hands."

"And requires your seed."

"Then be at peace. I promise to help His purpose by marrying again. Whether my efforts on your behalf produce male or female babes is something I cannot control."

Brightening, Fulke gestured toward the village. "That woman who owns the inn is comely and has a strong enough will she might even breed robust sons. If you insist on choosing a local wench, you would do worse than that one and even gain a profitable inn with the marriage."

Ralf shook his head. "You promised me your plotting would cease."

"Or, if you insist, the Saxon creature." He waved his hand. "She's young, has many years to breed, and should drop enough rams amongst the ewes." He frowned for a moment. "Or even your daughter's nurse. She's got wide enough hips to bear."

"Perhaps you would prefer that I take all three to the church door."

For an instant, Fulke looked as if he were considering the idea before finally asking, "Do any have land to bring you?"

Ralf grabbed his brother by the front of his robe and pulled him close. "You shall provide all land for my eldest son. Sibely inherits her mother's manor. I have bits of land purchased by selling my sword as a mercenary. For a dowry, those may suit a simple but honest man who wishes to marry any other daughter I may have. As for extra sons, should God be so generous, they will fend for themselves as I did. Now you have all the answers you need to any questions. Again, I demand your oath that you shall leave me alone to find my own wife."

"Release me! Have you forgotten who I am and whom I serve?"

"Was I choking you?" Ralf laughed and shoved his brother away. "Swear on any dim hope you may have for Heaven."

"You have my word, as long as you fulfill yours and give me an heir."

Ralf slapped Fulke on the shoulder. "I shall work diligently on that. In the meantime, go back to court, increase the wealth you have sworn to my son, give my greetings to your wife, a saint for tolerating you, and leave me to render justice here in your name and that of the king without your interference."

"I would cheerfully promise all, brother," Fulke replied, his expression suddenly turned grave, "except for the last. Remember that we have a new king. If he deems it in his interest, he may command me to get involved."

Equally somber, Ralf nodded. "Then let us hope he does so in ways that are honorable."

"He is God's anointed. To do other than obey him is treason."

The younger brother said nothing.

Fulke waited

Ralf folded his arms.

Fulke shook his head and mounted his long-patient steed.

Father Eliduc savored the fear he had seen in Prioress Eleanor's eyes. Although he had no proof that she lusted after Brother Thomas, he knew the frailties of men and women well enough to guess it. And from her reaction to his carefully phrased remark, he was certain his assumption was correct and that she knew he had guessed her secret.

It was always good to leave those whom you had cause to respect with the knowledge that you were capable of winning all battles against them. Although he had outwitted her this time, he knew Prioress Eleanor was possessed of a mind and will made of far finer steel than those of most men. To most she was already a formidable opponent; for him, she had the potential to grow into one. He had meant what he said when he expressed hope they would meet again. After all, struggling only against the unworthy dulled the sharpness of one's own wit.

As he watched the servants finish the packing of last items, he grew content. Soon they would be traveling back to court, and he was eager to return to other work on his lord's behalf.

This time, he was bringing a present with him, one he knew would surely please.

Simon was a far better prospect than the earl's by-blow he had rescued from prison. Although Brother Thomas had served well in his way, this lad had sharp passion where the monk was possessed of too tender a heart.

Men with those womanish inclinations were dangerous when blind resolve was needed to further sacred causes. With a king like Edward, a far more forceful man than his father, the Church might soon have a mightier struggle over dominion. Such a holy war would require unblinking obedience in those who served the Church. Simon would make a fine zealot.

Thus Eliduc was pleased to release the monk Thomas from further onerous duty, and, in so doing, he had learned of a useful weakness in the Prioress of Tyndal. All that, and knowing the lands from Baron Otes would pass safely to the hands of his lord, made the priest a very happy man.

He walked over to Simon.

The lad was gazing heavenward with an ardent look that would surely delight even the desert fathers.

"Mount your horse, my son. We leave in a short while."

"I shall always remember that I found God's purpose for me here," he replied.

"And since you will also never forget your vow to Him that you shall serve as directed," Eliduc whispered in Simon's ear, "then the secret of your unfortunate contacts with rebellious factions need never be mentioned to any mortal."

Simon seemed not to have heard him speak. The young man looked like a crusader going into battle, one whose thoughts were focused solely on slaughtering the enemy.

Chapter Thirty-six

Eleanor stood at the window of her chambers and watched the dust clouds, raised by the departing horsemen, settle. Never had she been so grateful to see men leave as she was these. They had brought violence to her priory and carried the plague of discord as well, worldly contagions that were difficult to cure once the infection was established.

His soul bound for Hell, Kenard's corpse had been tossed into a shallow pit in unconsecrated earth next to Brother Simeon's grave. No one would ever know how he had managed to lure Otes away from priory grounds or why he had chosen to kill him below the hermitage. Doubting that the servant had known about Brother Thomas, the prioress suspected the man had simply picked the spot because it was remote and blood would not be shed on God's land. Even though Kenard had committed self-murder within Tyndal's walls, an act some would call sacrilege, Eleanor did wonder if he had done so to be closer to God and thus to let Him know his soul longed to be good in spite of his violent acts.

"My lady?"

Willing enough to set heavy thoughts aside, the prioress immediately turned to acknowledge Gytha standing at the door.

"As you requested, Prior Andrew has ended his solitary penance and awaits your command. There is ale, cheese, and bread on the table. Shall I remain outside the door in case you need me?"

Eleanor nodded and walked into her public room.

A hollow-cheeked Prior Andrew entered. When he met her eyes, he fell awkwardly to his knees.

Gytha hurried out and closed the door behind her, leaving but a modest inch open.

Rarely did the prioress require complete privacy in her conversations with either nun or monk. This time she did. The opening in the door satisfied the letter of propriety's law. Although she trusted her maid's discretion and silence, the content of this discussion was one with which Eleanor did not want to burden anyone else. Her decision with respect to her prior, as well as all the errors he had committed, ought to remain between the two of them alone.

"Rise, Prior Andrew," she said and gestured for him to be seated near the food and drink.

"I am not worthy of this kindness," he whispered, looking at the bounty on the table.

"The queen's emissaries have left," she responded. "Perhaps you have not learned this. Baron Otes was killed by Lady Avelina's servant, a man who had a long-standing grudge against the baron. Later, he committed self-murder. Unfortunately, the lady herself, although innocent of blame, died as a result of the shock this news dealt her. Her son, Simon, has decided to take vows." More detail than this, she concluded, he had no need to know.

"And through all I was unable to give you the support and service that the Order and my vows demand. I am a foolish and a wicked man."

"Since you were locked away in a windowless room, as a penance you agreed to serve, there could be no doubt you were innocent of the second death, and, for that reason, most likely of the first as well. Yet, if the Lady Avelina had not been so willing to tell me the reason for the baron's murder, you might have remained a suspect."

"You were wise to anticipate how evil works and shut me safely away, my lady. Indeed, I did use the time to pray over my grievous sins, but I am most guilty of adding to the priory's troubles with my own actions. I deserve no mercy and beg none."

"Your only error was in not telling me the entire story of your brother and the argument with the baron. Your reasons for that failure were not founded in evil, and I believe you wanted to protect me from worldly horrors as honorable men are wont to do with women." She walked over to the table and served him the ale with her own hands. "Nonetheless, I fear that Satan often thwarts the efforts of good men." Turning to the window, she stared out at the bright sunlight bathing the priory grounds. "And so we frail women have learned to keep, as it were, cloaks of chain mail close to hand with which to arm ourselves on such occasions."

Bowing his head, he expressed sorrow that this had been necessary, then asked, "When I surrender my position as prior, my lady, how may I best serve you?"

"Have you given thought to the ways in which you might do so?" She kept her back to him and her voice even.

He did not reply for a long time.

She kept her counsel and said nothing.

"I was a good porter, my lady."

Noting the rasp in his voice, Eleanor wondered if he was weeping, but she did not turn around, preferring to allow him a man's pride. "That you were," she replied.

"Or, if Brother Thomas does not return from his hermitage, I might wait upon the sick in the hospital."

"Aye."

"If you find I am too unworthy for such work, I will gladly spend my days preparing the dead for burial, cleaning the stables, or any other..."

"I praise you for the humility you have expressed in this matter and will not keep you in suspense any longer. I have decided how you may best serve God in this priory."

She heard the bench scrape on the floor and knew he had fallen again to his knees. Even though she feared for his bad leg, she waited, resisting a woman's concern.

When she did choose to look at him, she noted he did not even try to hide the river of tears flowing from his reddened eyes into the rushes on the floor. "Stand and face me," she ordered, her voice breaking in spite of her resolve.

He struggled to his feet but kept his eyes lowered.

"You must retain the position of prior at Tyndal," she said. "Nay, do not protest for my decision is final."

"I am known to be a man who fought for de Montfort!"

"And many others have been long aware of that connection. Did you not confess it to me when I first arrived here?"

He nodded and looked longingly at the ale.

"Drink, for I have heard the hoarseness in your voice," she said, knowing full well that his need for the ale had little to do with a dry throat. Her heart ached when she saw how his hands shook.

"I am unworthy of this clemency."

"Let me be frank, Prior. Tyndal is a minor religious house, and we struggle to pay for our simple needs. Since we are not wealthy, we wield no influence in the world. I doubt King Edward will care that our prior served the Earl of Leicester in the distant past, and, in fact, you were pardoned by his uncle. Now you serve God, as does our new king, and surely he is wise enough to see that he has far greater threats to contend with than a man who has long foresworn the world."

"I cannot forget that Baron Otes threatened you because of my past."

"The baron tried to bribe me. Or else he only meant to offer Tyndal the lands so their worth might grow greater in the eyes of another and the latter inspired to increase his payment for them. In any case, he misjudged my greed. Where Baron Otes saw profit, I saw thirty pieces of silver." For the first time, she chanced a softer tone. "Nor would that Judas price buy this priory such a talented administrator as you, one who serves in God's name and without worldly recompense."

Then Andrew smiled, albeit weakly.

She poured herself a cup of ale and smelled the yeasty scent of the freshly baked bread on the table. Sadly, she had no appetite. "Whether or not the cause is righteous, war is a brutal thing, and many grow wicked in the heat of it even as they shout God's name. In our priory, it matters not that my kin fought for King Henry while you, and your brother, supported a man now called either saint or traitor. We each have begged, and received, clemency of the other as our beliefs demand."

"When I told my tale several years ago, you were merciful and kind. I know of no offense your family ever committed against any of my kin, but I would bear no ill feeling if such have been the case. I am honored to serve you, my lady, for you truly represent the Queen of Heaven in this priory with a mother's wisdom and compassion."

"Then go forth, Prior," she said with a smile, "and see to our sheep as you have always so ably done."

He bowed. "Gladly. Both the four-footed ones, blessed with wool, and the less well-covered of God's creatures that stand on only two feet."

Eleanor laughed and dismissed him.

Despite his lame leg, he was gone in an instant.

Eleanor stared at the door and clung to solitude for just a moment longer, although Gytha waited outside.

She was glad Andrew had been kept safe from suspicion and that he would remain to help administer priory business with his much needed skills. It was thanks to his stewardship that the debts of the past had been paid and Tyndal, in fact, showed promise of more prosperity than she had suggested to him. After all she had just seen over the last few days, however, she did wonder if there was too high a cost paid for that little prosperity.

Although she wanted Tyndal to have sufficient income to fulfill all of God's commandments regarding the care of the sick, poor, and helpless, she knew men grew selfish if there was too much of it. "We had best remain lean," she thought, "and ever grateful for whatever we receive of His bounty."

Eleanor walked back to the window and looked down once again at the land she ruled on God's behalf. It was beautiful in her eyes, even when snow and ice turned the earth glacial white.

Closing her eyes, she breathed in the scent of the earth and knew how precious Tyndal had become to her. "If God is merciful," she said, "He will give me the wisdom to recognize when we have sufficiency and keep me from wanting more."

Suddenly, she felt something press firmly against her leg, and, looking down, saw her great orange cat, Arthur. She picked him up and buried her face in his thick pelt.

He purred.

"I have not seen you here for far too long, my prince," she murmured. "Did Father Eliduc frighten you away?"

Crawling higher on her shoulder, he burrowed his head into her wimple.

"I may hope that neither of us shall ever see the man again." The words caused her to shiver for she had little faith in the truth of them. "If he should reappear, you must show me all your hiding places so I might join you until he departs."

He began to scrub the cloth around her neck.

"Indeed, he is too clever for me. Although he was not complicit in murder, he had a purpose here, was successful in attaining what he wanted, and was most satisfied by the time he left. Nor do I believe that I shall be spared a future meeting. I can only pray that God gives me the insight and calm to outwit him if our intentions conflict." She shook her head and wished, as she had oft before, that her aunt, Sister Beatrice, was closer than Amesbury Priory and could help her handle these matters with more understanding.

The chamber door groaned on its leather hinges.

Eleanor turned around.

Gytha peeked through the opening. "My lady, forgive me for disturbing you. A monk urgently implores an audience."

Perplexed over who this might be and what new trouble was facing her, the prioress eased the cat back down to the floor and gave her consent.

The young maid opened the door wide and stood aside.

A tall, freshly-shaven and tonsured monk entered. He knelt at the prioress' feet.

Her hand flew to her pounding heart as she gazed at him and wondered at the sun dancing in his red-gold hair.

"My lady, I beg permission to return to my former duties at Tyndal Priory," he murmured, his deep voice soft with longing.

"That plea is granted, Brother Thomas," she replied, not caring that her tone might well convey the caress she dared not give him. "You have been deeply missed by all here."

In truth, even the cat seemed pleased. Walking over to the monk, Arthur tentatively sniffed at the former hermit and began to lick Thomas' hands.

Author's Notes

Despite loving theater for decades, enjoying many musical forms, and having some experience with Christian rituals, I remained utterly ignorant of liturgical drama until early December 2003. This embarrassing gap in my knowledge was filled when the Aurora Theatre and the Pacific Mozart Ensemble presented *The Play of Daniel* at St. Mark's Episcopal Church in Berkeley, California.

Although the night was certainly dark and very stormy, I inched my way to the performance of the 12th to 13th century drama. Not only did I discover that it was an astonishingly delightful mini-opera, but the moment I heard the roaring lions off-stage, I knew it was also perfect for murder.

After the sun came out, my first visit was to the University Press Bookstore, which made sure I got Professor Dunbar Ogden's *The Staging of Drama in the Medieval Church*; the next was to the adjoining Musical Offering where I found CDs of *Ludus Danielis* by the Dufay Collective and Clemencic Consort. Later, a friend discovered E. K. Chambers' *The Medieval Stage* at Black Oak Bookstore. Thus a few Berkeley merchants were made minimally richer by my small purchases and I, immensely so.

From its earliest years, the Church condemned plays, equating them with the many varied depravities of a few murderous Roman emperors as well as the legitimization of non-Christian deities. Yet the love of "playacting" may be as much a part of our DNA as music, dance, and other ways of telling of tales in verse or prose. Whatever the antipathy for them, few can deny that enactments are powerful teaching tools.

When something is useful, we have always found a way to repackage and incorporate it into the culture even if it was objectionable in its original form. (Today, we might call this *spin*.) The Church leaders have been successful at this as well, and, as they have converted popular wood nymphs into Christian saints, they have also transformed theater into a method of educating those who did not understand Latin, did not read, or might be converted. And so a tenth century canoness, Hrotswitha of Gandersheim, was permitted to write well-regarded, instructional plays inspired by Terence. About the same time, brief dramatizations of the Easter tale (with the three Marys at the tomb) and the manger scene at Christmas (complete with shepherds, ox, and donkey) became commonplace.

The twelve days of Christmas were especially suitable for enactments. It was a harsh season in the northern latitudes, filled with illness, bitter cold, and diminished food supplies. People needed color and excitement to lift their spirits. One popular event was the Feast of Fools. As possible counter to this rather riotous amusement, which probably included a little warming alcohol, the Church put on more edifying performances like the flight into Egypt, Herod slaying the innocents, and the *Prophetae*. The latter were stories of prophets from the Old Testament, all of whom foretold a messiah. One of the most popular and well-developed of these was the *Play of Daniel* or *Ludus Danielis*.

Like many early enactments, there is much information we do not have about the play: what the actual costumes looked like; most details about stage directions and set; or the music. With *Daniel*, however, we do know that the first recorded version was written by Hilarius, a twelfth century pupil of Abelard, and further developed by "the youth of Beauvais" in the thirteenth century. The popularity of *Daniel* (with Darius, Belshazzar and the Persians) may be explained, in part, by the numerous crusades in those centuries. Not only did crusaders bring back spices and medical knowledge from Outremer, they also sparked curiosity about the cultures there.

Given such gaps of knowledge and even contradictory information, I saw that I might have some reasonable flexibility with the performance done at Tyndal Priory. After listening to more than one version of *Daniel*, I learned there were many interpretations possible for stage set, the type and number of instruments used, composition of singers, and even how to use the lions. One of the most intriguing omissions in extant manuscripts is an explanation of how the writing on the wall was done. Some suggest a monk did it, but I preferred more drama in the moment and so created the embroidered banner myself. The idea fits the time and might have actually been used.

The play is primarily written in Latin, but many vernacular phrases are sprinkled throughout. As for the narrator, this may not be strictly original but was used in the 2003 Berkeley performance. Since Queen Eleanor was not comfortable with Latin (nor was Edward), I thought she might like the thoughtful addition even though the story was quite familiar. Overall, I have kept details close to what is known of early performances of this or similar plays.

Most of the information we have on enactments are from those done in great cathedrals or wealthy religious houses, but, having seen *Daniel* in a little church, I can attest to the power of the tale in a small space with less elaborate settings. Since Tyndal Priory is modest in size and riches, I have kept the staging simple and limited the number of instruments to those easily learned by young boys and readily available in a rural setting.

To anyone who wants to know more about this subject than I could possibly write in short notes, I point to the wonderful sources listed at the end of this book.

To the best of my knowledge, Eleanor of Castile, wife of Edward I, never spoke of going on the pilgrimage suggested in this book. As a conventionally religious queen, she might have considered doing so but would never have been able to undertake it. Her only living son at that time, Henry, died in October

1274, and she was already pregnant with her next child, born in March 1275.

In fact, during her twenty-five year marriage, she had fifteen known pregnancies, the last in 1284 or six years before she died at forty-nine. She and her husband had a remarkably happy marriage, much like the one between Henry III and Eleanor of Provence, and Edward grieved deeply at her death. The famous Eleanor crosses are testimony to that.

Although her husband was not noted for his literary interests, Eleanor read the vernacular and owned a library containing both history and fiction. Embroidery and weaving were favored leisure activities, but she preferred hunting with dogs rather than falcons, the king's favorite. She did not especially fancy gambling but did enjoy chess and was serious enough about that to have studied a contemporary manual on the game. In addition, she loved gardens and was very fond of fruit, imported her own olive oil, and received the occasional cheese from her sister-in-law who was the dowager countess of Champagne and Brie.

Eleanor of Castile is also surrounded by legend and controversy. The story of how she sucked the poison from Edward's wound when he was almost assassinated on crusade is probably untrue. Another tale has Otto de Grandson doing the same thing, which may well be equally fabricated. But I also doubt she had to be gotten out of the room because of her weeping and lamenting. The known details of her life suggest a much tougher woman than that.

As for the controversy, there is some debate over how much she had to do with her husband's callous expulsion of the Jews from England in 1290. Her preferred religious were the Dominican friars, later closely associated with the Inquisition, and there is little to suggest she had much concern for the Jews, besides viewing them as cash cows whenever she wanted extra money. I have seen the argument that the strength of her faith was often questioned, because she was more highly educated than many women of her time, and thus she dared not show tolerance of non-Christians out of fear that she might suffer even harsher censure. At the moment, I have some doubts about that, but, since Eleanor of Castile is far too interesting not to show up in some future book, I plan more reading to grow better acquainted with the multi-faceted person she most certainly was.

The Seven Comfortable Acts were based on that highest of all virtues, charity. They included feeding the hungry, clothing the naked, quenching thirst, housing the wayfarer, visiting prisoners, nursing the sick, and burying the dead. Although they were intended to balance the Seven Deadly Sins, it is the latter we know best.

Kenard's loss of speech, a form of aphonia, is an actual psychological condition, often caused by trauma and known to occur in soldiers. The victim can cough and sometimes whisper but not speak normally. It is also curable. The modern methods of doing so, however, are definitely preferable to how Kenard recovered his ability to speak.

In September 1274, Edward replaced the majority of sheriffs who had grown corrupt under his father's lax administration. Oaths were required to keep the few retained and the new ones honest, but some were skeptical about the efficacy of this method. One clerk noted on an official document that he considered these oaths to be no better than *sheriffs' perjury.*

Edward himself had been an early de Montfort supporter and, once king, even instituted some governmental changes favored by the dead Earl of Leicester. It seems reasonable, therefore, that he should offer, in 1276, what we might call a general amnesty for all who had fought in the civil wars during the reign of his father. How this gesture might have affected someone like Simon in this story is unknown. Then, as now, a broad statement may sound good, but people often discover to their dismay that the devil inevitably lies in the details.

Bibliography

One of the joys in writing these mysteries is the opportunity to discover academic treasures that both spark the imagination and delight the mind. The following are a few I'd like to share for those who want to know more about certain details in this book. As always, I take full blame for any errors of understanding or fact.

The Medieval Stage (2 volumes) by E. K. Chambers, Oxford University Press, 1903.

Contemplation and Action: The Other Monasticism by Roberta Gilchrist, Leicester University Press, 1995.

Requiem: The Medieval Monastic Cemetery in Britain by Roberta Gilchrist and Barney Sloane, Museum of London Archaeology Service, 2005.

The Play of Daniel: A Thirteenth Century Musical Drama, edited by Noah Greenberg, Oxford University Press, 1959.

Simon de Montfort by Margaret Wade Labarge, W.W. Norton & Company, 1962.

The Staging of Drama in the Medieval Church by Dunbar H. Ogden, University of Delaware Press, 2002.

Eleanor of Castile: Queen and Society in Thirteenth Century England by John Carmi Parsons, St. Martin's Press, 1998.

To receive a free catalog of Poisoned Pen Press titles, please contact us in one of the following ways:

Phone: 1-800-421-3976
Facsimile: 1-480-949-1707
Email: info@poisonedpenpress.com
Website: www.poisonedpenpress.com

Poisoned Pen Press
6962 E. First Ave. Ste. 103
Scottsdale, AZ 85251